Goodbye, Miss Emily

Goodbye, *Miss Emily*

MARTHA SIBLEY GEORGE

First Edition

Design: Laurie Shock, Shock Design Books
www.shockdesign.com
Editing: Amy Bauman
Printed in the United States of America
ISBN-13: 978-1503246959
ISBN-10: 1503246957

CHAPTER ONE

MORGAN

Until the spring of 1934, no shadow of consequence had crossed Morgan Bigley's adult life. His pretty wife adored him, his law practice thrived, his home was comfortable and pleasant, and any aggravation two healthy children might engender was alleviated by the presence of a kind and capable nurse. Therefore, when the tide of his good fortune turned, it took him unawares.

It turned in April, that month in which azalea and dogwood transform southern neighborhoods into fairyland. It turned on the day his ten-year-old daughter got a new horse and his five-year-old daughter learned to pump on the backyard swing.

The day started off as any other except that Morgan was late in leaving the house. Ordinarily, he fixed his own breakfast—a piece of toast and a half grapefruit—and was already in town when the cook arrived at his home. However, on this particular morning, he ate with his family because his wife, Emily, was taking a trip, and he wanted to be there when she left. Emily's friend, Carlotta Howell, was picking her up after breakfast, and the two ladies were driving to Americus, Georgia, to spend the night with a former classmate from college.

He did not like the idea of Emily and Carlotta driving alone through the backcountry. And he did not like Carlotta. She was a rich divorcée whose lips were too red and whose fingernails were too lethal and whose voice had a carrying quality that fell gratingly on the ear. Her former husband had succumbed to the bottle, and this bolstered Morgan's conviction that behind every male alcoholic was a cold, cantankerous female. However, what really bothered him about the woman was her influence on his wife. Only a few days before, Carlotta had persuaded Emily to cut off her hair and wear it in a more "up-to-date" style. The new bob was not unattractive, but he preferred the graceful, familiar sweep of the long, dark hair pulled back in a bun. He had expressed such distaste for the new haircut that even now, as Emily sat at the breakfast table with him and the girls, she wore the little knitted cap that covered her ears.

"You don't have to wear a hat inside," he said. "I don't think it looks that bad."

"You complained so much. You've made me self-conscious."

"It's just that I miss seeing you take the pins out of your hair before you go to bed. And I love to watch you brush it."

"It will grow. It's always growing. They say it grows even after you're dead."

"Is Grandpa's hair still growing?" ten-year-old Josy asked. "Is it like a girl's by now?"

"Oh," Emily groaned. "I don't know. Well, yes. I suppose it is. Grandpa's in heaven, and I expect everybody has long hair there. And speaking of hair, if you don't keep yours out of your eyes, I can't see how lovely you are." She leaned toward Josy and gently pushed a wayward strand of curls away from the girl's face.

Morgan noticed Agnes, the pudgy five-year-old, quietly removing her own barrette and shaking her head until her straight brown hair covered her eyes. He stared hard at his wife in an unsuccessful attempt to catch her attention and direct her gaze toward their youngest daughter.

"Am I lovely?" Agnes asked.

Emily burst out laughing. "Why, honey, of course, you are. Both of my daughters are lovely," and she smoothed the short brown hair and refastened the barrette. Then she looked sheepishly at her husband. Because people so often commented on Josy's beauty, they had decided to avoid commentary on it themselves, especially in front of her little sister.

"You know," Morgan said, "if you will just wait until Saturday, I'll drive you and Carlotta to Americus, spend the night at a motel, and bring you home on Sunday."

"No," Emily said. "You would be bored to death on the trip down and back. Carlotta and I will want to talk women's talk, but knowing you would be bored, we won't, and then we won't have a good time."

"Well," he said gruffly, "If I would inhibit your pleasure . . ." His voice trailed off.

"I wish you wouldn't go, Mama," Josy said. "My new horse is coming this afternoon, and you won't get to see me ride."

"For goodness' sake! I'll be back for supper tomorrow, and I'll see you ride on Sunday."

"I need a horse," Agnes said.

"You don't need one," Josy said. "You have a new swing, and you can't even make that go by yourself."

"Today, I'm gonna make that swing go up to the clouds. I need a horse and a swing."

Their conversation was put to an end when Viola, Agnes's nurse, came in the room to announce the presence of a shiny red automobile in the driveway. Morgan, having resigned himself to the inevitable, picked up his wife's overnight bag, and the family, including Viola, went outside to say good¬bye.

It was a cool, crisp day, and the promise of a glorious southern spring was in the air. Emily paused for a moment on the front steps and surveyed her kingdom. The trees were almost in leaf, and the forsythia formed golden clumps along the drive.

She touched Morgan's arm and smiled up at him. "In a few weeks," she said, "my garden will be at its peak, and there'll be a muse behind every dogwood."

Morgan's heart gave a little jump of pleasure as it always did when Emily indicated how much she loved their home. However, he was more interested in the automobile Carlotta was driving than in muses. It was a brand new 1934 Packard Roadster, complete with whitewall tires and a rumble seat. Its huge headlights gave it a comical, bug-eyed look, but he knew that in these depressed times, the cost of it wasn't comical. It must have set her back at least $2,000 and maybe more. He gave a low whistle, strode over to the left side of the car, and propped his foot on the running board. "Mighty fancy!" he said. "Mighty fancy!"

"You like it?" Carlotta asked.

"Indeed I do. It's beautiful, but sometimes a sporty car like this tempts you to go too fast. Remember, south Georgia is cow country, and there's no fencing, so keep your speed down and your eyes peeled."

He paused for a moment, having noticed Carlotta's bright red lips turn upward into what he perceived as a poisonously tolerant smile. However, feeling that the enumeration of possible disasters might somehow prevent them, he did not let the smile deter him.

"And watch out for fools," he continued. "There's no end of crazy people driving cars, and you never know when one will show up and either hit you or run you into a ditch. And check your gas and your water down around Macon, and . . ."

His lecture was interrupted by the appearance of a huge, ungainly black dog who came bounding around the house, panting and wagging his tail. He had been a stray whom the children had adopted and Viola, in deference to his bad smell, had named Blossom. He raced toward Emily at full speed, stopped abruptly and threatened to jump.

"Get down! Get down, sir!" Morgan shouted, and the animal collapsed at Emily's feet, slobbering happily as she stooped down to stroke his head.

"Don't you want to put that creature in the rumble seat and take him with you?" he asked Carlotta.

"Not for all the gold in China," she answered.

The remark contributed to Morgan's lack of confidence in her. It was not a period in which one thought of China in terms of gold. He supposed that she had meant to say "tea," but he would be a gentleman and let it go.

It was time for leave-taking. Emily hugged Morgan, the girls, and Viola good-bye, and then seated herself in the roadster.

Suddenly Agnes began to cry. She grabbed the bumper of the automobile and wailed, "I want to go! I want to go with Mama!"

Viola pried the little girl loose and swept her up in her arms. As the car backed away, Morgan began walking alongside, calling to his wife, "Have a good time. We'll be all right here. Have fun."

He followed them out to Muscogee Road in order to instruct Carlotta in the art of operating a motor vehicle in reverse. However, they had not gone far in this manner, before Carlotta jammed on the brakes and leaned out the window. "Morgan," she said, "I know how to back up. I don't need help."

He threw his hands up. "Sorry," he said, hoping with all his heart that she would hit the mailbox. "I won't help any more—not for all the tea in China."

She maneuvered the shiny red roadster to the road, and he watched it move down hill and pause at the crossroad before taking a right. As the car turned, he saw through its window that Emily had removed the little cap and was fluffing out her new haircut with her fingers.

He shook his head and grinned. "Women!" he said out loud, as if the saying of it contained an explanation for all the world's contrariness. But he wondered if he had made too much over the new bob. It was just that he knew of no sight lovelier than a beautiful woman brushing out her long dark hair.

∞∞

That morning he did not arrive at this office until 9:30 a.m. The receptionist looked at her watch, smiled broadly, and said, "Mr. O'Brian is already here."

Bill O'Brian was Morgan Bigley's best friend and law partner, and the two shared a standing joke about office hours. Morgan maintained they began at 8 a.m., and O'Brian argued they began at 9.

"I guess he must be planning on leaving early," Morgan said, speaking loudly for the benefit of his partner whose door was partially open. "You might tell him to come in to see me if he can spare the time."

He hung his coat and his squashed up fedora on a coat rack in the corner of his office. Emily wanted him to buy a new hat, but he thought the beat-up appearance of the old one contributed to the illusion that he was a naïve country lawyer, easily befuddled by city slickers. He and Emily had both come from a small town in south Georgia, but realizing the opportunities of a bustling young city, they had moved to Atlanta.

He sat down at the big mahogany desk that had belonged to his grandfather and surveyed his surroundings with satisfaction. The walls were lined with law books and photographs of prominent men of the city, including one of O'Brian, holding a basket full of quail and looking very jaunty in his hunting clothes. O'Brian frequently paused before this particular likeness to admire it and to count the quail, sometimes coming up with twelve and sometimes coming up with thirteen. This morning, however, when O'Brian came into Morgan's office, he did not stop to admire the picture. Instead, he held his watch up to the light and scrutinized it. "What kept you?" he asked.

"Emily is driving down to Americus with Carlotta Howell, and I wanted to see her off," Morgan explained. Then he added, "Our women are getting too damn independent."

O'Brian assumed an expression both philosophical and droll. "How true. Today it's south Georgia. Tomorrow it's Paris."

"Sit down," Morgan said. "We've got serious things to talk about."

His partner pulled up a chair and swung his legs up so that his feet rested on top of the mahogany desk. Simultaneously, Morgan produced a pipe, which he chewed on but did not smoke. Then the two men got down to business, which, in this case, involved the defense of a well-known male Southern writer accused by a female writer of plagiarism. An hour later, as they wound up the discussion, Morgan commented, "We know she's lying. No woman can get into a man's mind and into his britches like this one does in this book. I just don't see any problems with this."

As O'Brian got up to leave, he flashed Morgan a big Irish smile. "With your brains and my charm," he said, "we don't have problems with anything."

"You've left out my hard work and long hours," Morgan retorted.

∽◌∽

In mid afternoon, O'Brian came back to Morgan's office, a different man. He was pale, and his countenance was utterly sober. Morgan noticed the change and thought his partner might have eaten something for lunch that made him sick.

"What's the matter?" he asked. "You look as if we just lost our richest client."

O'Brian spoke softly, "I wish it were that."

A prescient chill seized Morgan in the area of his heart. "What is it?" he asked.

O'Brian's voice dropped to a whisper. "I don't know how to say it."

Morgan spoke sharply. "For God's sake, Bill, just spit it out!" The chill inside him spread.

"There's been an accident outside Americus," O'Brian said. "It seems a lumber truck was passing on a curve and hit the roadster and . . ."

"And Emily . . . ? Is Emily hurt?"

O'Brian closed his eyes for a second and drew a deep breath. "She's dead. Both ladies are dead. I talked to the sheriff myself."

Suddenly, Morgan, on whom the gods had smiled throughout his adult life, felt the foundations of his world give way.

CHAPTER TWO

VIOLA

Viola ate her meals in the Bigley kitchen, but she slept in a narrow, one-room apartment above their backyard garage. Her bed, covered in a brightly colored patchwork quilt, was centered lengthwise under a window to give the room the illusion of width. A magazine picture of Joe Louis with his dukes up was thumbtacked to the wall on one side of the window. A framed picture of Jesus with the caption, "Prince of Peace," hung on the other side. A milk crate painted white served as a bedside table or, if the situation demanded, a coffee table. The remainder of the apartment was furnished in worn but comfortable Bigley furniture including a fine Brumby rocker that Miss Emily had given her when the girls got too big for rocking solace. A sink, an icebox, and a hot plate were located against the bathroom wall, and an orange braided rug lent an aura of cheerfulness to the surroundings.

The children were not allowed to visit Viola's apartment unless invited, but, frequently, after the day's work was done, Viola's women friends came to call. Pointing their flashlights on the driveway, they walked unobtrusively past the big house, and if anyone from within or anyone sitting on the veranda inquired who they were, they identified themselves in voices barely audible above the sound of katydids and crickets. Then, after climbing the steep stairs to Viola's apartment, they closed the door for an hour or two away from the white man's world.

Viola's friends knew how hard she had taken Miss Emily's death, and, after the accident, a steady stream of them brought pies and fruit to the little apartment to express their sympathy. Even the white folks, when they called at the big house to commiserate with Morgan Bigley, sought out the children's nurse to offer condolences. Everyone, black and white alike, was familiar with the unusual circumstances surrounding the birth of Agnes.

Those circumstances occurred on Viola's day off. She had been in town window-shopping when a white girl dashed out of Rich's Department Store and threw a scarf in her direction. The white girl disappeared around the corner just as the store detective charged out of Rich's and accused Viola of stealing the scarf. Morgan was out of town, so it was up to Miss Emily to set matters straight. Upon being notified by the detective that he had caught her "nigger" stealing, Miss Emily, despite her very pregnant condition, drove to town by herself and marched majestically into his office. After listening to both sides of the story, she lit into the detective with a ferocity totally foreign to her usual gentleness. However, in the process of dressing him down, she stopped in mid-sentence, gripped the desk, and let out a terrible noise. It was a loud, guttural, primal sort of noise, and it came up from somewhere deep inside her. The detective thought it signified how low down she thought he was, but Viola recognized it as an urgent announcement of the arrival of a new member to the Bigley family. An ambulance was summoned, but by the time it arrived, the office was askew, Miss Emily was on the floor, and Viola was holding a newborn baby in her arms. The birth of Agnes cemented a friendship and affection between the two women that was forever binding.

∞∞

A few nights after the funeral, Viola's best friend, Clara Belle, climbed the steep stairs to the little apartment over the garage. Huffing and puffing, she stopped to get her breath at the top of the landing and to peek in the window by the door. Viola was hunched over in the Brumby rocker, tears flowing down her broad cheeks and arms folded against her chest as if she needed to hold somebody who wasn't there.

Before knocking, Clara Belle cleared her throat and stomped on the landing. It took a few minutes for Viola to answer, but when she did, her eyes were dry. Clara Belle handed her a store-bought apple pie as a sign of her sympathy and then plopped down in an easy chair. "These stairs get any steeper," she said, "you ain't gonna have much company."

Viola, who was tall and heavy-set but not fat, pointedly looked her friend up and down. "Some folks have more trouble than others," she observed. Then she got two plates and forks from the shelf above the sink and cut two slices of pie. Giving her guest the larger slice, she sat back down.

"I sure do hate to hear about your trouble," Clara Belle said as she took a large bite of pie. "How's that poor baby taking it?"

Viola shrugged her shoulders. "Agnes is taking it pretty well, I guess, but she don't know what dead means. She thinks her mama's on a trip."

Clara Belle took another bite of pie before speaking. "Agnes is like a lot of little white girls around here. She thinks her nurse is her mama. What about Josy and Mr. Morgan? How they doing?"

"Hurting. Mr. Morgan's real quiet, and Josy goes off by herself and cries. She's like me. She don't want nobody to see her cry, and she says she's too big to sit on my lap. There ain't no way for me to comfort her."

"It looks to me like you hurting, too."

"I'm all right. I can stand most anything, but when I get up here all by myself and start thinking about Miss Emily and all she done for me, my eyes start leaking."

"If all white ladies was like Miss Emily," Clara Belle observed, "this world would be a fine place to live. But what you got to do is get your mind on something cheerful. You remember that time she saved you from going to jail?"

"Of course I do. I ain't never gonna forget that."

"Well, you remember what the doctor said when the ambulance came and took you and Miss Emily and the baby to the hospital?"

A slow smile traveled up the sides of Viola's face. "He said that Agnes was a fine baby girl and she couldn't be any finer if he had delivered her himself. Lord! Lord! That was my proudest moment."

"Well, let's think about that while we have another little piece of pie," Clara Belle suggested.

Viola's smile broadened. "You eat like you get paid to do it."

"Lord! Lord," her friend responded, "I wish I was." And the two ladies finished the pie and the conversation.

∞ ∞

Viola tried to maintain a cheerful demeanor as she went about her daily tasks. The two women had worked together well, dividing many household activities to suit their individual inclinations. Emily's great passion had been gardening, and, incongruously because she was delicate and light boned, was often found wielding a hoe or a spade. In contrast, the tall, broad Viola excelled in creating exotic floral arrangements in which she combined Emily's flowers with wild blossoms she found along the road. And when company came to dinner and Roxie, the cook, roasted quail Morgan Rigley had shot, and an arrangement by Viola was centered between two silver candelabras, what pride they all took in that table!

But since the accident, Viola didn't feel like picking flowers, and Roxie didn't seem to remember how to cook anything except chicken. The menu became so invariable that Viola took it upon herself to go into the kitchen and complain.

"You have chicken one more night," she said, "and this whole family is gonna start clucking."

Roxie was sitting at the kitchen table, stringing beans in a half-hearted sort of way. "I can't help it," she sighed. "I ain't got no heart for cooking, and this family ain't got no appetite, and we having chicken tonight."

Viola drew herself up to her full six feet. "Looker here," she said. "Nobody knows better than me what a fine lady Miss Emily was, but life goes on, and we need to eat something ain't never had feathers."

"We need lots of things," Roxie said. "Agnes needs a haircut, and Josy ain't got nobody to take her to riding lessons except them widows and old maids that come sniffing around here talking sugar and spice before Miss Emily's cold."

Just as Roxie was speaking, Agnes came in the kitchen bearing a tray of cookies. "Miss Louisa Jones brought these cookies over for dessert," Agnes said. "They're for me and Papa and Josy. You all can't have any because Miss Jones says she don't want the darkies to eat them all up."

Roxie scowled and put the tray on the table. "I'd rather be called a nigger than a darkie," she said.

"What's the difference?" Viola asked.

"A darkie's some low-down, dirty thing that white folks feel sorry for. A nigger ain't nothing but a low-down dirty thing."

Agnes knit her brows, put her hands on her hips and looked hard at Roxie. "Are you a nigger or a darkie?" she demanded.

"She ain't none of them things," Viola said, "and don't let me hear you using them words. You talk like that, and I ain't letting you sit on my lap no more, and if you try to crawl up on me, I'm gonna stand up and shake."

The little girl thought for a moment. Roxie was glaring at her and her nurse was threatening to take away the place she went for solace during life's dark moments.

"All right. I ain't gonna talk like that."

"And don't say ain't, Now go play with Blossom. That dog's got a lot of love to give, and he needs to get some back."

"I hate that dirty dog."

"Well, go outside and swing,"

Agnes eyed Viola quizzically. "You think my mama can see me swing from way up there in heaven?" she asked.

"Yes, baby. Your mama is watching you now."

"Well, I hope she thinks I'm a good swinger," Agnes said. She took several cookies and went outside.

⌀⌀⌀

As the weeks wore on, Viola began to worry about Josy. Agnes acted as if her mother had gone away on a trip, but Josy was suffering. Her face was pale, and after school, instead of playing with her friends, she would sneak up to her parents' room and curl up on her mother's side of the four-poster bed. Viola wanted to put her arms around her, but Josy wouldn't let her.

One rainy afternoon, Agnes wheedled Josy into a game of checkers, even though Agnes always lost and, in so doing, always cried. This afternoon, when Agnes lost and cried, Josy threw the checkerboard at her, sending the checkers flying all over the living room. "I hate you! You fat little crybaby!" she hissed. "You don't even care that Mama died."

She spoke with such venom that Agnes flew into Viola's arms, and Josy disappeared upstairs. Later, Viola found the ten-year-old in Morgan's bedroom, curled up on her mother's side of the four-poster bed. "I miss my mama," she sobbed. "I miss my mama." This time, Viola was able to put her strong arms around the grief-stricken little girl and hold her close until she stopped crying.

She knew Josy needed to keep busy and stay with the riding lessons, and it was too soon to turn things over to the widows and old maids. So on the night of the checkers incident, she approached Morgan Bigley with a solution.

"What we need around here," she said, "is a white lady who can drive and who can go places I can't go. We got no way to go to do nothing without being beholden."

It was after supper, and he had settled down in the living room with the evening paper, but he put it away and took off his glasses. "What would you have me do?" he asked, and his eyes were steely.

"Well," Viola began, "Miss Mattie Craig is selling her big house and moving in with her sister. She can drive a car, and her cook says she always tries to do right by people. I expect Miss Mattie would make a fine housekeeper."

"She must be sixty-five. She is too old to be looking for a job."

"She's old, but she's lively."

"Her husband was a doctor. He delivered Josy and Agnes. He must have left her comfortably fixed," Morgan reasoned.

"Miss Mattie's cook says he left her with a pile of bills and a big mortgage, and she don't want to move in with her sister."

Morgan's eyebrows shot majestically up and stayed there as he spoke. "Does her cook also say she wants to move in here?"

"We got the room," Viola said.

He took his time before answering. Finally, he said, "I will think on it." Then he put his glasses back on and opened up the paper.

The following Saturday, Viola looked out the window and saw a skinny little lady walking up the driveway. She wore white gloves, a navy blue dress, and a matching straw hat with flowers attached to its brim. Her hair was pulled back in a gray knot, and her face was covered with wrinkles, but her step was lively. Miss Mattie Craig was coming to call.

CHAPTER THREE

MISS MATTIE

Miss Mattie was dumbfounded when Morgan Bigley phoned her in regard to a job-related interview, and she was sure it would all come to nothing. She was sixty-five years old, had never worked, and had, for the better part of her life, lived in gracious sufficiency. Now she was broke and lucky to have a house to sell and a sister to move in with. But her sister luxuriated in ill health, and her house was full of dust motes, pills, and never-ending complaints.

Miss Mattie did not know Morgan Bigley well, although they had once been connected through a disastrous marriage between her cousin and his uncle. She was not sure he was aware of the connection but, because of it and because her husband had delivered the Bigley babies, she had followed his career with interest. He was deeply involved in community and church affairs, and his picture was frequently in the paper along with articles describing him as an outstanding citizen, a pillar of the Presbyterian Church, and a forceful orator.

As she stepped up to the front door of the red brick colonial residence, she squared her shoulders and lifted her chin. The prospect of discussing the possibility of becoming Morgan Bigley's housekeeper was unnerving, but, as she told herself, she was quality, too, albeit, down on her luck. She drew comfort in the fact that the Bigley home, though attractive with its simple, well-balanced lines, was not as grand as the English Tudor she was selling. It was nice enough, but with its upstairs windows so perfectly lined up with those below and with what appeared to be a sunroom or a den on one side balancing off the porte cochere on the other, it was similar to so many homes in the neighborhood. However, the beauty of the landscaping and a particularly fine fanlight over the front door saved it from mediocrity.

She had expected a servant to let her in, but Morgan himself greeted her at the door. He was wearing a beat-up beige sweater over a blue shirt, jodhpur britches, and boots, and she deduced he had spent the morning on horseback. He was not as handsome as she remembered, having a face that was a little too wide and a chin that was a little too large, but his eyes were extraordinary. They were bright blue, and they conveyed both kindness and acute awareness, so that she knew he understood the awkwardness of her situation.

He led her through the center hall to a wide veranda that overlooked his late wife's garden and the woods beyond. They sat down in white wicker rockers and, as the interview progressed, Miss Mattie's chair moved rapidly, whereas Morgan's rock was slow and deliberate.

Viola brought them Coca-Colas, and Agnes joined them, settling down on her father's lap as if she owned it. She was chewing a large wad of gum with her mouth open, and she glared at the guest as if she were a thief who might run off with the silver.

"My!" Miss Mattie exclaimed. "What a healthy-looking child."

It was the pleasantest thing she could think of to say in regard to this rather chubby and seemingly hostile little girl.

"Both of my children are blessed with good health," Morgan said. "There is no worry there. The worry is that they need a lady of quality to look after their needs. I thought that if we just sit here and chat a while, you'll get the feel of the family." He motioned toward the woods where Josy and her friends were playing. "We have always had a very open house. My wife was hospitable to everyone, and the neighborhood children always come here for their games."

He spoke slowly, exhibiting that imperturbable deliberation so common to the Southern gentleman. Dr. Craig had been the same way. When the crash came, and she had asked him what it all meant, he had answered, "Why, Mattie, it means we're broke. That's all."

Under the calming influence of Morgan's voice, Miss Mattie began to relax. "I, too, am a believer in hospitality and in friendships," she said. "I was a bridesmaid in twenty-two weddings before I married Dr. Craig. As a matter of fact, I was in Josiah Bigley's wedding to Henrietta McClure. I believe Josiah was your uncle."

There was a faint flicker of amusement in the bright blue eyes. "That union didn't hold."

Miss Mattie stopped her chair in mid-rock and spoke authoritatively. "That's because Henrietta went to Vassar College. After she graduated, she wanted to run the world and everybody in it. Neither the South nor Josiah could do anything right after Henrietta got an education."

"Sometimes," Morgan said, "our girls go off to the great Eastern schools and lose in charm what they gain in education."

Just as he spoke, Josy, followed by Blossom, came bounding up from the back woods. She stopped just long enough to be introduced and, even though her shirt and shorts were dirty and torn, Miss Mattie had never seen a lovelier child. She was like a fawn, long and light of limb with a delicate sensitive face and large brown eyes. Her companion, the dog, was unusually unattractive.

"We're playing Tarzan," Josy explained, "and I'm Jane. I just came in to get some Coca-Colas."

"I want to play," Agnes said.

"You can be a monkey," Josy offered.

"I don't want to be a monkey. I want to be Tarzan."

Josy rolled her eyes and, followed by the dog, went inside to the kitchen. When she returned, she had four Coca-Cola bottles on a tray, and she was balancing the tray on her head. The dog, close by her side, jumped and panted as if he thought the refreshments were for him.

After the Coca-Colas were successfully delivered, Morgan commented, "Children are like colts. They need a loose line and plenty of running room."

Miss Mattie suddenly felt her age. She wasn't sure she was up to children who did balancing acts with glass bottles.

"That's a most unusual looking dog," she said. "I wonder if he's any particular breed."

The glint of humor returned to his eyes. "You put that most delicately. He's a stray. He just showed up one day, and Emily adopted him. Viola, who has a fine sense of irony, named him Blossom."

"He smells bad, and he jumps," Agnes said. "Josy likes him, but I don't."

Miss Mattie wasn't crazy about large, smelly dogs either, but she refrained from comment. "And how old is Josy?" she asked, "and what grade is she in?"

She's in the fifth grade," Morgan said, "but I'm afraid she isn't a scholar. You needn't worry about her going to Vassar, but she rides a horse like an Indian."

Miss Mattie said nothing, but she thought to herself that a girl as pretty as Josy would benefit more from horsemanship or a good game of bridge than from scholarship. The little girl on her father's lap might need an education, but a true Southern beauty like Josy needed good manners and a few pleasant outlets to lead a fulfilling life.

Agnes stashed the gum in the corner of her mouth long enough to say, "If you buy me a pony, Papa, I'll ride like an Indian, too."

"I'll buy you a pony when your legs get a little longer." He patted her in an absent-minded fashion.

"Tell me about the servants," Miss Mattie asked. "I believe your Viola knows my cook."

"Viola has been with us a long time. She is part Indian, part white, and part Negro. My wife thought she exemplified the best qualities of all three races, and our children have derived a great store of comfort from that warm lap of hers. I think you'll find she is easy to get along with. In the neighborhood, she has the reputation of a healer."

"What does she heal?"

"Various and sundry things, but warts are her specialty. Her grandmother was a full-blooded Cherokee, and she taught Viola how to make a poultice using medicinal plants that is said to get rid of most skin afflictions. She also makes an herbal tea out of rose hips that my wife swore by. She said it cured a sore throat."

Miss Mattie, thinking how horrified Dr. Craig would have been at these primitive remedies, lowered her gold-rimmed spectacles and became, for a minute, the interviewer. "Do you and your children rely on this herbal healing?" she asked.

"No, we rely on a doctor and try very hard not to get sick, but we drink the tea."

"And your cook. Is there anything I should know about your cook?"

"Roxie has been with us twelve years. She is a fine cook and a hard worker. She and Viola, together, keep the house clean. The laundress and the yardman come in twice a week. The house runs smoothly, but I need a lady of character and kindness to see to the overall well-being of my children."

Suddenly, Agnes sat up straight, knit her brows, and pierced Miss Mattie with the bright blue eyes she had inherited from her father. "Are you a Presbyterian?" she demanded.

It was so unexpected that the two adults laughed, and Agnes, clearly hoping to be twice funny, repeated the question.

"I was brought up a Baptist," Miss Mattie said, not wanting to admit that under Dr. Craig's influence, she had not been to church in years.

The laughter eased the atmosphere, and Morgan began to speak less formally. "Miss Mattie, when I was seven, my parents went to China as missionaries and left me with my grandfather. I will always remember the anguish I felt at their departure. I like to believe that had they known the pain I suffered, they would not have gone. However, because of it, I understand my children's loss. My wife died over a month ago, and while this one"—he indicated the little girl on his lap—"doesn't understand the ramifications of death, Josy cries at night when she thinks no one will know. There is such a void in this house, and my children have needs that only a woman of kindness and quality can fill. I know how difficult it is to come into someone's house as a stranger, but will you try it?"

He stopped rocking and leaned toward her, and she saw the pain in his eyes. She thought of the adjustment it would take to come into this family's home, and she didn't know if she were up to dealing with other people's children and other people's servants. Then she thought about the pills and the dust motes and her sister's proclivity to speak at length of her throbbing head or her racing heart or her immovable bowels. Sister wallowed in self-pity, and Miss Mattie envied her the indulgence. She, however, was too hardheaded and too realistic to feel sorry for herself. Life had dealt her some stiff blows of late, losing Dr. Craig and losing her money, but other people had stiff blows and tough choices, too.

Morgan started to rock again, slowly and deliberately. She adjusted her chair to the motion of his.

"Mr. Bigley," she said, "all we can do is try it and see if it works."

He smiled, and she was impressed with his attractiveness. She was sure the housekeeping job would be a temporary one. The women about town would not allow this man to remain single for long.

"We will do our best," he said. "That's all we can do." Then his expression sobered. "These last few weeks have been so terrible for me and my family, but I have found solace in my religion. I would like to thank God for your coming and to ask for His guidance."

Miss Mattie was surprised. She was not used to godly men. Dr. Craig had not been religious. In fact, he had constantly criticized God for his construction of the human plumbing system—railing at the Almighty for making the "God damn apertures too small." He had maintained his criticism right up to his last kidney stone, and even during his final illness, when Miss Mattie had appealed to God for help, Dr. Craig had said, "Let it alone, Mattie. I didn't like Him much when I was well, and I don't much like Him now." Nevertheless, when Morgan suggested prayer, Miss Mattie bowed her head.

"Kind Father," he intoned, "Give us the wisdom to raise these motherless children to live happy and productive lives, and . . ."

Miss Mattie discreetly raised her head and opened her eyes. She thought how kind and earnest he looked while praying, and she was glad she was almost seventy and no longer romantically susceptible to attractive men. Then, to her horror, he opened his eyes in mid-prayer and observed her observing him. She quickly bowed her head again.

CHAPTER FOUR

THE FAMILY

Miss Mattie moved in with the Bigleys in June. She brought with her a radio, a 1929 Ford, and her clothes. The remainder of her possessions were either sold or stored with her sister. Whether her position as housekeeper worked out or not, she no longer needed much in the way of worldly goods.

She arrived on a weekday afternoon in time to unpack before dinner. Viola greeted her at the door and helped unload her car and carry the bags upstairs. Josy was nowhere to be seen, but the youngest Bigley, thumb in mouth, was lurking in the hall. Miss Mattie greeted her pleasantly, but Agnes ignored her.

"You gonna like it here," Viola said reassuringly. "It's gonna take getting used to, but you gonna like it. Mr. Morgan does right by people, and we gonna see you have a good time."

Viola's kindness brought tears to Miss Mattie's eyes. She could stand up to almost anything except kindness.

As they passed by the living room, she noticed a portrait of Emily hanging over the mantle. It was an unusually graceful picture, and she paused to admire it. Emily was wearing a deep blue dress and was seated on an antique armchair very much like the one by the fireplace. A small table by the chair held a vase of irises mixed in with what appeared to be wildflowers.

"How perfectly lovely," Miss Mattie said softly, referring to the portrait.

"That's my mother," Agnes said. "She's dead."

"It was painted from a photograph," Viola explained. "After Miss Emily passed, Mr. Morgan hired an artist to paint her picture. The artist come to the house and looked around at everything we got before he started to paint. He saw a vase of flowers I done fixed, and there it is, right there in the picture."

"You must be very proud," Miss Mattie said.

"Yes, Ma'am. I is."

Viola led the way upstairs, and Miss Mattie was pleased that her room was large and airy with a handsome bed and bureau, a comfortable easy chair, and a small desk. The bathroom, however, was at the end of the hall, and she was to share it with the girls. She was not used to sharing a bathroom with children but, fortunately, there was no contract that said she had to stay more than twenty-four hours if she didn't like it.

Viola and Agnes left her alone to unpack and settle in. She put away her clothes and fiddled in her room with the door closed until six o'clock, the Bigleys' dinner hour. When she emerged, Morgan greeted her at the foot of the stairs and escorted her to the dining room, which, like the living room, overlooked the veranda and Emily's garden.

Someone—Miss Mattie thought it must have been Viola—had put an arrangement of roses on the table. The flowers, the view of the garden, and three bright paintings of Parisian scenes above the sideboard, offset the pomposity of the massive Victorian table. The silver candelabras, she noted, were very nice but no nicer than the two she had just sold.

Morgan held out her chair and, after he and girls were seated, said the blessing. This time she did not look up and, in the event he was observing her and praying at the same time, she tried to look, at least, moderately holy.

As soon as he said "Amen," she commented on how happy she was to be dining with such an attractive family.

"We're glad you're here," Morgan said, and he did not elaborate. Unlike her late husband, he wore his suit and tie to the evening meal. The girls wore shorts and both of them looked sullen. She suspected they resented her presence and particularly her presence in their mother's chair. She didn't blame them, but their mother was dead. That was a fact, and facts were what you had to learn to live with as cheerfully as possible.

As Viola passed the chicken, Miss Mattie tried again. "My!" she said, beaming at everyone, "but this looks good. Chicken's my favorite!"

Morgan looked as if he were trying to smile but found the process too painful to complete. Josy said nothing, Agnes transferred a wad of bubblegum from her mouth to her butter plate, and Miss Mattie produced an Irish linen handkerchief from the sleeve of her blouse and twisted it.

A lengthy silence ensued until Agnes decided to test the newcomer with a few time-honored riddles. However, this was an area in which the housekeeper was so knowledgeable that Agnes, in a follow-up to "Why does the chicken cross the road?", turned to invention. Assuming an expression of great cunning, she asked, "Why does Papa wear a belt?"

"To hold his pants up, stupid," Josy said. "That's not a joke."

Agnes thought for a moment. "No, he wears it to hold his legs up." This answer tickled her five-year-old funny bone so convulsively that it took her a few minutes to regain equilibrium.

Miss Mattie broke the next silence by saying, "I know a riddle, but it's a real one, and it takes brains to answer it. Can anyone at this table tell me what you can hold with your left hand that you can never hold with your right?"

The girls made numerous stabs at a correct answer, but Morgan silently ate his dinner and seemed to withdraw to some remote place far away. Their efforts toward a solution lasted almost throughout the meal, and then, just as Viola was bringing in the dessert, Morgan smiled widely and said "Aha!" Doubling up his arm, he pointed his right elbow first toward Josy and then toward Agnes.

Miss Mattie, happy to see this side of his personality, laughed out loud, and suddenly the light of understanding radiated from Josy's face. "Your elbow," she shouted. "You can't hold your right elbow with your right hand," and she, too, was laughing.

"As I live and breathe," Miss Mattie exclaimed. "How did you ever figure that out so quickly? You're the smartest family I ever had dinner with." Viola, hovering in the doorway between the pantry and the dining room, beamed with happiness, and only Agnes wore a dark expression.

"It's not a very good riddle," Agnes said.

ℂℂ

That night, after everyone had gone to bed, Miss Mattie's sharp ears picked up the sound of low muffled sobs. She listened as long as she could stand it before tiptoeing to the girls' room. Agnes had gone to sleep, but Josy was lying on her stomach with her face buried in her pillow and her shoulders shaking. Miss Mattie sat down on the bed and gently stroked the girl's back as she spoke softly of sorrow and loss.

"When Dr. Craig died," she whispered, "I thought the end of the world had come. I thought I would never laugh again, or feel sunshine, or taste chocolate pie, or go to the movies. My hair turned gray overnight, and my face wrinkled up like a prune. But the world kept right on spinning and spinning, and after a while, it didn't hurt so much."

She kept on stroking and talking until the little girl's shoulders were still. When she appeared to be sleeping, Miss Mattie crept back to her room. Before she got back in bed, she heard Josy get up and pad down the hall to the bathroom. She stood motionless in her doorway and watched as the girl turned on the light and scrutinized her reflection in the mirror above the sink, examining her face closely and holding up a few strands of hair. A surge of affection for this lovely child suffused Miss Mattie's being as she observed the girl looking for telltale and unattractive signs of grief. Soon after that, the nightly crying petered out.

After a few weeks, the Bigley household resumed a little of its normal routine. Miss Mattie, who jerkily drove her '29 Ford as if she were applying rickrack braid to the road, performed all those household tasks requiring wheels. Roxie prepared a variety of dishes for the evening meals and conversation at the dinner table became so lively that Morgan frequently invited friends to Friday night suppers.

The housekeeper enjoyed entertaining but was often bewildered by the disciplinary aspects of her career. Should she tell Morgan that sometimes after school, Josy and her friends hid out behind the garage to smoke rabbit tobacco from pipes made from acorns and bamboo stems? She asked Viola's advice, and Viola said, "They ain't gonna burn nothing up. So long as they think they're doing something bad, they'll be careful." So she turned a blind eye to the smoking and also to the wads of gum that Agnes stuffed under chairs, having decided that if anybody crossed Agnes in matters other than life and death, it would have to be her father or her nurse.

Some of the little girls smoking in the back woods were from the town's wealthiest families while others wore the faded dresses of the depression child. Josy made no distinctions and got along with everybody except Agnes, who was an embarrassment to her. "To think," she complained to Miss Mattie, "I have only one sister, and she is a fat little sissy."

It was true. Agnes was a sissy. She cried if Blossom jumped on her and flew into Viola's arms at the sight of blood. This behavior irritated Josy to the point that she could barely stand to stay in the same room with her.

∞∞

On summer evenings, the girls played hide-and-seek with neighborhood friends in the wooded area behind the house. The high pitch of their voices reflected the excitement of dark shadows over familiar landscape. Agnes, the youngest player, always crouched behind the same big oak where, shivering with anticipation, she remained until discovered. One night, all the children went home and left her hovering behind the tree. When she realized she had been forgotten, an unmanageable lump formed in her throat, and she ran inside to the kitchen and threw herself into Viola's arms.

That night, when Morgan came to her room to hear her prayers, Agnes asked God to punish Josy and her friends for forgetting her. "Send them all to hell, God," she prayed, "and don't let them come back."

She had expected her father to express disapproval at this particular innovation to the nightly ritual, but to her surprise, he was laughing. It made her so happy to see Papa laugh that she forgot to be mad at Josy and her friends. Instead, she laughed herself, and in an attempt to prolong the happiness, she repeated, "Send them all to hell, God, and don't let them come back."

∞∞

The advent of fall put an end to the evening games. After supper, Agnes played checkers or Old Maid with Morgan or Miss Mattie while Josy rushed through her homework. After Agnes had settled down for the night, Josy went to Miss Mattie's room, climbed up on her bed, and the two of them listened to "Gang Busters," or "I Love Adventure," or the Lux Radio Theater on the radio.

Downstairs, Morgan listened to the ball game or read, always preferring to sit in the living room with the portrait of his wife than sitting alone in his den. He remembered the blue dress so well. The back had had hooks, and it had been his job to fasten them before a party. And then he remembered how at the end of an evening he had fumbled as he released them, and how, when he had kissed the back of Emily's neck, she had trembled.

∞∞

That fall, a pretty lady, who lived down the street, took Agnes to see a Shirley Temple movie and, at some point during the singing of "On the Good Ship Lollipop," Agnes underwent a sea change. She deserted her old direct ways and became a coy, flirtatious, and infinitely saucy little girl. It didn't matter that she was too fat or that her hair was straight and brown because, in her mind's eye, she was all blond curls, dimples, and smiles, and she acted accordingly. It truly annoyed Josy, and even Viola was heard to say, "Honey, you do better when you acts yourself."

It was the custom for the girls to perform when relatives or friends came to call. Josy stood on her head or did cartwheels, and Agnes, prior to the Shirley Temple movie, gave deadpan recitations of nursery rhymes. However, after undergoing the personality change, Agnes took to rolling her eyes, wrinkling up her nose, and swinging her arms rhythmically as she recited "Twinkle, Twinkle Little Star" to a captive audience. Josy found her little sister's performance so repugnant that she took her aside and taught her a new poem, one that was making the rounds of the neighborhood.

One Sunday, Ruth and Naomi Bigley joined the family for the midday meal. They were Bigley cousins who had just returned from spreading the gospel in the Orient. They had not seen the girls since Emily's death, and Naomi, the more effusive of the two, held out her arms and cried,

"Lambs! Poor motherless lambs!" She embraced first Josy and then Agnes, grinding one motherless head into her bosom and then the other.

During the meal, the missionaries spoke of their work in the Orient and the joy of bringing Christ to the heathen. They said that when the end came, their converts would reside in heaven right along side their own kith and kin.

As they were finishing dessert, Ruth asked if the girls had developed some special talent they would like to exhibit. "I know," Ruth said, "there must be some little something you girls do particularly well. Perhaps you know a poem or a verse from the Bible."

Josy vowed she didn't do anything well, but Agnes said, "I know a poem."

"That's wonderful," Naomi said. "Our little lamb is going to give us a recitation. Now stand up straight, Agnes, and speak out so we can hear every word."

Agnes got up from the table and moved away from it so she would have plenty of room for dramatic play. Then feeling, adorably saucy and dimpled, she began to swing her arms vivaciously as she launched into:

> Rickety, rackety, rust
> Papa don't like me to cuss.
> But damn it to hell
> I like it so well
> I got to do it or bust.

A shocked gasp and then a profound silence followed the recitation. Ruth was the first speak. "And where did you learn that bit of irreverence?" she demanded, pointing her finger at the performer.

And Agnes, looking the missionary dead in the eye, replied, "Miss Mattie taught it to me."

Another shocked gasp followed this obvious example of false witness, and Agnes was in deep trouble. Morgan gave her a lecture on misrepresenting facts, and Viola took her aside and demanded, "What you mean by spreading tales about a nice lady like Miss Mattie?"

Agnes did the only thing she could think of to do which was to cry loudly and lustily, building in volume as she went along. "I miss my mama," she sobbed. "I miss my mama."

Viola swooped her up in her arms, and the missionaries shook their heads sadly. "Poor, poor little lamb," Naomi crooned.

Later, in the kitchen, when all had quieted down, Roxie said to Viola, "That little girl is leading you down the garden path."

"Agnes is all right," Viola said. "She ain't used to Miss Mattie, and she don't like change, but she's all right."

"She's gonna have more change than Miss Mattie," Roxie said.

"What you mean?"

"I mean Mr. Morgan done ask that pretty lady that took Agnes to the movies to supper."

Viola put her hands on her hips and looked at Roxie as if she were crazy. "If you mean Miss Beverly Brown, Mr. Morgan ain't studying her. Miss Beverly ain't got but one oar in the water."

"Well, he done ask her to supper. And if he done ask her to supper, that means he's ready to court. And if he's ready to court, that means change." And with that, Roxie handed Viola a wet dish to dry.

MISS BROWN

Morgan was a bosom man. He had been one ever since a voluptuous Sunday school teacher had leaned over his shoulder to show him how to draw a cross. At the time, he was four, and forgetting about the cross, he had dropped his head against her soft fullness and closed his eyes.

"Why, Morgan," the kind lady had said. "I do believe you are tired." And she had stroked his hair.

This event of his youth served to whet his appreciation for bosoms to the extent that he was sure that a really full-breasted woman could be neither bad-tempered nor stingy. Therefore, when Miss Beverly Brown rang his doorbell one Saturday afternoon to pick up Agnes, he noted with approval that her face was lovely and her bosom enormous.

He did not know why this attractive woman was taking his five-year-old daughter to a Shirley Temple movie, but he supposed it had something to do with a loving spirit. He walked with her and Agnes out to her car where Clara Belle, her maid, was sitting in the driver's seat. He figured Clara Belle was driving because Miss Brown was one of those extremely feminine women who had never learned to handle a motor vehicle. This did not diminish his admiration and, as he held the back door open, he thanked her for her kindness and asked to, at least, let him pay for the movie and the popcorn.

"No," she said, shaking her head vehemently, "My mama told me that I am to pay."

He laughed appreciatively. What a humorous way to put aside a tedious argument over money, he thought. As he closed the car door, he realized that he really ought to do something to return her kindness, and he had a sudden brainstorm.

"I wonder," he said, speaking through the car window, "if you would have supper with us next Saturday? Nothing fancy. Just a little family style meal with Agnes, Josy, Miss Mattie, and me."

The second the invitation was out, he was sorry. He was forty years old, and she was probably fifteen years younger. It would most likely be an evening of inane small talk.

However, when she looked him in the eye and asked, "What are you having to eat?" he was again struck by her humor.

"What would you like?" he asked.

"Hot dogs and potato chips."

He laughed a little harder. The lady didn't just have a sense of humor; she was downright funny.

"We'll do the best we can," he said. "How about six o'clock?"

"Clara Belle will bring me at six," she said.

∞ ∞

Morgan asked Miss Mattie to plan a good but simple meal for the following Saturday. He explained that he had asked Miss Brown to supper only because she had been kind to Agnes and some expression of appreciation was appropriate. He said he didn't need a banquet to do this, just an ordinary family type meal that was particularly tasty.

Miss Mattie nodded to let him know that she understood there was absolutely nothing out of the ordinary about the invitation. She did not add that she knew Beverly's Brown's mother or that she was vaguely aware of some scandal connected with the family. However, when she sat down at the kitchen table with Roxie to discuss what to serve for a simple but particularly tasty meal, Roxie kept shaking her head. The Brown's maid, Clara Belle, had told Viola and Viola had told Roxie that Miss Beverly had melancholia and, consequently, was addle brained.

"I hear she ain't got good sense," Roxie said.

"Sometimes men don't care about that as much as they do about other things," Miss Mattie replied. "We'll just have a good meal and let him figure out whether or not her brain is in good working order."

☞☜

On the following Saturday afternoon, Miss Mattie's sister called her to say she had pains around her heart. "Don't worry about me," she said, her voice wavering. "I'll be fine all alone. Just check on me tomorrow. I'm so afraid of dying in the night and creating an odor. Dead people do that, you know. Even dead people who come from the best families create an odor. But don't worry about coming tonight."

"I'm coming immediately," Miss Mattie said. She packed her overnight bag and was just leaving as Morgan and Josy got back from a horseback ride fifteen minutes before the guest was due to arrive.

"I'm so sorry I'm missing the company," she said, "but Sister has had an attack of some sort. It may be nothing, but I would never forgive myself if it turned out to be serious, and I let her lie there all alone."

"Of course," Morgan said, but inwardly he groaned. Now he would have to make small talk without her help, and he was not looking forward to it. He had always relied on the ladies for that sort of thing, and without Miss Mattie, the evening took on tedious overtones.

He told Viola and Agnes to make the guest comfortable when she arrived. Then he hastened upstairs to shower and change.

Agnes greeted Miss Brown at the door. She led her into the living room and showed her the portrait. "That's my mother," Agnes said. "She's dead."

"She doesn't look it," Miss Brown said.

This remark gave Agnes pause. "It's painted from a photograph," she explained. "She was alive when they took it."

"Oh!" Miss Brown said. She sat down on the sofa opposite the picture, and Agnes sat beside her.

The afternoon sun shone through the living room double windows and lit up Miss Brown's curly, blond hair. The "V" in her lacy white blouse was low enough to show to advantage the prominent crevice, and the top button was unbuttoned. Agnes thought she looked like the cover on one of Josy's movie-star magazines.

Viola, wearing her best serving uniform, came into the living room then and explained Mr. Bigley's absence. "Now what can I get you all to drink?" she asked.

"Scotch," Miss Brown said. "I like scotch on the rocks."

Without changing expression, Viola nodded and went back in the kitchen. She realized she should have said, "May I bring you a Coca-Cola or ice tea?", but it had never occurred to her that Miss Beverly would ask for scotch. Mr. Bigley seldom partook of alcoholic beverages, but he did keep a little scotch and bourbon on hand for his male friends. And there had been times when Miss Emily had been so tired that Viola had given her a little nip on the sly, after which Miss Emily had always brushed her teeth and gargled.

"Lord! Lord!" Viola said to Roxie as she took the bottle from the cupboard, "I don't know what he's gonna think of this." She poured the scotch over ice and fixed Agnes a Coca-Cola.

"How she look?" Roxie asked.

"She gonna get pneumonia. She ain't but half dressed. I declare. It's right pitiful."

"How come it's pitiful?"

"Well, Clara Belle says that ever since Miss Beverly come back from the crazy house acting like a child, her mama been stuffing her in low-cut dresses and sending her up here so Mr. Bigley can get a good look at her tits."

"Looks like it's working; don't it?" Roxie said. "Now you better get in there and see how it's going. He's coming downstairs."

Morgan, pleasantly pink from his shower, entered the living room with his hand outstretched. "My! My!" he said, "It's so good of you to come. We appreciate . . . I mean I appreciate how kind you have been to Agnes."

Even though she was sitting down, Miss Brown's bosom bounced up and down with the force of his handshake. He tried not to watch.

Viola came into the living room to pass the drinks, and Morgan asked what Miss Brown was drinking.

"It's scotch," Viola said. "Miss Beverly wanted scotch."

Uncomfortable at the prospect of entertaining a strange lady, he decided to desert his Presbyterian principles. "Well," he said, "in that case, I believe I will have a little of the same."

Again, Viola did not change expression, but she went back to the kitchen and commented to Roxie, "It's gonna be a hot time in the ole town tonight."

Morgan's experience with alcohol had always been that it befuddled his thinking and was therefore to be avoided. Even cough medicine made him light-headed. Tonight, however, he needed something to help him through the evening. He was good at speech making but poor at chitchat, but he did not fault himself for this. Indeed, he felt it was only natural for an intelligent person to have difficulty talking about nothing.

Viola brought him his drink, and he gingerly took a sip. Almost immediately he felt light-headed. Nevertheless, he decided it might be a clever move to make a toast. He raised his glass. "To Shirley Temple," he said, "who brought us together."

"Who?" Miss Brown asked.

Morgan blushed. He sensed that his attempt at cleverness had been a mistake, and he endeavored to rectify the error. "Agnes tells me that she very much enjoyed the Shirley Temple movie you took her to or, to be grammatically correct, to which you took her."

Miss Brown refrained from comment. Morgan took a larger sip of scotch. "It was kind of you to take her."

"Yes," Miss Brown said. A long silence ensued in which Morgan almost finished his drink. "She is a remarkable little actress," he said.

"Who?" Miss Brown asked again.

Morgan felt that perhaps the scotch had done him in. "Why, Shirley Temple, of course."

"Yes," Miss Brown said.

Suddenly Morgan began to see a little dark humor in the situation. He, who hated small talk, had invited a pretty lady with a remarkable bosom to dinner, and she was practically a mute. Didn't she know about conversation? Didn't she know that after he threw her a sentence, she was supposed to throw one back? Did she think that all she had to do was sit there and heave her chest?

Well, he would wait it out. She could make the next move. He waited.

Finally, Miss Brown said, "She doesn't look dead."

"Who doesn't?" he asked.

"Your wife," Miss Brown said, looking at the portrait.

"It is a very lively picture," Morgan said stiffly, feeling that the situation was worsening. The woman obviously had no gift at all for conversation, a social grace he had heretofore undervalued. He supposed he would have to talk about the weather, but what could be said about early fall in Georgia other than it was still hot? He could not bring himself to be so trite. A long and painful silence ensued, which was finally broken by Agnes.

"You forgot to button your top button," Agnes said, looking at Miss Brown.

"My mother likes it that way," she responded, but she buttoned the blouse.

Morgan laughed uneasily. The lady had a sense of humor, albeit an unusual one. It was rude of Agnes to call her attention to the errant button, but he supposed that if the silences got any worse, they might ask each other any number of unmannerly questions.

Another silence followed that was so long that it broke Morgan's resolve. "It's still very hot," he said.

"Yes," Miss Brown responded.

Morgan excused himself, went to the foot of the stairs, and called Josy to come down and meet their guest. He then went to the kitchen, told Roxie to hurry it up, and asked Viola to give him another scotch.

When he sat back down and observed Miss Brown sitting across from his wife's portrait, he suspected that Emily might be having a good laugh in heaven. It would probably amuse her to see how difficult it was for him to make conversation with women. He was so pathetic that it almost amused him.

When Viola announced that dinner was ready, he shot to his feet as if a firecracker had gone off in his seat. Leaving his second drink by his chair, he led the way to the dining room where it was obvious Viola had gone to a lot of trouble in setting the table. She had arranged a centerpiece of garden roses, polished the candelabras, lit the candles, and put out Emily's best Haviland china. Before they sat down, Agnes said that she wanted to sit next to the guest and suddenly Miss Brown seemed to relax. "Agnes and I are friends," she said.

When everyone was seated, Morgan bowed his head and launched into a particularly leisurely blessing. He found it easier to pray than to talk, and he regretfully said "Amen" only after he had thanked God for every bit of good fortune he could summon to mind.

When he finished praying, Miss Brown leaned forward in her seat and said brightly, "Maybe she's a midget."

"What?" Morgan asked.

"Maybe she's a midget," Miss Brown repeated.

"Who?"

"Who what?" Miss Brown asked.

Morgan was sure the alcohol had completely destroyed his brain cells. "Who is a midget?" he asked.

"Shirley Temple, of course."

He could only nod.

"She dances so beautifully," Miss Brown said.

"Yes," Morgan replied.

The conversation about Shirley Temple wound down as abruptly as it came up, and there was no more small talk until Josy reminded her father that he needed to call the blacksmith.

"Oh," Miss Brown said, "Every time I hear the word blacksmith, I think of my favorite book which is Black Beauty. Have you read it, Josy?"

Miss Brown did not allow an opportunity for response. "I've read it over and over," she continued, "and each time I read it, I cry. I once had a horse that looked just like Black Beauty. I rode him all over the countryside, and sometimes we jumped ditches that must have been ten feet wide."

She paused for a moment and looked directly at Morgan. "Have you ever jumped ditches that must have been ten feet wide?" she asked, but again she didn't wait for a reply. She went on and on about her adventures with her horse, stopping occasionally to pose a question but never waiting for the answer. The monologue ended with the animal's death and the extent of Miss Brown's grief.

"When my horse died," she said, "I cried harder than I cried when Papa died." There was a long pause during which the guest looked intently at Morgan. "Did you cry hard when your wife died?" she asked, and this time she waited for an answer.

Morgan bowed his head. "Yes," he said.

A pall fell over the supper table. Morgan stared at his plate, and Miss Brown withdrew behind an invisible curtain.

"Ain't you gonna eat a little something, Miss Beverly?" Viola asked as she was clearing the table, but Miss Brown stared straight ahead, as rigid as a washboard.

After dessert, Morgan and Agnes walked the company home. It was a pleasant walk past comfortable houses, lovely lawns, and tall trees, but Morgan walked fast, anxious to discharge his guest as soon as possible.

Clara Belle greeted them at the door. "It was mighty nice of you to have Miss Beverly to dinner," she said. "I know she appreciates it." Then she added, "Tell 'em you had a good time, honey, and come on in."

From inside the house, a female guttural voice said, "Ask the gentleman in, Clara Belle."

"Good-bye," Morgan said, pretending he didn't hear.

It had cooled off enough to be balmy, and Morgan and Agnes took the long way home. The air smelled sweetly of neighborhood flowers, and the crickets and katydids and frogs were tuning up in preparation for their nightly symphony.

Morgan slowed down to a leisurely pace. "Agnes," he said, "I believe your friend has some problems."

"I know," Agnes said. "She has the lapses."

"What do you know about the lapses?" he asked.

"She just forgets things. Clara Belle told me all about it."

"Honey, it makes me nervous for you to go to the movies with somebody who forgets that much. She might forget to bring you home."

"She can't forget, Papa. Clara Belle drives us to the movies. Then we sit downstairs, and Clara Belle sits in the balcony. Clara Belle says for me to come get her if Miss Brown acts funny."

"I see," Morgan said. "I guess Clara Belle is pretty nice."

"She's real nice. She fixed us cookies and milk after the movies."

They walked for a while in silence. Then Agnes said, "Papa, old Mrs. Brown is mean as hell."

"Agnes, don't talk like that."

"Well, that's what Clara Belle told Viola."

"Agnes, when you hear that kind of talk, don't repeat it. That conversation was between Clara Belle and Viola."

"Yes, Papa."

They were almost home before Morgan reopened the conversation. "I do wonder what would bring Clara Belle to say such a thing and how you happened to hear it. I wouldn't think they would talk about that kind of thing in front of you."

"They didn't," Agnes said.

"Well, how did you hear it?"

"Viola and Roxie were changing the sheets in your room, and I heard Viola say that Miss Brown wanted to marry somebody that old Mrs. Brown didn't like. So old Mrs. Brown locked her up in the bedroom and wouldn't let her out. Then Miss Brown took too many aspirin and got real sick, so old Mrs. Brown sent her off to the crazy house in Milledgeville."

"Oh my!" Morgan said. "Oh my!"

When they got back to the house, Agnes went upstairs to look at her books and Morgan went in the kitchen. Roxie had gone home, but Viola was still there, putting away the last of the china.

"Viola," he said, "For a while there, I thought I had too much scotch."

"You didn't have much, Mr. Morgan. It was mostly water."

"You watered down my scotch."

"Yes, sir."

"Viola, did you know about Miss Brown?"

"Well, me and Clara Belle knowed each other for a long time."

"Why didn't you tell me about her?"

"I didn't think it was my place."

Morgan locked eyes with Viola. "I would never ask you to make quick judgments about a guest in my home, but if there is anything I ought to know, I should be told."

"Yes, sir," Viola said.

"And if ever again someone with a mental problem comes in contact with my children, please inform me."

"Yes, sir."

"And the next time I order scotch, assuming there is a next time, please don't . . ." He stopped in mid-sentence. "Never mind," he said. "Have a pleasant evening."

Later that night, Morgan went to Agnes's room to say good night and to hear her prayers. This was a practice he had established since Emily's death because Emily would have wanted him to do it and because Agnes needed direction in how to pray. She was all too prone to use the nightly ritual as an opportunity to beseech God to retaliate against anyone on her blacklist. On one occasion, she had asked Him to please help Miss Mattie fall down the stairs, and on another she had asked Him to please help Josy's horse throw Josy in the ditch. He had spoken to her about love and forgiveness and tonight, at his suggestion, they added Miss Brown, old Mrs. Brown, and Clara Belle to the list to be blessed. In so doing, he felt he was demonstrating a fine spirit and also bringing closure to a perfectly horrible evening. He doubted if he would ask another lady to dinner anytime soon even if he found one with bosoms the size of meal sacks. Then, feeling at peace with the world, he kissed Agnes good night and went downstairs to read the evening paper. He was deep into the news when Miss Mattie came home

"I didn't have to stay," she said. "Sister thought she was having a heart attack, but it was only indigestion. Has your guest gone home so soon?"

"Yes," he said, and he barely looked up from the paper.

"I trust the meal was satisfactory."

"The meal was fine."

"Beverly Brown is so pretty," Miss Mattie commented.

Morgan put down the paper. Then he took off his spectacles and wiped them off. Finally, before putting them back on, he spoke. "Under the circumstances, the evening went well. I think we did the right thing by having Miss Brown to dinner. It was the Christian thing to do."

"Yes, indeed, "Miss Mattie said. "I am sure it was."

CHAPTER SIX

THEODOSIA

Handsome and well-to-do, Morgan was easily the best catch in town. The single women came after him in droves, and Louisa Jones led the pack. Hardly a day went by that she didn't drop by the Bigley house to ask about the girls or to visit with Miss Mattie or, her cookies having failed, to bring Morgan a little divinity candy.

Viola and Roxie discussed the situation in the kitchen. "Them ladies is jumping over Mr. Bigley like fleas," Viola said.

Roxie disagreed. "They more like ticks than fleas. Fleas hop around and don't amount to much. These ladies aim on settling in and getting fat. And one of them is gonna do it because Mr. Morgan's got the honey britches for somebody, but he don't know who."

Roxie was right. Morgan wanted a woman in the worst way, but not a woman like the eager, eligible ladies who were hot after him. He wanted a girl like Emily had been fifteen years before—someone young, wistful, and unsettled—someone who would make him feel alive again.

He tried to speak to O'Brian about it at the office. O'Brian raised his eyebrows, put his feet up on Morgan's desk, and said, "My wife's got a good-looking cousin she wants you to take out."

"Isn't that the one with the false teeth?" Morgan asked.

"Have a heart," O'Brian said. "It isn't as if they rotted in her head. She had an accident when she was a teenager. However, if you prefer a woman with her own teeth, we'll find you one."

Morgan lowered his glasses and regarded his partner. "I prefer," he said, "a woman who has her own everything."

O'Brian shook his head. "With women you never know. But I hear there's a cathouse over in the next county where they have all of their body parts in all shapes and sizes."

But Morgan wasn't interested in brothels. His life revolved around family, church, work, and his horses. He had an itch, but it would have to remain unscratched.

Work was his salvation, and he drove himself at the office, allowing no time for brooding. For recreational purposes, he and O'Brian bought nine hundred acres each of adjoining property on the far side of the river. They wanted a place for hunting and riding that would be beautiful, private, and nearby.

His practice took him to New York City for a few days each month, where he hated the noise and the push and shove of people in the street. He couldn't understand how humans could live and work so close together, coming in and out of buildings like angry hornets. He was always anxious to get back home until one evening something happened to change his attitude.

That evening, Morgan had been invited to a large dinner party being held at a posh New York hotel. His host, Carter James, was a valued business client and, for that reason, he accepted the invitation. As Morgan was not a drinker and was not much at small talk, he steeled himself for a boring evening.

He arrived late and surveyed the scene. Waiters scurried about with trays of drinks, and a small band was unobtrusively playing "Begin the Beguine." A few couples were dancing, but most of the guests stood around in groups, sipping their drinks and conversing. He didn't see a soul he knew or wanted to know.

He was wearing an extremely expensive suit from Brooks Brothers. It was the first article of clothing he had bought since Emily died, and O'Brian had pushed him into shelling out the money. "If you're gonna represent us up there in the big city," O'Brian had said, "you've got to let them rich Yankees know the South is on the rise."

Morgan didn't like expensive suits. They made him feel like a dandy, so he blamed it on the new duds when an ugly woman, holding a cigarette in one hand and a martini in the other, approached him.

The lady was lean with a clever, predatory face. She wore a black, low-cut dress that revealed a serious shortage of bosom, and Morgan didn't see anything attractive about her. However she offered to escort him to the bar, so there wasn't much he could do other than tag along. Her interest waned after he ordered a Coca-Cola, and when he spotted his host and went over to speak, she declined to accompany him.

Carter James was talking very earnestly to a full-bodied woman with black hair. He saw Morgan approach and held out his hand, exclaiming "My God! I was afraid you weren't coming. I want you to meet your dinner partner, Theodosia Boyd. Tedde, meet Morgan Bigley. He's the lawyer from the South I was telling you about."

The woman turned toward him, and he looked into a face as bright and lively and appealing as any he had ever seen. Her large, clear eyes were bluish green, and her full lips turned pleasantly up at the corners, as if she were ready to share a good joke.

"Forget Theodosia," she said, "and call me Tedde."

He stood there awkwardly, trying to think of the right thing to say and trying to figure out if she was beautiful or just attractive, plump, or just well-rounded. Finally, he blurted out; "You look as if you laugh a lot."

Her smile widened. "I think perhaps I do. And you look as if you spend a lot of time outdoors." Her voice was low and husky.

"Morgan rides horses," Carter James explained. "He's one of those Southern landholders who has a stable of horses just so he can ride over his plantation and count the cows, or the cotton bales, or the slaves."

"Do you have very many?" she asked. The twinkle in her eye belied any seriousness to the question.

"No cows, no cotton, and certainly no slaves," he said.

"But I was speaking of horses."

"Only three. One for me, a nice little pony horse for my daughter, and a side-of-the-road horse as an extra."

Her eyebrows shot up. "A side-of-the-road horse. What kind of animal is that?"

"It's an animal you see on the side of the road that you buy from a farmer cheap. It's a horse that's short on heritage and who may or may not have good character."

"I've never been on a horse," she said, "but if I ever ride one, I hope he'll have good character."

"Tedde's an actress," their host interjected.

"I've never known an actress." Morgan said.

She lowered her gaze modestly. "I'm just a side-of-the-road actress."

He didn't smile, but his eyes imparted a glint of amusement. "Well, I hope you have good character, because I'm just a simple country lawyer."

She regarded him archly. "Ah, I suspected you were just a simple, country lawyer. I could tell by the demeanor and the dress. I imagine you ordered that nice blue suit from Sears and Roebuck."

She caught him completely off guard, and he laughed and blushed at the same time. It was the first time a woman had really made him laugh since Emily died.

"My business partner makes me dress up when I come to New York," he explained. "It has something to do with upholding the honor of the South."

"I bet you do that very well."

They were interrupted by a gentleman who began a conversation with Tedde about the theater. Others joined them and, as their circle widened, Morgan had a chance to stand back and observe. He noted the delicacy with which she sipped her wine, the womanliness of her figure, and the way she leaned forward and listened intently when she was particularly interested in the conversation. But the thing that fascinated him most was the way her lips turned just slightly upward at the corners. There was something about her mouth that was both good-humored and sensual.

"You can't take your eyes off of her; can you?" Carter James said in an aside.

"She's mighty attractive," Morgan admitted. "Mighty attractive!"

"I thought you would like her. That's why I put you next to her at dinner."

"Thank you," Morgan said. "I'm grateful," and he meant it.

By the time the guests sat down at their appointed tables, Morgan was so taken with the actress that he couldn't focus on the other six people who sat around them. He knew he ought to make some kind of general conversation, but he kept forgetting.

"Are you acting now?" he asked her.

Her eyes widened. "You mean right now?"

He blushed. "I mean—are you in a play now?"

"No, but I'm auditioning for a part tomorrow."

"It must be time-consuming being an actress. Do you have a family, too?"

"I don't have children, and my husband has been dead for six years."

"I'm so sorry," he said, and he tried to disguise his delight in the demise of a husband.

At some point between the shrimp cocktail and the entree, he asked her to dance; warning her first that he wasn't much of a dancer. "My grandfather raised me," he said, "and he was a Presbyterian minister who didn't take much to dancing."

"My grandfather was a rabbi," she said.

His jaw dropped. "You're Jewish?"

"No. My mother was a Christian. I was brought up in the Episcopal Church. But I have Jewish blood of which I am proud and a Jewish cousin in Germany whom I love."

He exhaled a sigh of relief. He had nothing against Jews, but he didn't want to fall in love with one. He wanted to fall in love with a woman of his own persuasion.

"Are you religious?" she asked.

"Yes, but I wasn't always. When I was a boy, I hated God. My parents left me when I was seven and went to China to save the heathen. I blamed God for their departure. It took me a long time to make peace with my Maker."

"It was the same with me," she said. "My mother hated my father's Jewish heritage, and when they married, she changed him into an Episcopalian. I adored my grandfather and was caught in between. But I was given the part of the Madonna in the church play, and I sang solos in the choir."

She paused for a moment, and the happiness drained from her face. "I married an Episcopalian, and we had a baby, a little girl, who died. And then, later on, my husband died, and I had to believe in an afterlife. I still have to believe in one. I'm no good at forever losing the people I love, so I'm a Christian."

She paused again and, in the process, regained her former brightness. "And guess what," she said, clapping her hands, "I even serve on the altar guild."

He was entranced. He had found a woman of character, beauty, and wit. He stood up and held back her chair. "Excuse us," he said, addressing the other six people at the table. "This kind lady has promised to dance with me."

The woman sitting opposite him looked amused. "Of course," she said. "We didn't think you knew we were here."

"I'm sorry," he muttered. "I'm so sorry," and he made a mental resolution to talk to everybody at the table when he sat down. However, the minute he took Tedde into his arms, his resolve faded.

Emily had loved to dance, and she had made him learn a few steps. He had a natural sense of rhythm and, as the music was good and his partner pliable, he moved her around the floor with a fair amount of ease. As he did so, he decided she was not the least bit plump, just well-rounded.

"You're not a bad dancer," she said, "for the grandson of a Presbyterian minister. Who taught you to dance?"

"My wife."

Her face clouded. "And where is your wife?"

"She died almost two years ago … in an automobile accident."

"I'm so sorry," she said, and she softened in his arms.

When they sat down, she asked about his children. He took out his wallet and showed her a picture of Josy, and she commented on the girl's delicate beauty. Then he showed her one of Agnes who was wearing her dead earnest, no-nonsense expression, and Tedde laughed and said, "Agnes looks very resolute."

He told her about the girls and how different they were and how, after Emily died, Agnes's nurse had put him in touch with Miss Mattie. "I'm lucky to have a housekeeper who truly loves my children," he said. "She's not as good as a mother, but she wants us all to be happy. She has a lot of common sense, but she doesn't hold much stock in education. Her worst nightmare is that the girls will grow up smart and go to Vassar College. She doesn't have to worry about Josy, but Agnes might make it."

Tedde put her hand on Morgan's arm to stop him. "What has she got against Vassar?"

"Her niece went there and came back wanting to change the South and all the old ways."

"I went to Vassar," she said.

Crestfallen, he apologized. "I'm so sorry. I'm afraid I put my foot in it."

Her shoulders were shaking with laughter. "It's alright. I'm not offended. Now tell me about your plantation."

"I don't have a plantation. I've bought some worn-out fields by the river and some woods that are beautiful." And because she seemed so interested, he told her how he was going to build up his pastures and cut trails through his woods for riding. Then he told her about walking along his creek and discovering a waterfall he didn't know was there.

Right there at the table, she touched his cheek with her hand. It was an intimate gesture, and it made him blush. "I love to hear you talk about your children and your land," she said. "It makes you look so young."

They danced again, and he held her closer. She seemed to like him, and he hoped she wasn't acting. If she was, she was good at it.

The floor was crowded, and they jostled another couple. Morgan stopped and apologized, but the other gentleman was surly in his response. When they resumed dancing, Tedde whispered in his ear, "I think that man is very side of the road. No heritage and very bad character."

"And a lousy dancer," he added.

When they sat down, he asked her to lunch on the following day even though he had a meeting in the morning and an early afternoon train to catch. She accepted even though she was auditioning for a part and might have to leave before she was called.

They were the last people at their table to leave. The lady who had sat across from them smiled knowingly as she said good-bye. "I hope you don't miss us too much," she said.

Morgan insisted on escorting Tedde home. He hailed a cab, and for some reason it was a little awkward sitting alone with her in the back seat. He figured that was because he wanted to kiss her so much, and it was too soon.

When they reached her apartment building, he got out of the cab and rode the elevator with her to the third floor. As soon as she opened the door to her apartment and turned on a lamp, he said good night.

His meeting the next morning lasted longer than he had expected, and he was late for lunch.

However, she seemed as good humored as ever, and he noted with pleasure that she was as pretty in daylight as she was in the evening. Her fitted blue suit brought out the brightness of her eyes and the roundness of her figure. She said she didn't think she would get the part in the play, and over lunch, they talked about when they would see each other again.

After that, Morgan's business trips became the high point of his life, and he saw Tedde at every available opportunity. They went to the theater, the ballet, the museums, and even the opera. They took long walks and rode on top of double-decker buses. And when she got a part in an off-Broadway play, he saw it three times, which was as long as it lasted. And at some point in their relationship, he didn't know just when, New York suddenly changed from a hive of angry people to a city of light and culture.

Chapter Seven

THE GIRLS

In the spring of 1936, almost two years after Emily's death, Morgan Bigley began reading poetry. Miss Mattie found out about it because he asked her to help him find a book he had misplaced. He thought he had left it in the living room and that Viola or Roxie, both of whom had gone home for the evening, had put it away somewhere.

"What's it called?" Miss Mattie asked.

"I think it's called *The Love Song of J. Alfred Prufrock*. It's a very small book of poetry by a poet named Eliot."

"Oh, that sounds lovely!" she exclaimed. "I used to read love poetry. I was crazy about that love poem called "Annabel Lee." It was so beautiful and romantic that I memorized it. Then Dr. Craig ruined it for me."

"How did he do that?"

"He said Edgar Allan Poe wrote it while he was swinging from a lamppost dead drunk."

"That would take a lot of talent," Morgan said. "I doubt if many poets can do that. However, I don't think this is love poetry. To tell the truth, I don't understand it. When we find it, I'll read you a few lines to see if you can make heads or tails of it. It's by a very modern poet."

The two of them began combing the bookcases on either side of the fireplace. There were hundreds of books, some of which had belonged to Morgan's grandfather, and they included the complete works of Charles Dickens, Shakespeare, and even Edgar Allan Poe. Morgan spotted what he was looking for next to some books of verse that had belonged to Emily and, retrieving it from the shelf, he advised Miss Mattie to take a seat and be comfortable while he improved her mind.

Miss Mattie sat down, but Morgan remained standing. He thumbed through the pages, and when he found what he was looking for, he cleared his throat and began to read. However, when he came to the second repetition of "In the room the women come and go—talking of Michelangelo," he stopped. "What's this fellow getting at?" he asked.

Miss Mattie raised her eyes to heaven. "I have no idea. Perhaps Mr. Eliot wrote that poem while swinging from a lamppost dead drunk. Wherever did you get that book?"

"A friend of mine gave it to me. Now listen to this line. 'I should have been a pair of ragged claws scuttling across the floors of silent seas.' Why does he want to be a pair of ragged claws?"

Miss Mattie thought for a minute. "I guess he doesn't think very much of himself. Maybe, he means he might as well have been a crab."

Morgan studied his housekeeper carefully. "I think maybe you are on to something," he said. Then he took the little book upstairs to read in bed.

That same spring, Morgan bought a fancy new gramophone and started a record collection. In the evenings, when he wasn't puzzling over poetry and when he thought no one was looking, he dipped and glided around the living room to the music of Cole Porter. Miss Mattie recognized the signs of a man in love but the question was—with whom? He spent a lot of time in New York and, when at home, did not seek female companionship.

One night, as the gramophone was playing "Night and Day," he glided into the hall with his eyes half shut and a dreamy look on his face. He was so carried away with the music that he failed to notice that Miss Mattie had just come out of the kitchen and was on her way to the stairs. He executed a graceful little dip, reversed course, and then slammed into the housekeeper, almost knocking her to the floor.

They were both shaken, but Morgan more so than the housekeeper. He blushed and stuttered as he apologized. However, once he ascertained she was unhurt, he decided to brazen it out. Hoping to appear debonair, he grabbed her hand and her waist and attempted a few dance steps down the hall. It took a split second for him to realize he had made a dangerous mistake. Miss Mattie was twenty-five years his senior and was in no condition, physically or emotionally, to glide gracefully down the hall with an employer who had evidently lost his mind. They knocked knees, locked ankles, and tripped each other until the housekeeper grabbed the stair railing and cried out, "Mercy! Mr. Bigley, if you don't stop this foolishness, you are either going to kill us or maim us."

Morgan readily agreed, and while she sat in the living room recovering, he brought her a glass of water.

"Tell me," she gasped, after she had regained her composure and could breathe steadily again, "who is the lady who has brought on all this exuberance, and where are you hiding her?"

Morgan turned red and grinned broadly. "I have no idea what you are talking about," he said. "I declare, Miss Mattie! You're as hard to understand as a modern poet, but I hope you get to meet her soon."

∞∞

Even though Morgan was obviously preoccupied with new endeavors, he set great store by his daughters, spending time with them whenever possible and enjoying them for their individual qualities.

The two girls were not alike. Josy was a tomboy and had no interest in her appearance. Miss Mattie was constantly reminding her to tuck her shirttail in or to comb her hair, and if the girl knew how attractive she was, she was indifferent to it.

Agnes inherited her father's vivid blue eyes, and her face, like his, was a little too wide and her chin a little too prominent. She had the sturdy build of a fireplug, and she wore her straight brown hair pulled back on one side and fastened with an outsized ribbon. The ribbon represented Viola's attempt at beautification, and Viola frequently boasted that her baby had the biggest bow and fattest legs in town.

Josy saw more of her father than Agnes did because they rode horseback together. A vast network of trails meandered throughout the wooded hills of northwest Atlanta and, whenever possible, Morgan took Josy to The Saddle Club where he stabled his horses.

One afternoon, as they were cantering through the woods, Josy's mare, Rosebud, stepped in a hole, fell to the ground and rolled over on her rider's arm. The girl scrambled to her feet, held the reins so the horse would not step in them, and encouraged Rosebud to get up. When it was clear that the mare was sound, Josy said, "Help me back on, Papa. My arm hurts, but if we go slow, I can make it back home."

Morgan saw that her arm was broken. He made a makeshift sling out of his sweater and helped her mount. They walked their horses back to the barn and then drove directly to the hospital. Throughout the setting of the bone, Josy never complained. However, she turned the color of chalk, and her face was clammy with sweat. From that day on, Morgan often referred to his oldest daughter as his "brave little Indian" and told the story of the broken arm at every opportunity. To Agnes, the tale became increasingly odious at each telling.

Agnes had been angling for a pony since she was four years old, and on her seventh birthday, she got a black, blue-eyed Shetland named Butch. He was purchased from a farmer who demonstrated how gentle the pony was by leading him around his back yard with a puppy in the saddle. Morgan bought him on the spot, and when he described the pony to Agnes, she was delighted.

"I love him, already," she said, "but I don't like his name. I'm going to call him Black Sapphire."

On the day of Black Sapphire's arrival at The Saddle Club, Agnes, Morgan, and Josy got to the stables early, and Agnes had time to strut around the barn in her new jodhpurs and boots. She took care to avoid the mud from the previous night's rain and to tell everyone she saw what she was getting for a birthday present.

It was a lovely day. The sun had come out and gentle breezes ruffled the bright green leaves of early spring. A spirit of lighthearted anticipation permeated the atmosphere as the silver trailer advanced up the muddy road to the barns and parked in the turnaround. A newly employed groom named Jackson ran out of the barn in order to put down the ramp and lead the pony out. Agnes, seized with almost unbearable happiness, watched as a grinning Jackson and a sturdy, blue-eyed Shetland pony stood in the open door of the trailer. A few people clapped as the groom, holding the halter rope rather loosely, started down the ramp. The pony, however, did not budge. He looked as if, having emerged from his confinement and having surveyed the surrounding territory, he did not like what he saw.

Feeling a second tug on the rope, he laid back his ears, bared his teeth, and lunged for the seat of Jackson's pants. The groom dropped the halter rope and catapulted down the ramp.

The animosity of the pony and the alacrity with which Jackson abandoned his post drew gasps of surprise from the onlookers. Jackson, holding the seat of his pants, mumbled something about how there was nothing meaner than a blue-eyed horse and ambled off as if his part of the drama was over.

"I'll get him out," Josy said, and with the aid of a piece of apple held flat in her hand and soft, comforting words, she led the stocky little black pony down the ramp.

"Do you think he'll bite me?" Agnes asked.

"No," Morgan said. "I think he's just nervous. This is a new place for him."

Morgan took the halter from Josy and stood by Black Sapphire as Agnes tentatively approached. Her blue eyes were troubled but full of love as they met the blue eyes of the pony. "I love you," she said. "You're going to be my best friend, but I don't like your name. I'm going to call you Black Sapphire because you're so beautiful."

She cautiously held out her hand in order to bestow a love pat on the new arrival. "I love you," she crooned.

Black Sapphire watched her approach, one ear forward and the other back. As soon as she was close enough to give him the love pat, both ears went flat, and he displayed a mouthful of very large teeth. As he lunged for Agnes, Morgan shouted "Cut that out," jerking him back just in time.

"He doesn't like me," Agnes wailed. "Black Sapphire doesn't like me. I don't want to ride today."

"Maybe, he doesn't like his new name," Josy said. "Maybe he prefers to be called Butch."

"His name is Black Sapphire," Agnes said. "And I'll ride next week."

Morgan suggested that Josy ride the pony around the ring and see how he behaved. Butch was bridled and saddled, and then Josy, letting her feet dangle below the stirrups, had him walk and then jog around the ring without incident.

"Now you get on," Morgan said to Agnes, "and I'll lead you until you get the feel of it. The man who sold him to me put a puppy on his back and led him around his yard."

Josy got off, and Agnes, with the enthusiasm of someone entering icy water, mounted. Morgan adjusted her stirrups and then led her and the pony six times around the ring. After the sixth time, they broke into a jog, splattering a little mud in the process. Agnes bounced painfully up and down, but did not complain.

"Good girl," Morgan said. "You're doing just fine. Now you take him around the ring by yourself."

"All right, Papa. I'll do it, but you stay close by."

Her father walked over to the gate to stand by Josy and watch. Butch went halfway around the ring and then stopped.

"Give him a nudge," Morgan shouted. "Kick him with your heels."

Agnes gingerly kicked. "Come on, Black Sapphire," she said. "I love you. You're my best friend."

The pony turned and jogged toward the center of the ring. In mid-jog, he gave a little buck that sent his rider flying off his back and into the mud, where she sat, loudly wailing, her new outfit covered with wet Georgia clay. Black Sapphire nonchalantly ambled over to the side of the ring and nibbled a little grass underneath the railing.

Morgan rushed over and knelt down beside his daughter. He saw no signs of injury, and judging by the healthy volume of her screams he surmised her feelings were impaired but not her body. When he tried to make a joke out of the situation by suggesting they inspect the pony to see if he were hurt, Agnes stopped crying long enough to express her outrage.

"I hope he broke his leg" she wailed, "and has to get shot!"

Her father countered with, "I'd like to see you get back on and show him you're the boss. I'll be right there beside you, leading you all the way."

"No!" Agnes screamed. "I hate that pony! Sell him, Papa. Sell him!"

Josy came out to the center of the ring to get Butch, and Agnes took a big hunk of mud and threw it at her. It spattered and fell yards short of its mark. Then she took another hunk of mud and aimed it at her father. It caught him on his shirtfront, but he ignored the insult.

"Come on," he said. "We'll put the pony up and go home."

Agnes blubbered the entire drive back, her wailing interrupted by only two sentences spoken between Morgan and Josy.

"I guess that puppy the farmer put on Butch's back can ride better than Agnes," Josy taunted.

And Morgan responded gruffly, "Leave it alone."

When they got home and Viola saw Agnes in her muddy new clothes, she threw up her hands and exclaimed, "What happened to my baby!"

Morgan silenced her with a look and said, "Let's not make too much of this."

That night at dinner, the incident was not mentioned until Agnes brought it up, herself. "That pony's mean. He scared Jackson and chased him out of the trailer." And then she added, "Jackson's a sissy."

"It takes one to know one," Josy said.

Agnes began to snivel, and Josy said, "Ha! Ha! You're soft, and I'm hard."

Later on, Morgan took his oldest daughter aside and said, "Except for your relationship with Agnes, you're a lovely person. I want you to work on that area; it needs improvement."

"I can't help it," Josy said. "There is something about her I just naturally detest."

"She's almost six years younger than you. Be a little kinder."

"All right, Papa. I won't call her names anymore, but that was a good little pony."

For weeks after Butch was sold, Josy avoided looking at Agnes. If circumstances forced a face-to-face encounter, she screwed up her face as if she were inhaling a particularly malodorous pile of manure.

Although Agnes was a failure as a horsewoman, she had one redeeming quality that was uncovered at school when her teacher, having noticed that her head was always buried in a book, asked her to share what she was reading with the class. To everyone's surprise, she stood up and read *The Little Mermaid* out loud, displaying as she did so, a flair for drama that amused her teacher and impressed the students. Her reading was so far above grade level that pretty soon she was reading to the students on a regular basis.

When Morgan found out about this accomplishment, he grinned with pleasure and pride, and even Josy had to admit her sister was good for something. Viola, however, was proudest of all and was fond of saying, "My baby is so smart her teacher's got her teaching all them other children."

◌◌◌◌

The household ran smoothly under the guidance of Miss Mattie and Viola, and the days and months went uneventfully by. No one knew if or how much the girls missed their mother. Although Josy sometimes tended Emily's garden, she was a stoic and kept her own council. Agnes seemed to have forgotten Emily altogether, but she was curious about the role of a mother in a family.

A frail, timid little girl moved into the house next door. Her name was Joanna, and she and Agnes became best friends. One day in early summer, when just the two of them were playing out back, Agnes asked Joanna if she liked her mother better than her father.

The question seemed to distress the new little friend. "I don't know," she stammered. "I think I like them both the same."

Hands on hips, brows knitted, and looking Joanna dead in the eye, Agnes demanded a better response. "You better tell," she said. "If you don't tell, I'm going to make a big, bad, ugly man come and get you in your bed at night."

The little girl went home in tears, but she never told.

One hot afternoon later in the summer, Joanna went home early because she wasn't feeling well. Nobody thought anything about it until Miss Mattie received a phone call the next morning. After that call, a sense of impending doom enveloped the house like an unhealthy fog. Miss Mattie, Roxie, and Viola spoke in whispers and communicated fear with their eyes. Joanna had contracted polio.

"When will she be back to play?" Agnes asked.

"I don't know," Viola said. "I don't know."

"Will I catch it?"

"No, baby. Viola ain't gonna let you catch it," and she rocked Agnes on her lap.

Viola prepared a special tea made of rose hips and mint, which she said would protect the girls. Miss Mattie was always nervous when Viola practiced medicine, but she, too, drank the tea.

The fear and the heat intensified as more and more cases of polio were reported in the city. The public pools closed down, and children were encouraged to stay away from crowded places. Joanna was very ill, and there were rumors she might never walk again.

One night Morgan came home from the office and called Miss Mattie, Roxie, and Viola into the living room for a conference. "I want to get my girls out of the city," he said, "so I have rented a large cabin on an island in Maine. It's a big cabin, and I'll be having a guest join us soon after we get there. We leave next week."

CHAPTER EIGHT

MAINE

A week later, Morgan installed the family, plus Jay Hightower, a great nephew of Miss Mattie's, on a windswept island off the coast of Maine. There were no cars on the island, but twice a week a boat delivered mail and took the islanders to the mainland for supplies. Morgan stayed just long enough to help the family stock up on essentials, and then, having concluded that the setting was conducive to his children's good health, took off for New York.

The house was large and rustic with a huge front porch overlooking the craggy shoreline. Behind it was a small cottage for Viola and Roxie. The nine-mile island was inhabited by five other families and seagulls.

Right off the bat, Josy and Jay, who were both thirteen, befriended a pair of fourteen-year-old twins named Muffin and Molly. The four of them sailed every day in the twins' boat or played tennis on a cement court in their backyard. Agnes was always left behind.

As usual, she fell back on Viola for companionship. The water was too cold for swimming, so the two of them explored the woods and scoured the beaches for little pieces of salt-stained glass. Whenever they sat down, Viola made up a new rabbit story until one day Agnes yawned and said, "I'm sick of rabbits. Tell me a story about a lion that got loose and ate up a baby."

"I ain't gonna tell you no nasty story about no nasty lion," Viola said, and she stuck with the rabbits.

Occasionally, Agnes followed Josy and Jay over to the tennis courts and watched. She could tell they were having a wonderful time by their exuberant laughter. When she asked if she could play, the answer was always "No."

One day after tennis, she tracked the foursome into the woods. She found them lounging around on a big rock, smoking cigarettes and drinking wine stolen from the twins' kitchen. She couldn't play tennis, but smoking and drinking looked easy. With high hopes of inclusion, she approached the group and asked if she could smoke, too.

Muffin was the first to answer, "Anybody who still has a nurse is too young to hang around with us," she said. Then she pointed a stubby finger toward the cabin and shouted, "Go home!" as if she were addressing a particularly obstinate dog.

"Don't yell at my sister," Josy said. "I'm the only one who can do that."

"Except me," Jay said. "I can yell at her. I'm one of the family."

Agnes felt a great lump form in her throat. She didn't know how to deal with it, so she began to wail. She wailed and blubbered all the way back to the cabin where she found comfort in Viola's lap and Roxie's cookies. But when she told Viola about the dreadful things that Josy, Jay, and the twins were doing, Viola said, "Now don't go bringing home tales about your sister. Ain't nobody likes a tattletale."

The evenings were not as boring as the days for Agnes. After dinner, someone always lit a fire in the great stone fireplace in the living room, and Miss Mattie either read out loud or the family played checkers or Monopoly. Sometimes Agnes even won at checkers, which always triggered a feeling of well-being and happiness. And on those evenings when Miss Mattie read out loud from a humorous book called *Penrod*, Agnes laughed as hard as anyone. All in all, the evenings were quietly pleasant until mid-summer, when a package brought over on the mail boat changed everything.

When the package arrived, Miss Mattie did a little skip and clasped it to her bosom. "It's here," she said. "It's finally here." She was referring to a brand new novel, written by a friend and fellow Southerner who loved and perceived the South just as Miss Mattie and the Bigleys loved and perceived it.

That night, after dinner, Miss Mattie read out loud from the new book, and the family met Scarlett, Melanie, Ashley, and Rhett for the first time. Roxie and Viola, stationed in the doorway halfway between the living room and the kitchen, leaned forward in their chairs to listen. Josy and Jay hardly moved, and nobody remembered to tell Agnes to go to bed, so that finally she dragged herself upstairs and got under the covers with her clothes on.

After the arrival of *Gone with the Wind*, the daylight hours were charged with anticipation for the night's reading. As the story progressed, the family got more and more into it and more and more enamored with their Southern heritage. Miss Mattie reminisced about old beaus, Josy cinched in her waist to twenty inches, and Jay developed a chivalrous attitude toward all females except Agnes. Muffin and Molly, who came over every night to listen, began calling Viola "Mammy," and Agnes took up hunting "damn Yankees."

"What you looking so mean for?" Viola asked one afternoon as Agnes skulked around the woods in back of the cabin.

"Looking for a damn Yankee," Agnes said.

"What you gonna do when you find one?" Viola asked.

"Shoot him in the head," Agnes replied.

"Well, watch out he don't shoot you first."

One afternoon, when Agnes was tracking down Yankees out back, she heard a familiar voice call her name. She turned around and saw Morgan standing in the yard with a beautiful woman by his side. She ran straight to him and jumped up on him so she could hug him good.

He lifted her up in his arms, and after they were through bear hugging, he said, "I want you to meet Miss Boyd. She's a good friend of mine."

Agnes stared at the beautiful lady and noted she had jet-black hair and the merriest face she had ever seen.

"My name is Theodosia," the lady said in a deep, husky voice, "but my friends call me Tedde."

Agnes wanted to be polite, so she said, "Yes, ma'am, Miss Boyd."

The lady's laughter, full and generous but without a trace of mockery, filled the air. She put her arm around Agnes, and the little girl was suddenly overwhelmed with happiness.

"I mean, yes, ma'am, Tedde," she said.

"Tedde is an actress," Morgan said.

"Was an actress," the lady said. Then, after breathing deeply of the Maine air, she added,

"This place is like a tonic. I think it will heal my gaping wounds."

"You were good," Morgan said. "It was the play that was bad. That play would bring down Helen Hayes."

"It doesn't matter, darling. I'm through with all that now," and she leaned closer to Morgan.

∞⌒∞

Everyone in the family was struck by Theodosia Boyd's beauty.

"She looks like a real movie star," Josy said to Miss Mattie. "She's got the blackest hair I ever saw, and something about her face makes you think she smiles a lot."

Miss Mattie agreed. "Yes," she said, "there is humor written on her face as well as beauty."

Viola and Roxie had a private conversation about the visitor's hair. "What you think she puts on it?" Roxie asked.

"Shoe polish," Viola said.

"She's got the blackest hair and biggest tits I nearly ever saw," Roxie said. " Looks like Mr. Morgan favors women with big tits."

"She's got big tits, and she drinks wine," Viola said. "Mr. Morgan done bought a bottle over from the mainland, and you know what that means."

"What's it mean?" Roxie asked.

Viola's grin spread from ear to ear. "It means good times are here again."

∞⌒∞

The first night of Tedde's arrival in Maine, Miss Mattie had a moment alone with her employer, while the actress changed into something "comfortable" for supper. She used it as an opportunity to comment on the beauty of his guest.

"Yes," he agreed, "She is certainly beautiful. We met at a party in New York, and I was immediately struck by her attractiveness, but I had never met an actress before. Then I discovered she was as lovely inside as on the outside." He paused for a minute, his eyes twinkling, before adding, "I know you will appreciate the fact that she is well educated. She went to Vassar and speaks three languages."

"Oh, dear!" Miss Mattie said. "Well, at least, she doesn't look like the type to rub our noses in it."

Morgan lowered his voice. "She is an Episcopalian, but her grandfather was a Jew."

Miss Mattie kept her eyebrows in place and said nothing.

"She is extremely proud of her Jewish heritage," Morgan added.

"I think that speaks well of her," Miss Mattie said. "I like people who stick by their own folks."

"It seems," Morgan continued, "that her father converted to Christianity after marrying her mother. Tedde was brought up in the Episcopal Church, but she feels a strong loyalty to her Jewish grandfather."

"Will that interfere with your feelings for each other?" Miss Mattie asked.

"Certainly not! She is a baptized Christian and as devout as either you or I."

"Well," Miss Mattie said, smiling slightly, "That's good enough for me."

☙❧

Before dinner, Morgan, Tedde, Miss Mattie, and the young people sat on the porch to enjoy the view and to engage in polite conversation. Tedde wore orange lounging pajamas that set off her dark beauty and, due to a low neckline, revealed more bosom than the Southerners were accustomed to seeing. Agnes was so fascinated that her furtive glances prompted the actress to gather a shawl around her upper torso.

Morgan poured a glass of wine for Tedde and offered one to Miss Mattie, who, to everyone's surprise, said, "I believe I will."

"I drink two glasses of wine every night of my life," Tedde said. "It kills any infection that might be lurking around the vocal cords. An actress has to be careful of her vocal cords."

"Will you tell us about being in the theater?" Josy asked.

"Well, I've had my ups and downs," Tedde acknowledged, "but it's been a lot of fun. I had a bit part in a French movie in which Charles Boyer kissed my hand. They had to do several takes. That was one of the ups."

"Oh my!" Miss Mattie exclaimed, "I do like Charles Boyer. He's my type."

"But," Tedde continued, "my last play was a flop, and one evening a man in the audience began snoring very loudly just after my character declared her undying love for the leading man. I had to say this terrible line, which was: 'My passion for thee boils up from deep within and exceeds a storm at sea in its ferocity.'"

She spoke the line very dramatically to illustrate how she had said it in the play. Then she reproduced several loud, repugnant, and piglike snores that sent Jay, Josy, Agnes, and Miss Mattie into fits of laughter.

Tedde laughed with them and then added ruefully, "The only thing in that theater resembling a storm at sea in its ferocity were those terrible snores," and for the benefit of Agnes, who had fallen to the floor in a paroxysm of giggles, she did a few more imitations.

The family was much taken by the actress. She was new and different, and they were captivated by her merry face and lively stories. But she was more than just a good mime and good talker. She was also a good listener and, during the evening meal, she drew out each one of them, so that she learned as much about each of them as they learned about her.

After supper, Muffin and Molly came over, and Miss Mattie brought out *Gone with the Wind*. When her voice grew a little raspy, Tedde said, "Mattie, dear, why don't you rest your vocal chords and let me take over?" And from that moment on, the family knew they were in the presence of true talent. She could do Georgia, Charlestonian, Irish, and Yankee accents like a native, and she turned a fast moving Southern saga into pure theater.

At one point, she looked up from the book and noticed Roxie and Viola stationed in the doorway between the living room and the kitchen. "Why don't you come closer," she suggested, "so you can hear better?"

The two servants grinned and carried their chairs to the back of the room.

That night Muffin and Molly went home and told their mother about the beautiful lady with the magic voice. Word got out to the other islanders, and from then on there was a full house from eight to ten p.m. in the Bigley cabin.

During the day, Tedde often read fairy tales to Agnes. Once, when she was reading *The Little Mermaid*, Agnes asked if she thought the little mermaid did the right thing in giving up her voice in order to meet the prince.

Tedde paused and looked at Agnes closely. "How astute you are!" she said. Then her eyes widened and grew misty, and her voice became huskier than ever. "Yes," she answered, "but only because he was a true prince. A true prince is worth any sacrifice."

"But Tedde," Agnes said, "remember the ending. The prince marries someone else, and the mermaid throws herself into the sea."

Tedde put her arm around Agnes so that the little girl's heart jumped with happiness. "I guess he wasn't a true prince, after all," she said. "A true prince would never do that. I guess the mermaid should have had second thoughts before she gave up her finest talent."

In the afternoons, Tedde, Morgan, and Agnes took walks along the shore or in the woods. The actress had a fine singing voice, and she taught them Broadway tunes to sing as they walked. She loved the island, and she was always breathing deeply of the salt air and exclaiming how glad she was to be away from the theater. "Thank you, dear Agnes and Morgan," she said, "for inviting me to visit you in this marvelous place."

And Agnes, holding on to Tedde's hand and basking in the warmth of her touch, was more than happy to take credit for the invitation.

One morning, Morgan rented a boat and took Tedde, Josy, Jay, Miss Mattie, and Roxie out fishing. Viola and Agnes stayed home because Agnes had a history of seasickness. The two of them took a walk along the shore, and they were both in a sour mood. Viola told a story about a rabbit that was too sick to go to a party and whose best friend had to stay home to nurse him.

"I hate that story," Agnes said. "If you can't think of anything better than that, just don't tell any more stories."

"Now looker here," Viola said. "If you could hold down your breakfast, I could be on that boat fishing."

They walked home in a huff, and then Viola went to her cabin, leaving Agnes to her own devices.

Agnes got out her books and looked them over. Some of the pages were missing, but it didn't matter because she knew them all by heart. Then since she didn't have anything else to do, and since nobody would ever know, she stealthily removed *Gone with the Wind* from its special place in the bookcase.

It was a big, heavy book, and Margaret Mitchell had written "To Mattie, with love, Peggy" on the first page. Agnes didn't see anything so wonderful about that. She took the book outside and walked to the end of the dock. Then she lay down on her stomach with her head propped up on her elbows and tried to read, but there were too many big words.

The sun was hot, and she began to feel drowsy. She lay all the way down on her stomach and closed her eyes. She thought about the family out there fishing. She knew they were having a wonderful time. Without opening her eyes, she gently elbowed *Gone with the Wind* toward the edge of the dock. Nothing happened, so she elbowed it again. This time, with a quiet splashing sound, a thousand pages of blood and guts, grace and beauty, cheating, lying, and stealing slipped into the sea.

That night at supper, the family was more interested in discussing Scarlett's behavior than bragging about the fish they caught. Jay thought that Scarlett did a bad thing by marrying her sister's beau, but Josy thought that since she did it to save Tara, her actions had some merit to them. Miss Mattie and Tedde agreed that, above all, Scarlett was a spunky little rebel, but Morgan thought that, albeit she had some fine qualities, her character, on the whole, was wanting.

"She seems to totally disregard her religious training," he pointed out, "and this is surprising in that her mother set such a fine example."

"I think," Tedde said, "that Scarlett represents the physical survival of the South and Melly represents the spiritual."

"I expect you are right," Miss Mattie said. "I never would have thought of it, but I expect that's just what Peggy meant to convey."

"The two can never be separated," Morgan said. "Without our love for God, our families, and our land, and without our sense of hospitality and the courteous exchange of ideas, the South would lose its identity."

"And become just like the North," Miss Mattie added. Then, remembering that the guest lived in New York, she apologized and said, "I mean become just like the carpetbaggers after the war."

That might have ended the conversation except that Tedde looked at Agnes and said, "The real reader in this group hasn't told us what she thinks, and I would like to hear that."

"I don't like *Gone with the Wind*," Agnes said. "I liked it when we read *Penrod*," and she slunk down in her seat.

At eight o'clock, the neighbors arrived, and everyone sat down in the living room. There were not enough chairs, so the young people sat on the floor. When Tedde reached for the book, and it wasn't on the shelf, everyone thought someone was playing a joke on them. After a few minutes of guessing who took the book, Miss Mattie suggested the jokester reveal himself, and all would be forgiven. Then, after another few minutes of fooling around, a search of the house began.

Agnes searched harder than anyone. She looked under the sofa and under the chairs and in all the corners. Then she went upstairs and searched her own room. While she was there, she closed her door, turned out the light, and got in bed.

As she listened to the others still scrambling around downstairs, she wondered if a big wave would wash *Gone with the Wind* to shore, and if her fingerprints would still be on it. Finally, the neighbors left, and she heard Morgan talking, but she couldn't hear what he said.

Viola came upstairs and stood outside the closed door. "My! Oh My!" Viola said to no one in particular. "I sure am glad I'm not the one who took that book." Then she went downstairs again, and Agnes pulled the covers over her head.

The next morning, Agnes considered being sick. However, she was so hungry that she stole downstairs not knowing what to expect. She heard Viola talking to Roxie in the kitchen.

"She's different, but I like her," Roxie said.

"She's got her own ways," Viola said, "and she sticks by 'em."

Agnes went in the kitchen. Nobody seemed mad.

"Go sit down at the table," Roxie said. "I'm gonna fix you something special."

Agnes sat down at the table with Miss Mattie, Josy, and Jay. Miss Mattie said good morning very pleasantly. Her lips weren't pursed, and she didn't look mad. Everyone seemed preoccupied with the cinnamon toast and the blueberries that Viola put on the table.

Morgan and Tedde came in from their morning walk, holding hands. They sat down at the table, and Morgan looked at Agnes with his clear blue eyes that saw everything.

"You went to bed mighty early," he said.

"I was tired, Papa."

"You missed the news," he said.

"What news?" Agnes asked, knowing almost for sure that *Gone with the Wind* had washed up on shore.

"Tedde and I are getting married. She is going to be your new mother."

And at that moment, Agnes thought the news was very good, indeed.

CHAPTER NINE

RELATIVES

When the Bigleys returned to Atlanta in September, the polio epidemic was over, and life resumed its normal, easy pace. Agnes's friend Joanna had a slight limp, but she was sufficiently recovered to play the ape to Agnes's Tarzan out back behind the house.

That fall, Morgan spent more time in New York than ever. Tedde had a commitment as an understudy through November and was unable to come South until December, and then, when she came, it would be for only two weeks. Lola, her German cousin, was expected in New York for the holiday season and, as Tedde explained to Morgan, she had lived with Lola in Berlin and felt an obligation to show her around the big city.

In the interval between the return from Maine and Tedde's arrival South, Morgan hired carpenters to add a bay window and full bath to his den downstairs. He moved his desk to his bedroom and with Miss Mattie's help, he bought a pretty new bed for the den and did some decorating. "I want her to have a nice, private place to sleep," he explained to Miss Mattie as they were planning the new room, "and after we are married, I can make your room into a den and you can move downstairs."

"I don't imagine you will need me anymore after you're married," the housekeeper observed.

"Well, don't make any plans to leave me anytime soon. Tedde and I will do some traveling after we're married, and we certainly will need you then. We will just have to see how everything works out."

On the morning of Tedde's arrival, Morgan plucked a camellia from

Emily's garden and, when no one was looking, put it on the pillow of the new bed. Then, suspecting that he would have little time with Tedde just to himself, he tried to sneak out of the house and go alone to the station. However, Agnes caught him before he got to his car and badgered him into letting her come.

They shared a moment of anxiety after the train arrived and Tedde did not immediately appear. Then, preceded by three handsome suitcases and looking absolutely smashing in a blue cashmere suit, she stepped down to the platform. He wondered, as he ran toward her, how he had ever thought she was plump when, in fact, she cut such a graceful figure with her small waist and well-rounded breasts and buttocks.

Agnes waited patiently as he took his time embracing her. Then it was Agnes's turn, and in a sudden rush of shyness, the little girl held back until the actress threw out her arms and pulled her blissfully close. Then the porter picked up the suitcases, and they climbed up the steep steps of Brookwood station to the street, Agnes hanging on to Tedde's hand as if she might lose it.

Driving down Peachtree, Tedde exclaimed over the gracious homes and magnificent trees. "At last, I'm in *Gone with the Wind* country" she said, and, looking at Agnes, she added, "I can't wait to see your house."

"Now remember," Morgan interjected, "it's not very grand. It's not Great Oaks or Tara. Not by a long shot, but you'll have your own room and bath, and I think you'll be comfortable."

"I'm going to love it," she said. And she appeared to do just that when they turned in the drive.

Josy, Miss Mattie, Roxie, and Viola, their faces covered with grins, rushed out of the house to welcome her. She embraced each of them. Blossom bounded up from the woods and tried to jump on her. Something about her scent seemed to intoxicate him because Morgan had to shout and jerk him away by the collar to make him behave. The dog finally contented himself by running around them in circles, panting heavily.

As soon as she entered the front door, Tedde turned toward the living room and saw the portrait. "That must be Emily," she said. "She has such a kind and gentle face."

"That's my mother," Agnes said, "but she's dead, and you're going to be my mother now." Then she took the actress by the hand and led her around the house, showing her every nook and cranny. After that she accompanied the engaged couple on a walking tour of the neighborhood, and after that she joined them for a drive around the suburbs of northwest Atlanta, where Tedde seemed more than dutifully impressed with the towering pines, huge magnolia trees, and spacious homes.

Morgan had hoped to make the drive without Agnes, there being a house for sale on Tuxedo he had wanted to point out to his fiancée. However, the zeal with which his youngest child gripped Tedde's hand indicated that she would not relinquish it readily. It was not until mid-afternoon, when Joanna came over to play, that he had a moment alone with the actress. They sat on the living room sofa and discussed plans for the wedding, and Tedde, leaning back in the crook of his arm, expressed her satisfaction with his house.

"I really love it," she said. "I love the fan light over the front door, and I love your furniture and this flowered chintz on the chairs. There is very little I would want to change."

"I tell you what," Morgan said, "Let's don't change anything. I'll buy you any house on the market your heart desires, or I'll build you a new one if that's what you had rather do. I think it's better if we start fresh. This house has so much of Emily in it."

"Of course," she said, and for a moment she looked a little taken back. However, she recovered quickly, and, smiling up at him, she asked, "Something with big fat columns? Something that will knock the socks off visiting Yankees?"

"Honey, that's your department. The man brings home the bacon, and the woman gives the family distinction. You choose the house that is right for us and fix it up. Decorating is women's work."

"But the furniture?" she said. "We can't get rid of the antiques just to start fresh." She leaned forward and ran her hand over the mellow glow of the coffee table.

"Of course not. Most of our furniture was passed down from either my family or Emily's over the years, and someday we will pass it down to Josy and Agnes. I can't think of anything more discomforting than brand new furniture."

"It's wonderful to pass furniture down from generation to generation," she said. "It's so different from my family. My grandfather left Europe without a possession."

Morgan, smiling, pulled her closer to him. "Sweetheart," he said, "I'm giving you a heritage."

She straightened up and looked him dead in the eye. "I don't have any family furniture from my grandfather's home. He escaped from a pogrom in Russia. But, sweetheart, I do have a heritage."

∞·∞

Later that week, Tedde confided in Miss Mattie that the portrait over the mantle made her nervous. "I feel she's watching me," she said, "and wondering if I'll measure up."

"I know," Miss Mattie said. "I felt exactly the same way at first, but Emily's ghost, if there is one, is friendly. However, it's eerie how lifelike the picture is."

The two ladies were seated on the sofa in the living room. From the rear windows, they could look past the veranda to the garden and the woods behind. The garden, since Emily's death, was tended by a yardman, although Josy, when the season warranted, did a little weeding or looked for beetles in the roses.

"What was Emily like?" Tedde asked. "Was she as lovely as the portrait?"

"Yes, she was lovely. She had the same soft, beauty that Josy has. I didn't know her well because she was so much younger, but I saw her, occasionally, at the garden club. She grew wonderful flowers."

Viola, who had come into the room to see if the ladies wanted a cold Coca-Cola, picked up on the conversation and added, "Miss Emily was crazy about growing things."

"I'm afraid," Tedde confessed, "that all of my plants have very short life spans,"

"Miss Emily was a mighty fine gardener," Viola continued. "She used to say that we was going in the flower business. She was gonna grow, and I was gonna fix."

"Viola," Tedde said, "I know there are a number of ways I can never live up to her, but I can appreciate the beauty of your flower arrangements. You are a true artist." Then, having drunk an interminable amount of Coca-Cola since coming south, she asked if there was any coffee left over from breakfast.

After Viola had brought in the beverages, the two ladies settled back into their conversation. "I wish I could tell you more about Emily," Miss Mattie said, "I saw her only at the garden club, but I know she would appreciate how kind you've been to Agnes. She certainly hangs on you. It must be a little like having a benevolent growth."

Tedde smiled at the analogy. "I'm only kind because I love her. But if you can't tell me about Emily, tell me about my darling Morgan. Does he always say such a long blessing before meals?"

"Always," Miss Mattie said, and the two women laughed indulgently.

"I love his piety," Tedde said. "He does what he thinks is the right thing to do, and that's such a rare quality. I meet so many phonies in the theater."

"He's very much in love," Miss Mattie said, "and his piety is genuine. I'm sure you know his grandfather was a Presbyterian minister of great prominence."

Tedde smiled and shook her head in wonder. "Oh, Mattie," she said, "Isn't it rich! Isn't it wonderful! Granddaughter of an itinerant rabbi marries the grandson of a Presbyterian minister. What a country we live in!"

☙❧

Morgan asked family members to keep the wedding plans under their hats until the engagement was officially announced at a party he was giving at his club. Everyone exerted great effort to comply with his wishes. Miss Mattie told only her sister. Josy told only three of her very best friends, and Agnes told only Joanna. Viola was true blue. She didn't tell a soul, but every time Clara Belle asked about the visiting Yankee lady, Viola hummed the wedding march. Somehow everyone in town got wind of the impending wedding, and everyone was anxious to meet the actress.

Louisa Jones met Tedde at Morgan's club where the engaged couple were dining with Bill O'Brian and his wife. The four of them were laughing uproariously at one of O'Brian's stories and Louisa and her escort came over to their table to hear the joke.

Louisa was wearing a pale blue evening dress that enhanced her cold blond beauty—O'Brian always referred to her a the ice maiden—and something about her manner put a damper on everyone's mood. O'Brian did not retell his story, but he pulled out chairs for the intruders, while Morgan did the introductions.

On meeting Tedde, Louisa was all sugar. "I heard you were lovely," she gushed, "and it's all true. You're perfectly beautiful, and your gown is exquisite. Of course, shopping in New York is so marvelous."

"We do have great shopping." Tedde said. "Thank you for liking my dress."

"I so envy you those stores," Louisa continued. "In fact, I would love to live in New York, but the Jews have taken it over. There's hardly an Anglo-Saxon to be found on the streets."

The O'Brians, knowing Tedde's heritage, dropped their eyes, and Morgan turned red. The actress, however, smiled sweetly and asked, "Do you go there very often?"

Louisa, impervious to the sudden chill, continued. "Yes, I go once a year. I love the theater, but I must admit that most of all I adore those stores. Shopping is my greatest vice."

Tedde's smile became even sweeter. "Why, Louisa, I don't believe that for a moment,"

Before Louisa could respond, the band struck up a tune, and Morgan and Tedde got up to dance. As soon as she was in his arms, he kissed her forehead and held her close.

"I'm sorry about her," he said. "I guess we've got a fair number of bigots in the South, but you took care of her so beautifully."

She nestled closer to him. "It's all right, darling. Remarks like that bounce right off. And we have a fair numbers of bigots in the North, too." They continued dancing until Louisa and her escort left their table.

∞ ∞

Later in the week, Morgan's cousin, Abigail Bigley, invited Tedde and Miss Mattie to tea and the actress underwent a few beforehand pangs of anxiety. "What do I wear, and how do I act?" she asked Miss Mattie.

Miss Mattie didn't hesitate. "You don't wear your orange lounging pajamas, and you act just like you are crazy about little cucumber sandwiches."

"I shall look as demure as a convent girl," Tedde promised, "but I don't know about the sandwiches. My theatrical training may not be that advanced. And, Mattie, I want to be introduced as Theodosia. It's a little more substantial than Tedde and goes well with sipping tea."

∞∞

Abigail Bigley was a maiden lady who lived with her ninety-year-old mother in an antebellum house outside of town. The house had been built by Morgan's great-grandfather, and Morgan had lived there as a child. It had none of the columned formality associated with old Southern homes, but its wide porches and large rooms provided a welcoming charm. Abigail, a tall, handsome woman with an impeccably straight back, stood by her mother in the entrance hall to welcome Tedde, Miss Mattie, and four other guests.

The mother, old Mrs. Bigley, was confined to a wheelchair. She was a small but elegant woman with a hawk nose, high cheekbones, and eyes as blue as Morgan's. Her white hair, pulled back in a bun, matched in luster the strand of baroque pearls that fell, opera length, below her bosom.

"Welcome to the cottage," she said in her ancient croaky voice, as each guest bent to kiss the parchment cheek. And, as Tedde approached, she added, "This must be the pretty little Yankee who is going to marry Morgan."

There was a titter among the ladies, and Abigail said, "Hush, Mama! It's supposed to be a secret."

"I think everyone knows," Tedde said.

Abigail ushered the guests into the parlor where a small fire burned in the grate and a Confederate officer's portrait hung over the mantle. The ladies sat down and assumed, throughout the afternoon, a ramrod seated posture due to tight girdles and the prickly horsehair upholstery. Abigail poured tea, and a maid delivered it to each guest before passing a tray of small sandwiches.

The conversation was carried on at top volume in deference to the old lady who was quite deaf. The subject matter ranged from the activities of the Daughters of the Confederacy to the latest antics of Mrs. Roosevelt who, someone observed, might at that very moment be serving tea to negroes in the White House. Tedde, sitting demurely on the horsehair sofa, hands folded in her lap, remained silent.

Eventually Abigail got down to brass tacks. "Theodosia," she said, "I was so glad to see you at Morgan's side at church last Sunday. Are you a Presbyterian?"

"No," Tedde said, "but I'm going to be one. I want to go to church with Morgan."

"We will be so glad to have you. But tell me, what is your present religious affiliation?"

"I am an Episcopalian."

Abigail exhaled a profound sigh of relief. "Praise the Lord," she said. "I am so glad to hear it. Frankly, we were all terrified you might be a Catholic."

Tedde's laughter was rich and full. "Oh! My goodness, no!" she exclaimed. "There are no Catholics in my family."

"What did she say?" the old lady asked.

"She said there are no Catholics in her family," Abigail shouted.

"Well, that's a blessing!" the old lady said.

Miss Mattie, who was sitting on the end of her chair, fervently hoped that Tedde would let her ancestral tree lie dormant, but that was not to be.

"Actually," Tedde continued, "my grandfather was a rabbi. He came to this country from Europe."

"A rabbi!" Abigail exclaimed. "I don't believe it."

"Oh, yes! He was a rabbi, and also a very great man." Her eyes grew wide and misty with the memory of her grandfather's greatness. "I only wish Morgan could have known him. I wish all of you could have known him. He had a long black beard, and he looked so distinguished. In fact, he looked a little like the Confederate officer above your mantle."

"What did she say?" the old lady asked.

"She says," Abigail shouted, "that she wishes you had known her grandfather."

"Was he a Yankee?" the old lady asked.

"No," Tedde shouted. "Absolutely not!"

"Praise the Lord," the old lady said.

"He was a rabbi," Tedde shouted.

"Stop!" Abigail barked out the command and held up her hand as if to ward off a blow. "The Bigleys have always been Presbyterians. Mama must never know that Morgan is marrying into a rabbi's family. She's not strong enough. It would break her heart."

Tedde's eyes went from wide and misty to cool and narrow. "That's nonsense," she said. Then she leaned toward old Mrs. Bigley and shouted. "My grandfather was a rabbi."

"A what?" the old lady croaked.

"A rabbi!" Tedde shouted. "A rabbi."

"A rabbi," the old lady repeated. "Isn't that a Jewish preacher?"

"Yes," Tedde shouted. "My grandfather was a Jewish preacher."

"I went to school with a Jew," the old lady said, and this time it was her eyes that went wide and misty. "He was the smartest boy in school. Always wished I'd known him better. Might have gone sparking with him, if I'd known him better."

Tedde looked Abigail triumphantly in the eye. Then she leaned toward old Mrs. Bigley. "I knew I was going to love you," she said.

At that point, Miss Mattie entered the conversation at a gallop, telling about Tedde's visit in Maine and how she had read *Gone with the Wind* to the whole island. Then she inveigled Tedde into recounting some of her theater experiences, so Tedde told them about her bit part in the movie in which Charles Boyer had kissed her hand. All the ladies, except Abigail, were fascinated and giggled appreciatively. But Abigail drew herself up very tall and said, "I dislike Frenchmen, and I would not proffer my hand to any one of them."

Tedde, wearing an expression of total innocence, inquired, "What kind of man do you like, Abigail?"

The maiden lady searched her mind. "Well," she said, "I don't like Frenchmen, and I don't like Italians, and I don't like Yankees. I suppose that if I must like a man, it would be an English gentleman."

Tedde racked her brains and came up with a story, mostly invention, about the English actor, Ronald Coleman, and even Abigail seemed interested. "He's short, but he's attractive," she admitted.

By the end of the afternoon, the ladies were thoroughly captivated by the blue-eyed actress with the merry face and very black hair. And when Tedde leaned over to kiss the ancient matriarch good-bye, the old lady's face brightened. "You are mighty pretty, honey," she croaked, "and you've got the world by the tail. Don't you ever let it go. You hear?"

And Abigail, standing very straight, extended her hand and said, "I didn't know ladies north of the Mason-Dixon line were so charming."

Once they were outside and out of earshot of their hostess and fellow guests, Miss Mattie exclaimed, "You had them eating out of your hand."

"I'm glad they like me," Tedde said, "as long as they like me on my own terms. I was closer to my grandfather than my own mother and father, and I will never forget him nor deny him."

CHAPTER TEN

DIFFERENCES

The wedding, originally planned for February, was upped to January, as Tedde no longer needed time to show her German cousin around New York. A letter from Lola, forwarded from New York to Atlanta, announced the postponement of her visit.

One evening after dinner, while Tedde and Morgan were sitting in the dining room making plans, Morgan looked at his fiancée sharply and asked, "Sweetheart, why do you look so worried?"

"Because I'm worried about Lola. She writes that the German government is feeding itself on prejudice. The hatred is so intense that Jews can't walk down the street without fear of getting beaten up. I want my cousin out of that country and into this one."

"The trip has only been put off. She'll be here soon."

"Well, when she comes, I want her to visit us here for a long time."

Morgan cleared his throat. "Does she practice her religion?"

There was an edge to her voice when she answered. "I don't see how she could practice it. I haven't seen a temple since I left New York. She is a very glamorous and talented singer. I don't think she will embarrass you."

For a moment his blue eyes were steely. "Now hold on. This isn't the dark ages, and I will always stand by your people, Christian or Jew, as if they are my own blood."

Her expression softened, and she took his hand and kissed it. "I know that, my darling. I know that. I was only cross because I am so worried about my cousin. After college I spent a year in Berlin. Lola was like a sister to me, and her last letter is frightening. Just listen to this," and she pulled the letter out of her pocket and translated a passage describing the burning of a temple.

He examined the envelope as she was reading. "This comes from France," he said.

"I know, I know. It's almost as if it were smuggled out of the country."

He spoke patiently. "Sweetheart, if you are implying that the letter was mailed from France because the Nazis might intercept all out going mail from Jews, I doubt it. I hardly think they have the time."

"But Lola is different. She is a well-known entertainer and has always held strong political views."

He groaned. "Another female agitator."

"No, another concerned citizen. And she wants me to be one, too." Then she read a passage in which Lola wrote, "The situation here grows more intolerable every day. It may be that because of your background and your great heart, you will be called upon to serve."

"Serve," Morgan said. "What does she mean by 'serve'?"

"Help out in some way."

"Does she know you are getting married next month?"

"I don't know if my last letter has reached her. All I know is that when I am with you and your girls, I feel safe and loved. Don't you ever let go of me." And she took his hand and kissed it, adding in a fake Southern accent, "You hear!"

∞◦∞

The weather was unseasonably warm that December, and Morgan and Tedde frequently took walks around the neighborhood, enjoying the pretty houses, tall trees, and lawns that were still green. Agnes usually tagged along, walking in the middle so she could hold both his and her hand. However, one Saturday, Miss Mattie inveigled Agnes into an afternoon movie, and the lovers were able to slip off by themselves.

They drove out to his land across the river, parked the car on the dirt road, and took a rough path that followed a ridge overlooking the creek. He had told her to bring old clothes appropriate for hiking, and her attire brought a smile to his face. Her sneakers were spotless, and her jeans were new and stiff, so that she resembled a plump and pretty teenager ready to bike in Central Park.

As soon as they entered the woods, she scampered over to a particularly large tree and leaned against its trunk. Holding out her arms, she said, "I love the woods, and this looks like a kissing tree."

"It is," he said. "It's called a Southern Kissing Oak," and he pressed his body against hers.

When they could bring themselves to leave, they walked the path single file, he leading so he could protect her from briars and branches. Even though it was a mild and gentle day, the landscape was austere. The hardwood trees had lost their foliage, and the pines, like the gates of heaven, stretched straight and narrow into the sky. Only the sound of their footsteps brushing against dry leaves or the cry of an occasional crow broke the silence until he stopped and said, "Look quick!" as a fox streaked across their path.

"How beautiful!" she exclaimed. "Do you see them often?"

"Mostly around ladies' necks," he said. "I prefer to see them in the wild."

They continued walking until they reached a clearing where the remains of an old chimney poked out from a heavy cluster of vines. Off to one side and surrounded by ancient boxwood was a graveyard containing six rough-hewn stones. As they tried to decipher names and dates, two large black birds flew down and settled on a limb.

"Look," she whispered," ravens." And she pointed toward the limb.

He smiled. "They're only crows."

"Well, whatever they are, they're guarding the graves. This is a beautiful but solemn place."

He looked around him. "I wouldn't mind resting here through eternity. In the spring the dogwood and wild azalea will be in bloom, and if you listen well, you can hear the creek."

"And," she said, "a New York actress will lie beside you, and ravens will keep watch."

"Crows," he said.

He pointed toward one of the graves. "There's only one word on this one." He stooped down to get a better look. "I think it ends in y. It might be Betty, but I can't be sure."

"Do you think it's the grave of a child?" she asked.

"I don't know. Betty might have been a slave. The others died before 1860, but this one has no last name and no dates."

"Strange," she said, "to think of slavery in this beautiful wild country where foxes run across your path."

"That was a long time ago. Come on. It's getting late."

As they turned to go, the birds cawed and flew off.

"They think they're ravens," Tedde said, "They're trying to say, 'Nevermore. Nevermore.'"

Below the clearing, they caught a glimpse of the creek, glistening in the afternoon sunlight. Leaving the path, they made their way down hill until they reached a large rock overlooking the water. She declared it was a perfect place for a picnic, so he put down his coat for her to sit upon, and they shared an apple he had put in his pocket. Then he stretched out full length on the hard surface with his head on her lap. She ran her fingers through his hair, stroked his face, and asked what qualities he most treasured in a wife.

"Oh," he said, "I want someone who has a strong inclination to be happy. I don't want some old prune taking her frustrations out on me and my girls. It's your merry face that I first fell in love with. You always look as if you want to laugh."

"Yes," she said. "I like to laugh, and I think I have an inclination to be happy. The only thing that keeps me from singing is that letter from Lola about the Nazis. I have bad dreams about Germany."

He turned his head toward her body. "Sweetheart," he murmured, "I would kill any Nazi that tried to harm you or your cousin." She leaned over and kissed his forehead.

"I know," she said. "I know. You and I are alike that way. We would cut out our heart for those we love."

"Yes," he said. "I would cut out my heart for you and my girls. But try to forget that dream. It's still possible the good people of Germany will kick out the Nazis."

They were quiet for a moment. Then she asked, "Tell me, my darling, what else besides an inclination to be happy do you look for in your bride?"

"I want her to be faithful and loving, and I want her to stand behind me when I need her and to believe in the things I believe in."

She picked a weed and ran it lightly across his face until she made him sneeze. "But suppose," she asked, "you have an intellectual disagreement with this lady who has an inclination to be happy. Suppose you think two hundred angels can stand on a pin and she thinks it would more likely be two hundred and fifty. What then, my love?"

He smiled. "I would act like any man of good sense. I would concede the other fifty."

"Be serious. Suppose your wife believed in evolution, and you didn't. What then?"

"Do you believe in evolution?" he asked.

"I don't know."

"Well, I don't know either. I don't want to believe in it, but I don't know. But if I were William Jennings Bryan arguing against it in the Scopes trial, I would not consider it good support for Mrs. Bryan to come out for it. There are more ways of making a monkey out of a man than through evolution."

"But," Tedde persisted, "suppose Mrs. Bryan was a scientist, and she came out for evolution because she believed in it passionately."

"I would turn her over my knee. Come on. It's getting cold."

They got up stiffly, the rock having chilled their bones, and climbed back up the hill. He held out his hand to help her over the steep part, but she declined. When they reached the clearing, the sun was low in the sky and the crows, guardians of the graves, had not returned. They hurried back to his car, not stopping at the kissing tree.

∞∞

He knew there would be differences, but he was sure he could give Tedde a life that was both fulfilling and enjoyable. He frequently went to New York, and she could go with him and renew old friendships. And if she wanted, they could travel, and she could put to good use her ability to speak French, German, and Spanish. And if travel didn't thrill her, and if she didn't like women's groups, and if the local theater was too amateurish, well then, he would teach her to ride and to hunt with him. He had taught

Josy to shoot, and she was as good as any man.

∞◌∞

He took Tedde riding the day before the engagement party. Josy came with them, but Agnes stayed home.

"Why don't you come?" Tedde asked Agnes.

"I'm a coward," Agnes replied. "I'm afraid of horses."

"You are not a coward, I know you too well for that."

"Yes, she is," Josy said. "She's a born coward."

"I really am," Agnes said, nodding her head in agreement.

In the car, on the way to the saddle club, Tedde expressed a little apprehension about riding.

"There's nothing to worry about," Morgan said. "All you have to do is relax and let the horse know who's in charge."

"Horses smell fear," Josy added, "so try not to be afraid. That's important."

"I am an actress," Tedde said, "and although this is a challenging role, I will act as if I am the boss, and I will exude no odors."

"You'll be fine," Morgan said.

When they arrived at the barns, Josy saddled and bridled Rosebud and rode her out to the ring in front of the stable. Morgan saddled Charley and hitched him to a post. Then he led a Roman-nosed, swaybacked, rather listless looking horse out of the stable. "Tedde," he said, "meet Old Tom."

"Oh!" Tedde exclaimed. "I am so glad to meet him. I know we are going to be great friends." The horse did not acknowledge the introduction. He looked as if he were falling asleep as Morgan ran the currycomb across his back, Other than an occasional flick of a rather large ear, he showed no signs of unnecessary movement.

After he had bridled and saddled Old Tom, Morgan made a stirrup out of his hands so that Tedde could easily spring into the saddle. However, she neglected to spring, and he was left bearing her full weight in his palms. His knees buckled, and he almost sat down.

"Get a leg up!" he shouted, his voice losing its usual calm.

She responded by executing such a mighty swing that Morgan

went reeling back until he landed on his backside in the dirt. He leapt to his feet immediately, and if she noticed that she had pushed him down, she gave no sign.

"Whew," she said, settling into the saddle, "That was a lot of work. Now I am just going to act as if I know what I'm doing."

He looked at her and noted that her whole body seemed to open up. Her knees and elbows stuck out and her bottom expanded. Somehow, he doubted Old Tom was going to fall for the act.

"Honey," he said, "Try and tighten up a little bit."

"I thought I was supposed to relax."

"I want you to relax, but I want you to pull in your knees and your elbows and shift your weight forward a little. There, that's better!"

As he turned toward his own horse, Old Tom wandered off to a tall clump of grass and put his head down to chew.

"I think I am on top of a sliding board," Tedde said, "and I'm on my way down."

"Pull his head up, honey. "Show him who's boss."

She pulled on the reins, but Old Tom kept on chewing.

"I think he's hungry," she said.

"He gets plenty to eat. You're not supposed to let him do that."

Tedde pulled again, and Old Tom lifted his head and meandered toward the woods.

"Where are you going?" Morgan asked.

"I have no earthly idea, but I am trying to act as knowledgeable as possible."

Morgan started toward Old Tom. But every time he approached him, the horse took off at a little trot and Tedde bounced precariously up, down, and sideways.

"Why don't you grab him by the tail?" she suggested.

His voice took on a decided edge. "That wouldn't work."

Finally, the horse, looking bored, stood still long enough to be caught. Morgan led him back to the barn and hitched him to a post. Then he mounted Charley, unhitched Old Tom, and led him to the trail. "You go where ever you want," he called to Josy. "We're going very slowly through the woods."

"This isn't very dignified," Tedde complained. "I feel like a child."

"As soon as we get away from the barn, I'll put you in charge again," he promised.

Five minutes later they were in a forest of tall Georgia pines. Morgan, dismounted, straightened Tedde's reins, and handed them to her. "I think he will just follow along," he said, "but if you have any trouble, just holler."

A few minutes later, Tedde said, "Morgan, I'm having a little trouble. He doesn't want to go."

Morgan stopped and looked around. Old Tom was standing stock still. He had lifted his tail and was depositing manure on the path.

Morgan smiled. "It's all right. He's just answering a call from nature. He'll move in a minute."

"Oh!" Tedde said, "I had no idea. Forgive me, Old Tom, I didn't mean to be rude."

They continued along the trail in silence. Then Tedde said, "This is lovely, Morgan. The woods are so pretty, and Old Tom thinks I'm a wonderful rider."

"That's good, honey." He turned his head to look at her and noted that she was slouched all over the saddle. He tried to remember if he had ever known any really full-bodied women who were good riders. Whatever the case, she was the most attractive naturally bad rider he had ever seen.

"Try to tighten up a little in the saddle, honey," he said.

"All right, darling."

As he rode, he thought about what a marvelous creature she was—so bright and pretty, and so loving to the girls and so willing to get along with everybody. All of his friends liked her, and even old Abigail Bigley had unbent enough to admit she was charming.

When he came to a long flat place in the trail, he turned around in the saddle to ask Tedde if she would like to try a little slow trot, but she wasn't there. She had disappeared without a word. He wasn't alarmed. He supposed there were some people Old Tom would take just so far, but he put his horse in a canter and headed back. Josy was standing outside the tack room when he got there.

"Where is she?" he demanded.

"Papa," Josy said, "Old Tom came roaring home about two minutes ago. Tedde fell off, but she got back on and tried to make him go back on the trail, but he just went in his stall. I think Tedde is crying. She told me not to help her, She wanted to get him out of the stall herself."

He dismounted and handed Josy his horse. Then he went over to Old Tom's stall. The horse was quietly munching hay, and Tedde was still astride. Her hair was in her eyes, her blouse was torn, and tears ran down her face.

"Morgan," she said, "I don't think very much of your horses, and I don't think you have very good control over them." She gave Old Tom a mighty kick. "Get out, damn you!" she shouted, but Old Tom continued to munch hay.

Morgan couldn't help smiling. He led the horse out of the stall and helped her dismount. Then he got on himself, and as soon as he was away from the barn, he flailed Old Tom with his crop. They galloped away with the rider still flailing.

When they returned, the horse was in a white lather. Morgan made him walk a good way past the barn again, and then he brought him back to Tedde.

"Now, honey," he said, "you get on again, and everything will be fine."

"I don't want to get on again," she said. "I've had enough riding."

"If you don't get right back on," Morgan said, "it makes it harder next time."

She folded her arms and glared. "There's not going to be a next time."

"Why, honey, I'm surprised at you. Letting a horse get the better of you. It's not like you."

She continued to glare. "Be that as it may. I'm not getting back on. Now or ever." And with that, she stalked over to the car, got into the front seat, and stayed there while Morgan walked Old Tom to cool him off.

The ride home was marked by long silences. Josy tried to lighten the situation by congratulating Tedde for remounting after Old Tom first threw her, but it didn't work. Morgan said that a person had to fall off at least three times before even beginning to be a good rider and, bearing that in mind, Tedde had made great progress. He got only the bleakest of smiles.

When they got back home, Blossom charged around the house to greet them. He planted himself in front of Tedde, panting and slobbering, in anticipation of a kind word and friendly pat. However, the actress glared at him and said something in a foreign language that no one understood.

But later, when Agnes asked about the ride, Tedde put her arms around her and whispered in her ear, "You're not the only coward in this family. I'm one, too."

The look Agnes gave her was pure adoration.

That night at dinner, Tedde's good spirits returned, and she was able to laugh about the afternoon's events. "I wasn't so much scared as humiliated," she explained. "I wanted to do so well, and I felt like a sack of potatoes, and that old villain made a fool out of me. Next time I'll do better."

"You did fine," Josy said, and Morgan smiled happily.

That night Tedde excused herself right after Agnes went to bed. She said she was tired and a little sore from her horseback ride, and she wanted to soak in a hot tub and then get a good night's sleep. Her good humor was perfectly restored, and she returned Morgan's chaste kiss with a hearty hug.

Morgan turned in early, too. He had some things to attend to the next day in preparation for the party, and he, too, wanted a good night's rest. He undressed quickly, showered, and then knelt down by his four-poster bed. After saying a short prayer in which he thanked God for his many blessings and prayed to be worthy of them, he climbed into bed and fell into the deep sleep of the pure in heart.

Several hours later, he felt a hand shaking his shoulder. "What? What?" he murmured.

"Shush" the voice said. "You will wake them up."

Foggily, it came to him that the voice was Tedde's. She hoisted herself up on the bed and put her fingertips lightly over his mouth. He brushed them away and whispered, "Why, honey, you shouldn't be here."

"Oh, Morgan," she said. "I had to come. Something terrible happened."

His voice was full of concern. "Sweetheart, what is it?"

"Oh, Morgan, I had the most terrible nightmare, and it seemed so real."

He sat up in bed and put his arm around her. "Was it the Nazis?

Did you dream they were after you?"

"It was worse than that. Much worse."

"Well, then, did some mean old horse run you in the barn?"

"Even worse than that."

"What was it then?"

"Oh, Morgan, I dreamed you didn't love me anymore."

He could feel her almost bare and almost too-large breasts lean into his chest. And though he could not see her face in the darkness, he was sure, as she looked up at him, that her almost-too-full lips were parted. He sent a prayer to God that was as straight and direct as an arrow, in which he acknowledged his manifold wickedness and his desire to, at some unspecified future date, put his house in order. Then he put both arms around the wonderful soft fullness of Theodosia Boyd and pulled her down into his bed.

Chapter Eleven

THE NIGHTGOWN

Morgan was awakened by something at dawn. He was not sure by what. He lay still and let the events of the evening filter through his mind. The pleasure of recall brought a blush and a smile to his face. He couldn't believe how loving she had been. Never before had he known such un-inhibited ardor. Remembering her passion and the feel of her body re-kindled his desire, and without opening his eyes, he put out his arm to pull her to him. The cold empty spot beside him was an affront to his senses, but he realized she must have gone back to her room to avoid being found out. That made sense. After all, they would be in a devil of a fix if Agnes or Josy were to catch on to them.

He heard a motor running outside his bedroom window and the click of high heels on the driveway. It must have been the sound of the motor that had awakened him. He got out of bed, stretched, and went to the window. It was still dark, but he could see Tedde in the headlights of a taxi. She was wearing the suit in which she had arrived, and the driver was putting her suitcases, all three of them, into the trunk.

He couldn't believe it. She was pulling out, lock, stock, and barrel.

"Wait!" he called out. "Wait! Come back!" His voice sounded so hoarse and tragic that, in some distant reach of his mind, he was reminded of a fat opera singer in the throes of an ill-fated passion. The cab moved out of the drive and into the street.

He sat down on the bed and put his head in his hands. What had he done wrong? My God! Was he that bad a lover? Had he driven her away?

And where was she going at this hour? Had she hired a cab to pick her up at sunrise and drive her a thousand miles to New York? There must be some logical explanation. Someone must be ill, and she had been called away.

As he started to dress, he noticed a piece of paper on the floor by his door. He picked it up and with a heavy sense of foreboding, he read:

My darling Morgan, what a lover you are, once you have gotten the sand out of your eyes. I shall never forget or regret last night. I went to my room early to pack my bags. I stayed awake until I knew it was safe to come to you. And when I was with you, it was better than I had ever imagined.

It will not work my darling. There are so many reasons why it will not work. Forgive me and come to see me when you are in New York. I have ordered a cab to take me to the station. Good-bye, my darling. I love you.

Tedde

P.S. Joel called a few days ago. There is a part for me in his new play. It is a play written to show the American audience what is happening in Germany. Forgive me, wish me luck, and bring the girls to see me on opening night.

So that was it. She was going back to New York. She was going back to the theater, and all this in a miserly little note. She had not even had the decency to tell him face-to-face. All night long they had lain in each other's arms, and she had led him to believe it would be like that forever. Then she had dismissed him with a little note as if he were a butcher or a yardman.

Well, she was wrong about one thing. This wasn't the big city, and trains didn't just come and go every fifteen minutes. It would be 6 p.m.—not 6 a.m.—before The Southerner worked its way up from Florida and pulled into the station. He had all day to go down there and demand an explanation, and, by God! he would take all day.

He began to pace up and down the bedroom floor as he reviewed the facts in his mind. Being a lawyer, he was comfortable with facts. Had she left on an impulse? No, she had not. She had gone to her room early in order to pack her bags. Then she had come to his room and his bed and given him a night of love that had answered the needs of his poor, deprived, flesh in a way he had never dreamed possible.

And the lovemaking? What had it meant to her? Unless she was better than Sarah Bernhardt, it had meant a lot. It was a fact that both participants had enjoyed the lovemaking, but it was also a fact that the lady did not enjoy it enough to change her mind about leaving. She had called it a gift that each had given the other, but the thought of the gift being given and then taken away made him so mad that he took his fist and punched the wall as hard as he could. A picture of Emily fell to the floor, its glass shattering, and Agnes, on the other side of the wall, let out a wail.

He saw Tedde's little white nightgown on the bed. He picked it up in order to tear it up or step on it, but before he could vent his fury on the flimsy little cotton gown, Agnes appeared at his door. Her face was tear streaked, and she was wringing her hands.

"Papa," she said, "I thought I heard you holler."

"I had a bad dream," Morgan said gruffly. "Now go back to bed. It's too early to get up."

"Papa, Tedde wrote a letter to me and Josy and put it under the door."

Well, that was another fact. She had written Agnes, too. She wasn't just fooling around if she had brought his children into it. She wouldn't play around with their feelings on a whim.

"Papa, the letter says she was called away. Papa, who called her away?"

He wanted to shout, "Let me alone, for God's sake. Give me a decent interval before you question me!" But he pulled himself together and said, "She has business that has just come up. She has been offered a part in a new play. Now go to bed!"

And that was another fact he had to deal with. She had been offered a job in the theater. She had written, "Joel called a few days ago. There's a part for me in his new play." And that was the fact that was cutting him up. Would she have left if Joel had not called? And if they had already been married and Joel had called, would she have left? Now, he was dealing with questions, not facts.

Agnes persevered. "Is she still going to be my new mother?"

"I don't know. It doesn't look that way. I just don't know." He wished with all his heart that she would let him alone.

Agnes started to cry, jamming her thumb in her mouth so that her breath came in short, choking sobs. "Papa, she must like the theater better than she likes me."

"Mostly," Morgan said, and he reached down to pat her head, "she likes it better than she likes me. I got a letter, too."

"Papa," Agnes gasped between sobs, "Why do you have Tedde's nightgown in your hand?"

He looked down and saw that he had just switched the lovely little white gown from his right hand to his left. He stared at it with shock and horror. He would rather have been holding a black widow spider or a copperhead. He felt like a man apprehended in a theft or a murder, and he wanted very much to wring the neck of his youngest daughter.

Swearing under his breath and speaking between clenched teeth, he hissed, "In the name of Jesus, can't you mind your own business?" Then he jerked Agnes's thumb out of her mouth and, leaning over to eye level, shouted, "Keep that thumb out of your mouth and get your fat little bottom into your room."

Agnes let out a wail as she left the room. Morgan didn't know what course of action he was going to take, but he knew he had to find some way to get hold of himself. He put on his riding pants and jacket and stuffed the damning little nightgown into his pocket. Then, in the first light of day, he drove at record speed out to the saddle club where he grabbed his crop, saddled and bridled his mount with the haste of a fireman answering a call, and swung into the saddle. He raised his crop and brought it down hard on Charley, a horse who had never needed encouragement to gather speed. They sprang forward into a gallop that took them hurtling down hills, across fields and streams, and into the next county. Morgan, leaning low in the saddle, was bent on riding that woman out of his system, forever.

⚮

Miss Mattie had heard Morgan shout out the window at Tedde, and she had heard him yell at Agnes and slam the door as he left the house. She, too, had received a note under the door, and not knowing whether it signified a lover's quarrel or a final departure, lay low in her bed until she heard Viola and Roxie stirring around in the kitchen. When she smelled coffee brewing, she put on her clothes and went downstairs. Josy was in the kitchen, and she had told Roxie and Viola about Theodosia's departure. The little group was sadly philosophical.

"It was Old Tom that did it," Josy said. "He scared her right back to New York."

"Well, I hope it wasn't my cooking," Roxie said.

"I sure do hate it," Viola said. "She was such a fine little lady."

Miss Mattie wrung her hands. "We are all very sad and confused, and I don't know what we are going to do about the party tonight, but poor Agnes is heartbroken. She is in her room crying her eyes out right now."

"That baby doesn't deserve this kind of treatment," Viola said.

She put down her dishtowel and went upstairs to Agnes's room. The little girl was lying on her bed and sobbing into her pillow. Viola sat down on the bed. "Now look here," she said, "you better crawl up on my lap before you get too big." Agnes climbed onto the big lap and buried her face in Viola's shoulder. "Everybody I love," she sobbed, "either goes to heaven or goes to New York."

Viola rocked back and forth. "Now that ain't so," she said. "Not everybody. Not by a long shot. Viola ain't going to New York or to heaven or nowhere else."

After a while, Agnes felt sufficiently comforted to crawl out of Viola's lap and look at her books. She reread her favorite, *The Little Mermaid*, and puzzled over the ending. She remembered she had asked Tedde if it were right for the little mermaid to give up her finest talent for love of a prince. Tedde had said a true prince was worth any sacrifice. It occurred to Agnes that Tedde had gone back to New York because Papa was not a true prince.

That morning Roxie helped Viola strip the bed in the new guest room. "I declare," Roxie said as she examined some black smudges all over the pillow. "Looks like some of that black on Miss Theodosia's hair done come off on the sheet."

"I told you she put shoe polish on it," Viola said, "and we better hope it comes out." The two women went upstairs to the master bedroom. Viola was the first to spot the picture and the broken glass. "Look here," she said, "there's my sweet little Miss Emily on the floor. I sure do wonder how come she fell off the wall like that." She put the picture aside for Miss Mattie to have reframed and held the dustpan while Roxie swept up the glass. Then they stood on opposite sides of Morgan's bed to pull up the sheets. They were fluffing up the pillows when suddenly they both stopped in mid-performance.

A big grin spread over Roxie's face. "Who would believe it!" she exclaimed. "Who would believe how that shoe polish travels."

Viola was grinning, too. "Hush up!" she said. "This ain't none of our business. This here's between you and me and the shoe polish." She paused for a moment before adding, "But don't you wonder how come the shoe polish went from Miss Theodosia's room to Mr. Morgan's room and then took off to New York so early in the morning?"

"You're right," Roxie said. "It ain't our business." They continued making the bed. Just as they were tucking the spread around the pillow, Roxie said, "You reckon he broke the picture before or after that shoe polish hit the pillow."

"I don't know," Viola said. "I just work here."

☙❧

Morgan was rubbing down his horse with Tedde's nightgown when O'Brian drove up to the saddle club. The nightgown was not absorbent enough to make a good rag, but it gave Morgan a sort of spiteful pleasure to rub the traitorous little garment over the sweat.

O'Brian got out of his car. "That's a mighty hot horse," he said.

"Mighty hot," Morgan agreed.

O'Brian went right to the point, "I take it that you and Theodosia had a falling out."

Morgan looked at him sharply. "Did she leave a note under your door?" he growled.

"I saw her down at the station," O'Brian said.

"Is that so?"

"I went down to the station early to pick up some tickets, and she was sitting in the waiting room. I said, 'I'm looking forward to seeing you this evening, Theodosia.' And she said, 'I'm sorry Bill, I've been called away.'"

O'Brian paused a minute to let Morgan speak, but Morgan remained silent.

"Then I asked her what train she was catching, and she replied, 'The Southerner.'"

O'Brian paused again, but Morgan maintained his silence and kept on wiping down Charley with the useless little nightie.

"So I told her that if she were taking the Southerner, she had a good ten-hour wait. She looked me dead in the eye and said that she had brought along a good book."

Another silence ensued.

"She's a damn fine-looking woman," O'Brian said, "and I have always liked her. But, you are my best friend, and if there is anything I can do, I am here to do it. If I can help mend a fence or . . ."

"Did you drive all the way out here just to rejuvenate our friendship?" Morgan asked.

"I did."

"Well, thank you for your trouble, but there is nothing anybody can do."

O'Brian turned to go. "In that case, I'll be on my way."

He started to get into his car, but Morgan called him back.

"Bill," Morgan said, "I appreciate what you are trying to do. And you are absolutely right. She is a damn fine-looking woman. So fine looking that I asked her to be my wife, and she agreed. But this morning I received a note under my door that too many difficulties stood in our way. She didn't spell them out, but I suspect the South, and the way of life down here, and the way I am, turned her off. Even so, I would go down to the station and have it out with her, and maybe she would come home with me. But she wrote my children a note, too, and by so doing she burned her bridges. I can't keep my family in a state of turmoil, and I know the lady would not want to do that either."

He stopped talking long enough to lead Charley over to the trough. Then he turned to O'Brian and said, "I am a Southerner and proud of it, and because the rest of the country looks down on the South and despises it so, I love it all the more. This is my home, and this is where I can do the most good as a lawyer and as a citizen. Emily understood that and felt the same way. I suspect that Tedde understands but doesn't feel the same way."

"A fat lot of good it will do either of us," O'Brian said, "but I sure as hell understand and feel the same way, too. We got to find you a good Southern woman."

Morgan smiled ruefully, "I suspect," he said, "that I have left out the most salient reason for Tedde's departure. A friend of hers has written a new play with a part in it for her. I guess I'll never know whether or not she would have left without that opportunity since I'm not going to chase down to the station to find out."

"She's not worthy of you," O'Brian said.

"I don't know about that," Morgan said. "I just know that the man has to be head of the household. He's got to take the responsibility and make the decisions, and he needs a good woman to back him up. I was raised that way. It's in the Bible that way, and I believe it. And if I ever marry again, I will cherish that woman the way I did Emily—as if she were an angel."

"I only got one question," O'Brian said.

"What's left?" Morgan asked.

"It's none of my business," O'Brian said, "but I can't help myself."

Morgan waited patiently.

"I just wondered," O'Brian said, "where you got that little piece of lace nightie you're wiping off Charley with."

For the second time that day, Morgan looked with horror at the little nightgown, now soggy with horse lather. But before he could come up with a reply, O'Brian had turned, walked over to his car, and started the engine. "See you later," O'Brian called as he pulled away from the barn.

Morgan took a deep breath and blew it out slowly. It was becoming increasingly apparent that he was not cut out to be a womanizer. He didn't know how to dispose of the evidence. He walked Charley around the ring until he had cooled off enough to put him in the stable. Then he got into his car and drove home. The first thing on the agenda was to make it up with Agnes.

∞∽∞

He wore his new suit to the engagement party, the one Tedde said brought out the blue of his eyes, and he pasted a congenial smile on his face. It didn't help any that, upon arriving at the club, he heard the faint, seductive whistle of the Southerner as it pulled out of town for New York. He greeted the guests in the dark paneled bar where two original Audubons, gift of a wealthy member, graced the walls. Everyone wanted to know the whereabouts of the beautiful lady, but Morgan offered no explanations.

"She didn't come," was all he would say. "Now get yourself a drink and make yourself at home."

In the beginning, a feeling of uneasiness and unanswered questions dampened the atmosphere, but it didn't take long for the bourbon to wash it away. Besides, other gossip was in the air. King Edward VIII of England had just announced that he was giving up his throne for Wallis Simpson, whom he loved, and there was much discussion involving the pros and cons of such an act. Some, mostly women, felt that the king had done a noble thing. Others, mostly men, felt that he was shirking his responsibilities.

Miss Louisa Jones, looking elegant in a black velvet gown, turned her beautiful face toward Morgan and asked, "What does our host think about the king's abdication?"

"I think England is well rid of him," Morgan said. "A man who puts his attraction for a divorced woman before his duties to his country wouldn't make much of a king."

Louisa nodded her head in total agreement.

CHAPTER TWELVE

THE ITCH

Morgan fumed over Tedde's departure for over a week and then decided to take the high road. He wrote her a short letter in which he implied he understood her decision to leave him.

"You are a beautiful and talented woman," he wrote, "and I suspect I attempted to turn you into a country mouse. Forgive me, dear Tedde, and knock 'em dead in the theater. As for me, I belong in the backwater. The South is the poorest part of this great nation, and I want to be a part of those forward-looking people who turn it around."

He did not mention the awkwardness of the engagement party or the hardship her departure had imposed on his youngest daughter. Agnes was always on the verge of tears, and the slightest criticism set her off. Just recently at dinner, he had asked her why she wasn't eating, and she had replied, "Because I'm sad," and she had fled the room.

"Why is she so upset?" Josy asked. "It was Papa who got jilted."

Miss Mattie looked at her plate, and Morgan did not speak.

After that meal, Viola had taken Josy aside and, in an effort to strike a tender spot in her heart, explained Agnes's behavior. "When Miss Emily passed, your sister was too little to know what it meant. Now she knows."

After Viola's lecture, Josy tried to be kinder.

It was not necessary for Josy to mollycoddle Agnes for long. A few days later, the postman delivered an airmail letter from New York addressed to Agnes Bigley in which Tedde wrote about her new play and her part in it. "I don't know if I will be any good," she wrote, "but I want you to come see me when we open, and I want you to bring Josy and Miss Mattie with you."

Agnes was ecstatic. She immediately sat down and printed her answer. The writing went all over the page, but the message was clear.

> Dear Tedde,
> I hope you are well.
> I am coming.
>
> Love, Agnes.

Morgan also received a letter from New York, in which the actress thanked him again for the wonderful moments they had shared. She never mentioned the twelve-hour wait at the railroad station, but she did say the girls had become like daughters to her, and she had no intention of giving them up.

"Agnes and I are particularly close," she wrote. "Josy has her startling good looks and her talent for friendship and for riding. Agnes's great gift is her marvelous imagination. I feel that she needs someone who understands this as I do. You must send them to New York when my play opens. I expect Mattie would love to chaperone."

She made no attempt to explain her departure.

"I know how it looks," she wrote, "my running off like that. All I can do is tell you that things are not always as they seem. Appearances do deceive." And in a postscript she added, "Lola is unable to get away. I am meeting her in Paris at the end of the month."

Something about the letter made him a little uneasy. He remembered how she had clung to him and how she had begged him to never let her go. A strange, nagging feeling, almost like guilt, tugged at the corners of his mind. Had she suspected she might leave him when she said, "Never let me go."

He saw that the break with Tedde would not be clean. The more Agnes prattled away about her friend, the actress, the more obvious it became that Miss Mattie and the Bigley girls would head for New York when the play opened. As for himself, he would wait and see, but his present disposition was to close out the relationship completely. She was a mighty attractive woman, but he did not intend to give another engagement party for a lady who did not show.

The incident of the nightgown would not die. Agnes brought up the subject at the dinner table. "When I go to New York," she announced brightly, "I can bring Tedde's nightgown to her."

The room was consumed in silence. No one asked for an explanation, but Agnes clarified her remark by adding, "I mean the one Papa keeps in his room. He had it in his hand the day Tedde left."

A long difficult moment followed. Miss Mattie regarded her plate with acute interest, and Josy stopped chewing her food. Then Viola, who was passing the roast beef, spoke up. "Lord knows I'm sorry about that," she said. "Sometimes I get so mixed up in my head that I get the laundry mixed up, too, and I reckon I put Miss Theodosia's nightgown in the wrong place."

Morgan felt a surge of gratitude toward this wonderful woman who had done so much for his family. He even managed a slight but rather hollow chuckle that was intended to close out the incident, forever.

Viola brought in the vegetables and continued the apology. "Yes sir! I done ironed that skimpy little nightgown with my own hands and then took it up to Mr. Morgan's room. I don't know what I was thinking about."

Morgan winced internally. Now that she had saved him, he wished, with all his heart, that she would drop the subject. In his mother's day, servants were better trained. They would never carry on a conversation while serving the dinner. What very little gracious living is left in this world, he thought to himself.

"I don't know how I happened to fold that skimpy little nightgown and put it in the wrong place," Viola continued, as she brought in the potatoes. "I must have had something mighty big on my mind."

"Your apology is accepted," Morgan said curtly. "We need never speak of the matter again." He gave Viola a sharp look that she returned with an expression of total innocence.

"Yes, sir!" Viola said, "but it sure do beat all how I put a lady's nightgown in a man's room."

That night, while she was drying the dishes, Viola said to Roxie, "I reckon I was put on this earth for three reasons: one is to get walked on all over by white people whenever they feel up to it, two is to give everybody as much love as they can handle, and three is to have a little fun whenever I gets the chance. And tonight I had a little fun with Mr. Morgan."

∞∞

Morgan did everything in his power to put Theodosia Boyd out of his mind. He worked harder than ever at the office and dedicated his leadership to numerous outside causes. He was, except in the management of nightgowns, successful in all that he undertook. He reorganized civic charities, headed a drive to build a new Sunday school for the Presbyterians and, in short, did everything in his power to enhance the quality of life in his community. As for the quality of his own life, it lacked only one thing—that being a good and lovely woman to grace his home, love his children, and warm his bed. The old itch was back, and, since that night with Tedde, it was more pronounced than ever.

The months passed. He entered a citywide golf tournament, came in second, and then hung up his clubs in favor of spending more time at his farm. There was something about the sweat of good, honest labor that satisfied a need. "Everybody ought to keep in touch with the land," he told Josy, who was his constant riding companion on the weekends. "A person's not complete unless he's growing something."

"You think I could be a farmer when I grow up?" Josy asked.

"You would make a good one," Morgan said. "Remember how your mama grew roses? There's a great deal of pleasure in growing something beautiful."

"Yes, but I would rather grow something to eat."

Morgan smiled. He did not tell her that every time he looked at her, he thought of those biblical lilies of the field who neither toiled nor spun. Her beauty was as natural as the wild flowers, yet she was either unaware or unimpressed by it, and she had a practical streak that endeared her to him. Agnes was bright and amusing, but Josy, because of her courage, companionship, and love of the outdoors, was the light of his life.

He and his caretaker, Sam Laudermilk, planted his washed-out fields in a vine designed to prevent erosion and restore nutrients to the soil. It would take a long time, but one day his pastures would come to life again. He would like to live long enough to see the muddy old river run clear.

Sam Laudermilk was a down-on-his luck artist. He was college educated, and therefore an unlikely farmer, but he brought a dedication to his work that delighted Morgan. Sam and his family had moved into a little ramshackle house on the property near the barn. Sam painted the house white and planted grass, and his wife, Jane, created a flower garden. Morgan was happy with the improvement and highly amused when they painted a rose on the outhouse door.

"I declare," he said, "that rose on your bathroom door is so pretty that it must be a pleasure to spend time there."

"It looks like a rose," Sam said, "but it don't smell like one."

Morgan knew that Sam and Jane would not be with him long. When the country got on its feet again, they would move with it.

He brought his horses from the saddle club to the farm and Tim, the Laudermilk's son, took care of them. Josy gave Tim riding lessons, and he became proficient enough to make even Old Tom put out. Morgan took great pleasure in watching his daughter and his caretaker's son racing their horses along the river path—two healthy, happy youngsters having the time of their lives. Sometimes, he joined them in the race, and at such times he felt that the pleasure of his farm and his work and his children were enough to sustain him.

∽∾

Agnes preferred her own backyard to the farm. She had inherited Josy's tree house, and she and Joanna used it when playing Tarzan. Agnes could get to it via a rope hanging from a limb above, but Joanna used an old ladder as a means of entry.

One morning, Morgan went out back to inspect the tree house. Viola had advised him the floorboards as well as some of the rungs on the ladder were rotting. He took his tools with him and spent a quiet morning making repairs.

It was early October—very still—with only a few cooling breezes and drifting leaves to mark the advent of fall. No one was about, and Morgan enjoyed his solitude amidst the towering pines. But as he repaired the tree house, he couldn't help thinking about Tedde. She had loved the

Georgia pine trees.

"They are so tall and straight," she had said to Morgan. "They remind me of you."

It had been almost a year since he had seen her, and like a schoolboy, he closed his eyes for a moment, leaned against the tree house and allowed himself the pleasure of recall. Remembering the feel of her flesh, he was consumed with longings and regrets. Guiltily, he shook himself and returned to his work.

Then out of the silence of the woods, a voice spoke his name. He turned and saw a woman partially concealed behind a tree. When he faced her, she came out in the open and stretched out her arms toward him, her palms open. She was blond and slim, and her dress was pulled down from her shoulders so that her bosom, beautiful and opulent, was exposed.

He felt he had gone back in time and become a player in some mythical drama. Some benevolent god had witnessed his need, taken pity on him and sent a nymph of the wood to woo him. Bewitched, he stepped forward.

The nymph lowered her eyes, covered her breast with crossed hands and spoke. "Where's Agnes?" she asked, and Morgan recognized Miss Brown.

The spell was broken. Who he was and what he stood for came rushing back to him. He was not a prince in an enchanted forest. He was a Christian gentleman and a lawyer, and he was in his own backyard and a half-naked lunatic was trying to seduce him. It was an unsavory situation that smacked of all sorts of incrimination and lawsuits.

"Miss Brown!" he said. "Pull up your dress."

Miss Brown uncrossed her hands, displaying the magnificent bosom again, and began to pull up her skirt. In so doing, she displayed a pair of equally magnificent thighs.

"No! No! No!" he shouted. "I mean put back on your clothes. Put them on this minute!" He turned and, breaking into a run, made a beeline to the house, leaving the lady and his tools behind. He ran to the kitchen, looking for Viola, but she was nowhere to be found. However, old Mrs. Brown was sipping tea with Miss Mattie in the living room.

Morgan didn't wait for an introduction. "Madam, your daughter is in a state of disrepair in my woods and needs your immediate attention," he said.

The old lady's voice took on a mean, ominous tone. "Did you touch my girl?" she growled.

Morgan spoke between clenched teeth. "I have touched no one, but you had better get yourself out back and attend to your daughter, immediately."

Later Miss Mattie told him that old Mrs. Brown and her daughter had dropped by to chat and to ask the whereabouts of Agnes. Miss Mattie had explained that no one was at home except Mr. Bigley who was fixing a tree house. Ignoring this bit of information, old Mrs. Brown had sent her daughter outside to look for Agnes.

"That old woman is out to get me," Morgan muttered, "and she almost did."

That night he had a talk with his youngest daughter. He said Miss Brown and her mother had severe problems that made friendship with them impossible. They acted strangely and when people acted strangely, it was better for other people to stay away from them. He ended by advising Agnes to decline any invitations to the movies or any other overtures of friendship Miss Brown might make.

"Papa," Agnes said, "I haven't been to the movies with her since last year. She's nuts."

Morgan sighed with relief. Agnes had a way of cutting through the trappings to unadulterated truth. He thought back over the events of the morning and smiled grimly. The old lady was doing her best to dump her troubled daughter on him. She had probably sent her out back and told her to pull her dress down. The horror of it was that he had almost fallen for it. He had reached out for that lunatic like a baby for candy. By God! He needed a woman bad. He was going to have to find some good Southern lady who understood his values and marry her fast.

Almost without thinking, he went in the kitchen and took one of Louisa Jones's candies. He had not liked them at first. They were too sweet, but she had pressed them on him ever since Emily died, and he was getting used to the flavor.

CHAPTER THIRTEEN

NEW YORK

Tedde's play failed, but a year later, she opened to good reviews in a hit comedy. Therefore, in February of 1938, and after much correspondence back and forth, Agnes, Josy, and Miss Mattie departed for New York. Morgan did not go with them. He had a prior commitment to take Miss Louisa Jones to a party.

The girls wore new outfits on the train. Agnes enjoyed being dressed up, but Josy was full of complaints. "My garter belt is falling off," she said, "and it's dumb to waste our good clothes just to ride on a train."

Miss Mattie, whose coat was draped with two little foxes and whose hat was adorned with a bird in simulated flight, was not sympathetic. "As soon as we get out of town," she said, "no one will know who we are. If we want to be treated like quality, we must dress like it."

Miss Mattie had been to New York forty years before with Doctor Craig. Then she had been pretty and young and carefree. Now she was old and wrinkled and had wrapped a money belt around her waist and stashed a fifty-dollar bill in the toe of each of her shoes. Nevertheless, when the whistle blew and the train began to move, her eyes blazed with excitement.

The girls waved good-bye to Morgan from their compartment window. He started to run with the train, but he couldn't go very fast because Louisa Jones was holding onto his arm. He broke away and sprinted down the platform, waving and smiling until he was swallowed up by the distance.

The compartment was tiny, but they had double seats that faced each other and a slim little sofa that faced the window. They even had their own little bathroom.

"There's everything here to sustain life," Miss Mattie remarked, "except a kitchen, and we don't need that because Miss Jones has made a picnic for us."

"We don't want a picnic," Josy said. "We want to eat in the diner. Eating in the diner is the best part of riding on a train."

The housekeeper agreed and, after warning the girls not to tell their father, she asked the porter if he could dispense with a cold fried chicken dinner for three, stuffed eggs, some fruit, and pound cake. He seemed delighted to oblige them, and the travelers happily gave away Miss Louisa Jones's cook's cooking and began the seemingly interminable walk to the dining car.

Miss Mattie led the way, and when the train lurched, she grabbed an oncoming, attractive male stranger to right herself. Josy and Agnes watched in amazement as she fluttered her lids, smiled sweetly, and said, "I do beg your pardon, but I must watch out for my bones. They are in a simply abysmal state of ossification."

Josy, in the middle, always jumped ahead in time to hold open the heavy doors that separated the cars. Agnes, bringing up the rear, noticed that when they walked down the aisle, men put aside their papers, their eyes lingering on her sister.

Once they reached their destination and sat down at the table with its immaculate white cloth, all three agreed that the walk had been worth the effort. Miss Mattie said that eating a good meal on a moving vehicle must be one of the high-water marks of modern civilization. "Girls," she said, "looking out that window reminds me of my life. Each scene is gone before I have time to digest it. We must all remember to savor this trip. We mustn't let it get away from us."

"This is probably the best part," Josy said, eyeing the menu. "I love to eat on a train."

"'Oh, but the play is the thing,'" Miss Mattie quoted from *Hamlet*.

Josy sighed. "I hate the theater. *Hamlet* is supposed to be the best play in the world, and I hate it. The people in it talk funny, and they talk too much. Hamlet says 'I die, Horatio, I die,' and twenty minutes later he is still talking."

"Ah," Miss Mattie said, "but twenty minutes later, Horatio says, 'Good night, sweet prince, and flights of angels sing thee to thy rest.'"

"He should have died when he said he would," Josy said.

"That may be," Miss Mattie conceded, "but it's a very good thing for a young lady to know a few Shakespearean phrases with which to enrich her conversation. To illustrate her point, Miss Mattie closed her eyes as if caught up in the spirit of literary exultation and repeated reverently, "Good night, sweet prince, and flights of angels sing thee to thy rest."

"What was wrong with *Hamlet*," Agnes said, "is that Tedde wasn't in it. Tedde's going to be in this one."

∞ ∞

That night the travelers retired early. Agnes, who had never slept on a train before, was amazed when the porter pulled down a berth from the ceiling, created another one from the two seats facing each other, and fashioned still another from the little sofa. Miss Mattie said she wanted to sleep on the sofa because it was only two steps from the bathroom, and the girls drew straws for the lower berth. Agnes won and spent a sleepless night with her nose pressed against the window. There was something magical about speeding through a moonlit shadowy landscape while at the same time lying prone in her pajamas with the covers pulled up. The sound of the whistle and the rhythm of the engine sent a thrill of anticipation through her being so that she felt intensely alive. Sometimes she dozed a little, but when the train jolted to a stop, she was immediately awake, and she scrutinized the people on the platform with great interest. They looked lonely and tired under the yellow station lights, but Agnes felt a strange excitement in being able to watch them from her dark and secret place.

Late in the evening, at another stop, just one person stood on the platform—a handsome young man who appeared to be waiting for someone. Agnes was so captivated by his good looks that she indulged herself in a little fantasy in which the young man was waiting for her. Then, just before the train pulled out of the station, he did something horrible. It was so horrible that she slammed the blind down and sat upright in bed. Never had she felt so personally insulted. The young man had unzipped his fly and begun urinating on the track. She sat for a moment, smoldering in indignation. Then she cracked the blind and peered out. As she would probably never again witness such a deplorable act, she decided to get a good look.

∞∞

Miss Mattie's comparison of the fleeting landscape to the events of life proved appropriate. The trip was so full of new sights and sounds that it was difficult to hold on to the moment and squeeze it dry.

They took a cab to the same small but elegant hotel on Lexington that Morgan frequented when in New York. The concierge, bellboys, and people behind the desk all knew him and inquired after his health. The management sent a basket of fruit to their rooms, and there were roses from Tedde who could not meet them because she was performing that afternoon.

They spent the day shopping on Fifth Avenue, and Miss Mattie let Agnes charge a white fur muff to Morgan. It cost three dollars, and although Miss Mattie thought that was a lot for a little piece of rabbit skin, she sanctioned the purchase. Then, after they bought presents for Viola and Roxie, Josy put two fingers in her mouth and, in the manner of a hardened New Yorker, whistled for a cab.

∞∞

They ate an early supper at the hotel and arrived at the theater in time to look at the posters on the outside walls. One of them featured Tedde, wearing a short, low-cut maid's uniform and passing drinks to guests at a dinner party. As she leaned over with her tray, the poster showed one gentleman ogling her from the front while another lasciviously eyed her from the rear.

As the theater began to fill, they went inside and were given a program and ushered to sixth row center seats. The program contained a short biographical sketch of Tedde, which stated that she had majored in drama at Vassar College, spoke three languages fluently, and had appeared in several off-Broadway productions.

Since the sketch made no mention of Tedde's trip South and her special friends there, Agnes turned around in her seat and announced to the people in the row behind that she knew Theodosia Boyd. "She came to visit us in Maine," she said, "and to our house in Georgia, too."

"Hush!" Josy exclaimed as she slunk down in her chair.

Agnes remained silent as long as she could stand it and then turned to impart the same information to the people beside her.

Finally, the magic moment came, the curtain rose, and there was Tedde. She played the part of an Irish maid with an engaging brogue. Although she was not the star, she had many humorous lines at which Agnes, Josy, and Miss Mattie laughed heartily.

The plot was complicated by a murder that the Irish maid inadvertently witnessed. The murderer was infatuated with the maid but felt it in his best interest to do her in. He wanted to accomplish this as painlessly as possible, so in one of the last scenes he followed her around with a silk scarf with which to strangle her when her back was turned. Every time he unfolded the murder weapon, the maid turned toward him and he, with eyes filled with adoration, put the weapon away. The timing between the turn and the unfolding of the scarf evoked much mirth in the audience.

During this scene, something strange happened to Agnes's mind. She forgot the play was a play, so that when the murderer pretended the scarf was a gift and commenced to wrap it around the maid's neck, Agnes felt that her beloved friend was in actual danger. Without realizing what she was doing, she rose from her seat and issued a warning in the form of a highly audible, abortive scream. The scream was abortive because, in the middle of it, she realized where she was. Therefore, cut off in mid-bloom, the warning had a choked quality that rivaled anything happening on stage.

There was a moment's pause in which three things occurred. The murderer dropped the scarf, Tedde's eyes bugged out as if she actually had been strangled, and Agnes sat down.

The pause was followed by a sprinkling of guffaws that outlasted some of the play's better lines. The only sober-minded people in the theater were Miss Mattie, who bowed her head and fingered her pearls; Josy, who slunk down so far in her seat that she almost disappeared; and Agnes, who wished to die.

When the play ended, Miss Mattie and the girls remained in their seats until the theater emptied. Then Miss Mattie put on her coat, gathered up her purse and gloves, adjusted the foxes, and said, "She is expecting us backstage."

"Can't we just go home? " Josy groaned. "It's so late, and she probably hates us."

"Nonsense!" the housekeeper said. "Of course, we can't." And noting the heartbreak on Agnes's face, she added, "It's not the end of the world."

Agnes dumbly trailed behind as an usher showed them to the rear of the stage. The door of Tedde's dressing room was open, and the actress saw them coming in the mirror she used to remove her make up. Turning, she held out her arms. "Agnes," she said, "Come here to me!" And Agnes walked straight into the outstretched arms of Theodosia Boyd.

∞∞

While they were in New York, Tedde's play was moving to a larger theater and would not reopen for three days. She used the time to show her visitors around town. They rode through Central Park in a horse-drawn buggy, ate with chopsticks in Chinatown, and stuck quarters in the Automat machine for a sandwich. They saw all the things tourists are supposed to see and almost burst with pride when, on the way to the ballet, the cab driver recognized the actress and wanted an autograph.

Agnes took her little fur muff with her everywhere. Tedde said it looked like ermine, and Agnes, grinning happily and displaying a missing tooth, felt like a movie star.

On the last afternoon, Miss Mattie took Josy shopping to look for a prom dress. Agnes spent the afternoon with Tedde in her apartment on Fifth Avenue.

It was a handsome apartment with colorful paintings, views of the park, and lots of books. The walls of the den were covered with autographed pictures of actors and actresses, some famous and some not. Family photographs were kept in the bedroom, and Agnes noticed a very prominently displayed likeness of herself on the table by the bed.

The actress let Agnes go through her closet, inspect her fancy clothes, and even try them on. Agnes was prancing around the bedroom in a red feathered evening gown when the doorbell rang and she heard someone say, "Theodosia, darling, I was in the neighborhood, and I had to drop by and say hello. But if you're busy, I'll just go quietly away without singing you my new song."

"It's a perfect time," Tedde said. "Come in, and we will have a cup of tea. I have a little friend here I want you to meet." She raised her voice and called for Agnes to come out and give them a fashion show.

Agnes dashed a little of Tedde's rouge on her face. Then, holding up her skirt in one hand and clutching the little fur muff in the other, she made her entrance. She was smiling her gap-toothed smile, when something about Tedde's friend wiped the pleasantness off her face.

The guest was seated in an easy chair by the fire. She wore a mink hat, and a mink coat was carelessly thrown behind her on the chair. Diamonds as big as dimes sparkled in her ears, off her fingers, and around her neck. Her dress was low cut and black, but what shocked Agnes was that the lady was the same color as the dress, which was blacker than Roxie or Viola.

"Agnes, come meet Miss Amory," Tedde said, as if it were perfectly natural for a colored lady to be sitting in the living room.

The little girl could only nod.

"That's a lovely little ermine muff," Miss Amory said.

"It's rabbit's fur," Agnes said.

Miss Amory laughed. "I wish I had that bunny."

Something about the remark made Agnes uncomfortable. She excused herself and went back in the bedroom and took off the red dress. She wiped the rouge off her face and very slowly put on her own clothes. She was in no hurry to have tea with Miss Amory. In fact, she was consumed with the same kind of indignation she had felt toward the young man who had urinated on the railroad track. It was hard to believe Tedde didn't know that white people sat in the living room and colored people sat in the kitchen. She thought everybody knew that.

When she returned to the living room, Miss Amory was sitting at the piano, fingering the keys with one hand and holding a teacup with the other. She didn't look like anybody's cook or maid.

Agnes picked out a straight chair and gingerly sat down. Nothing about the situation was right. But when Tedde brought her a cold Coca-

Cola in a bottle, which was the way she liked it, she began to feel better.

"I'm introducing a new song at the club," Miss Amory said, and she put down the cup and began to play and sing at the same time.

It was a lively tune, and the singer had a husky, teasing kind of voice. Tedde stood by the piano and swayed to the music and did a few dance steps in place.

"It's marvelous," she said, when Miss Amory had finished. "It's going to be a hit. The whole country will be singing it."

"I wanted you to be the first to hear it," Miss Amory said. "Now I've got to run. I'm due at the Plaza at four."

"Just one more tune," Tedde begged, "something like 'Tea For Two' since we are having it."

Miss Amory began to play again, and Tedde, who had taught Agnes a little soft shoe while they were in Maine, danced a few steps and then held out her arms for Agnes to join her. Agnes shook her head, but Tedde continued to hold out her arms, and since God had shown no visible signs of objection to Miss Amory's presence in the living room, she got up from her chair and danced, too.

Miss Amory played and sang a few verses. Then she jumped up from the piano stool, grabbed her mink, hugged Tedde and started to leave. "Take care of that muff," she called to Agnes before closing the front door.

"That lady," Tedde said, "is one of the finest musicians around."

"But she's colored," Agnes gasped.

"Yes," Tedde said gently. "I know that. And I know that in the South, black and white don't mix socially. But in my profession, it's different. People are judged by their talent. It would be wrong for me not to sit down with her. It would be both wrong and insulting."

"But couldn't you both sit in the kitchen like I do with Viola?"

"No. That would imply that Miss Amory wasn't good enough to sit in my living room. Besides, I don't have a piano in the kitchen."

The little girl paused for a minute before speaking. There was something about Tedde's answer that didn't quite fit. Finally, she asked, "How can a thing be wrong in one place and not in another?"

Tedde sat down in the easy chair by the fire and pulled Agnes down on her lap. "Honey," she said, "You ask the most astute questions of anybody I know. It's one of the reasons I love you so much. Your questions are too good for most people to answer. What you are going to have to do is keep your ears open and your eyes open and answer them yourself. Don't ask me and don't ask your Papa. Just ask yourself and then do your own thinking. It's as good as anybody's."

"Tedde," Agnes asked, "Do you love Papa?"

"Yes."

"Better than the theater?"

"Yes, but I know it doesn't look that way."

"But you don't think Papa is a true prince?"

"Of course, I think he is a true prince. What makes you say that?"

"Well, when you read me the story about the little mermaid, you said it was all right for the little mermaid to give up her beautiful voice for a true prince. But you didn't give up the theater for Papa."

"Someday," Tedde said, "I'm going to tell you why it didn't work out for your Papa and me. But right now, I can't tell you, and I can't tell him. So instead, I'm going to pull you down beside me and snuggle up because pretty soon you are going to be too big to snuggle."

"You sound like Viola."

"Yes, Viola and I have a lot of love to give."

Sitting on Tedde's lap within the circle of her arms, Agnes was sure of two things. One was that she wanted Tedde to be her new mother, and the other was that Tedde could have anybody she wanted to sit in her living room and it would be all right.

⟁

Going back home on the train, Agnes told Miss Mattie about Miss Amory. "Do you think it was all right to have tea with Miss Amory in the living room?" she asked.

"Why yes, honey. People do different in different parts of the country, and theater people are different by nature."

"Could we have Miss Amory to tea at home?"

"No, it wouldn't be acceptable at home."

"Why is something right in one place and wrong in another?"

Miss Mattie's face split in a huge yawn. She leaned her head back on the train seat and closed her eyes. "Honey," she said, "I'm an old lady, and it's been a strenuous trip. Right now my brain cells need a rest. Ask your Papa when we get home."

CHAPTER FOURTEEN

FIRES OF SPRING

Whenever Morgan thought he had recovered from Emily's death, something happened to bring him up sharp. On the evening he and Louisa took Miss Mattie and the girls to the station, Josy had looked so much like her mother from the window that he had sprinted after the train like a schoolboy, unwilling to lose the vision.

Certainly, his romantic life after Emily's death had run a pathetic course. Theodosia's rejection and the unfortunate incident with Beverly Brown had rendered him vulnerable to the romantic overtures of Louisa Jones who, on the surface, was the perfect mate. An expert horsewoman, beautiful in a cool, aristocratic fashion (O'Brian called her the ice maiden), and steeped in Southern tradition, she seemed preordained to take Emily's place.

Louisa had inveigled a dinner invitation from Miss Mattie a few days after the travelers returned from New York. As soon as she sat down at the Bigley table and the blessing had been said, she expressed an interest in all aspects of the trip.

"I want to hear every little detail," she said, "but first of all I want to congratulate Mattie on holding up so well." She turned toward the housekeeper. "You must have been terribly tired, my dear. Sightseeing is fun, but it can be grueling. I hope I can be as active as you when I'm your age."

"Really, Louisa," Miss Mattie said, "I wasn't tired at all. I may be old, but my health is good."

"That's what I mean," Louisa gushed. "You're absolutely remarkable.

But tell me everything, starting with what you enjoyed most."

"Eating on the train," Josy answered, and Miss Mattie gave her a hard look to remind her they had given Louisa's picnic supper to the porter.

"I liked the play," Agnes said, "because Tedde was in it."

"Agnes was in the play, too," Josy said. "She had a major role in the last act."

The story of the abortive scream was retold. Even though he had heard it before, Morgan leaned forward in his chair and listened attentively as he was prone to do whenever Tedde's name was mentioned.

"It just goes to show Agnes is very appreciative of the theater," Louisa said. "But what else was enjoyable?"

"I enjoyed meeting a famous singer," Agnes said. "She came to Tedde's house for tea."

"It's always fun meeting famous people," Louisa said. "I met William Jennings Bryan when I was a child, and I got goose pimples when he shook my hand."

"I shook hands with Mrs. Roosevelt when she came here to speak," Miss Mattie said. "She was absolutely charming, and it was a thrilling experience."

Louisa raised her eyebrows. "How," she asked, "can a Yankee woman with buck teeth be charming?"

"When she spoke, she was so charming I forgot about her teeth and—"

Miss Louisa didn't let her finish. "And further more, Mrs. Roosevelt hobnobs with negroes."

"She is a negro," Agnes said.

Louisa laughed delightedly. "No. No, Honey Bunny. The country hasn't come to that. Mrs. Roosevelt is white."

"I don't mean her. I mean the lady who came to tea at Tedde's."

Viola came in the dining room to pass the potatoes. Silence prevailed until she went back in the kitchen. Then Agnes turned to Louisa and asked, "Do you think it was wrong for Tedde to have a colored person to tea?"

Louisa finished chewing her roast beef and wiped her mouth delicately with the linen napkin. "I know there are some Yankees who hobnob with negroes," she said. "But I will not comment on it except to say we don't do that kind of thing here in the South."

Miss Mattie, who did not like to talk about race when the servants were about, turned the conversation to world events. "I heard on the radio that the Austrian chancellor was duped by Hitler, and German solders are marching into Vienna. Some people think Hitler is planning on taking over all of Europe." She turned toward Morgan. "What do you think?"

"I think Mr. Churchill has him pegged. The man has to be stopped."

"Let's don't talk about anything unpleasant," Louisa said. "Let's just hope those German soldiers know how to waltz. Now what else did you girls do in New York?"

"We shopped," Josy said. "Agnes got a fur muff, and I got a prom dress."

"I adore shopping," Louisa said. "And I want to see that prom dress as soon as we're through eating."

∞∞∞

After dinner, they retired to the living room, and, at Louisa's insistence, Josy modeled the dress. Even though her hair was in her eyes and her saddle shoes poked out from under the skirt, the pink off-the-shoulder gown enhanced her beauty.

"I think the color brings out the roses in her cheeks," Miss Mattie said.

Louisa narrowed her eyes. "Yes, it is a very becoming color."

Morgan asked to see the little muff, and Agnes had to tell him she had left it on the train.

"That was very careless of you," Morgan said, whereupon Agnes went upstairs to sulk.

Soon afterward, Miss Mattie excused herself on the pretext of having to call her sister, and Josy, having vowed she had finished her homework, went out to get a soda with a sixteen-year-old neighbor's boy who had just gotten his driving license.

Morgan hated the fact that Josy was now old enough to go out with boys. "I wish I didn't worry so," he said to Louisa as he sat down beside her on the sofa facing Emily's portrait.

"Of course, you worry. It's so difficult bringing up girls. Every red-blooded man worries about his daughter."

"Louisa, I know you are up on these things. What did you think about the prom dress?"

She heaved a long, seemingly reluctant sigh, folded and unfolded her lovely hands, and looked him resolutely in the eye. "I think Miss Mattie was out of her mind to let that child buy that dress. It would be fine for a nineteen-year-old debutante, but it is much too revealing for Josy. Miss Mattie is the dearest lady alive, but she is too old to remember—how shall I put it—she is too old to remember how fiercely the fires of spring burn."

"You think the dress is too revealing?"

"I think she is much too young to wear a gown that is held up by two tiny straps. It's asking for trouble."

"I'm glad I talked to you about this," Morgan said, "and I agree with you completely."

He stood and began pacing up and down. "The dress is out of the question, but I can't do anything about the ermine fur piece Agnes left on the train. I got a bill from the store today for $300. Miss Mattie got the decimal point mixed up and mistook an ermine for a rabbit."

"Miss Mattie let Agnes buy an ermine muff, and she left it on the train. Oh, Morgan, you must get it back."

"I doubt that I can. The porter has probably given it to his daughter or his girlfriend."

"Oh!" Louisa wailed. "It makes me sick to think of some darkie wearing Agnes's muff, but don't blame Mattie. She's very frail, and she's getting old."

"I haven't mentioned it to her, and I don't think I will, but Josy must find a more appropriate dress."

He sat back down, and Louisa immediately moved close to him.

"You are as kind as you are wise," she said, "and I appreciate what a difficult position you are in. Miss Mattie served you well when you were in great need, but, Morgan, she must be more than seventy, and she simply doesn't know what's going on."

Dismay showed in his voice. "Louisa, what exactly is going on?"

She leaned forward and patted his leg in a comforting manner. And then, for just a second, her hand rested lightly on the inside of his knee.

"Nothing to worry about at the moment," she said.

"Louisa," he demanded. "What is going on that I don't know about?"

She nestled closer, her breath falling lightly on his ear. "It's just that the neighborhood children always meet in your backyard. They used to play such innocent games. Now it's Spin the Bottle and Post Office. Even little Agnes plays. I don't think Mattie is aware of it, but there are so many places they can go. That little room off your garage, for instance."

The thought that his children might be indulging in sexual activity was maddening, but he was also aware of the incongruity of discussing their morals while Louisa was burrowing her thigh into his. The touch of her hand inside his knee had fueled a desire he wanted very much to keep in check.

"You see," Louisa continued, leaning toward him and dropping her voice to a whisper, "I know how fiercely the fires of spring burn." She paused for a moment before softly adding, "I feel their heat."

He needed time. He needed to stall. He cleared his throat and muttered, "You are a very beautiful woman."

It was true. Her face, tilted toward his, was composed of perfect features. Yet even at that very moment, there was a coldness and invulnerability in her blond beauty.

As if she read his mind, she slipped the pins from her hair so that it fell in pale, shimmering waves to her shoulders. The change was immediate. She looked almost like a schoolgirl.

"Morgan," she whispered, "turn off the light and kiss me."

Obediently, he reached for the light switch. He would kiss her once and kiss her good, and then he would take her home. With Agnes and Miss Mattie just upstairs and liable to put in an appearance unannounced, he didn't care to fuel any flames at that particular moment. But after he took her in his arms, he didn't want to let her go. She was soft and yielding, and as he kissed her, he forgot that she was a boring and predicable woman.

He tore himself away long enough to say, "I see what you mean about those fires," and then he was kissing her all over her face—her eyes, her neck, and back to her mouth.

A voice from upstairs shattered his passion. "Papa," Agnes shouted, "How do you spell photography?"

He removed his mouth from Louisa's lips, got up, switched the light back on, and walked to the foot of the staircase. "Look it up in the dictionary," he shouted back, his voice clearly impatient. "That way you will remember it."

"I did. It's not in the dictionary."

"P-H-O-T-O-G-R-A-P-H-Y," he said, grinding out each letter between his teeth.

"Oh. I thought it started with an F."

Looking at Louisa, he managed a rueful smile. "Come on," he said, "let's get out of here."

They held hands as he walked her home, but the magic of the evening was gone. When they reached her house, she claimed it might disturb her elderly mother if she asked him in. Before closing the door, she kissed him lightly on the cheek and whispered, "Don't forget about those fires."

He took a long circuitous route home in order to sort out his feelings. The big surprise had been Louisa's declaration of passion, and it was interesting to know about those flames. However, it was probably a good thing Agnes had interrupted their attempt at romance. Louisa was a beautiful woman and a fine person to take to an occasional party, but he didn't want to get too heavily involved. He knew she was after him and that she was deliberately trying to make Miss Mattie look old and incompetent, but he wasn't going to fall for that. Miss Mattie may have made a regrettable mistake on a decimal point, but she was as lively as a person half her age. He was lucky to have a woman with her spunk and good sense to run his house.

It was a chilly winter evening. The stars were out, and the air was crisp and clear—a good night for walking and a good time to think things through. As he moved briskly along, he began to enjoy the outdoors and relish the exercise. He was not good at whistling, but he managed a thin little tune as he headed toward home.

The whistling came to an abrupt halt when he reached his own driveway. A car was sitting out front, and two dark figures in the front seat leaned into each other. It was Josy kissing her date goodnight. His blood ran cold.

Chapter Fifteen

SEX TALK

When Morgan saw Josy kissing her date goodnight, he cleared his throat loudly, walked by the parked car and, upon entering his house, blinked the outside light continuously. It didn't take long for her to get the message; however, when she came inside, she looked so innocent and demure that he was loath to confront her with accusations. The girl needed a straightforward talking to about proper behavior between the sexes, but it was a delicate matter, and he wanted to do it right. He said a gruff good night and waited for a better moment.

He spent Saturday morning inspecting his property considering how he could sex proof it. There didn't seem to be much he could do other than get rid of the cot in the room off the garage. Even though its hinges were rusty, and it was obvious it had not been unfolded in years, he decided to trash it. As he continued to examine his property, he cursed his own susceptibility to all that was sensual. Textures, colors, shapes, and even old rusty cots stirred his imagination.

He hoped that he and Louisa were not making too much of the dress. He had seen his friends' daughters wear that kind of gown when they were presented to society at the Christmas ball. All that debutante business was a lot of nonsense, but, at least when Josy was old enough to do it, he would have the satisfaction of presenting the prettiest girl in town to the finest families. As for now, he just wanted her to do the right thing at the right time until she was old enough to marry a Southerner of good morals, good blood, and good prospects.

As for his youngest daughter, she presented him with new problems. On the Saturday after the dinner with Louisa, he and Agnes were having lunch when she startled him by saying, "Papa, I think we ought to ask Viola and Roxie to eat in the dining room with us."

He gave her a sharp look, and her clear blue eyes, innocent and steady, met his.

"They are servants," he said, "and I pay them to serve us. They can't serve and eat at the same time."

This seemed to satisfy her, but when they finished their lunch and were about to rise, she asked, "Could they have dinner with us on their day off?"

"No. They are servants, and they have their own friends. They don't want to have dinner with us on their day off. They want to relax and have a good time with their own people."

They got up from the table, and he went to his room for a short nap. Agnes followed, climbing up on the four-poster bed and sitting cross-legged at the foot.

"Papa," she asked, "do you think it was wrong for Tedde to have tea with a colored lady?"

He closed his eyes and feigned a faint snore. She was leading him into murky waters where he did not wish to tread.

She was not fooled by the snore. "Papa," she said. "Tedde still loves you. She loves you more than the theater."

He opened one eye. "What makes you say that?"

"I asked her, and she told me that you were a true prince and she loved you more than the theater or anything or anybody."

He closed his eyes again and pretended sleep.

∞∞

Later that afternoon, he and Josy drove to the farm in order to ride. They took Blossom with them even though his presence often excited the horses. However, on this day, Blossom immediately took to the woods and, while the two horses were walking quietly side by side on the dirt road leading to the river, Morgan decided it was a good time for a frank conversation.

He began by clearing his throat. He wanted to get just the right note of reasonable persuasiveness in his voice. "Sweetheart," he said, "I want to talk to you about your heritage. You know that your mother and your grandmothers were all women of high moral character."

"Of course, Papa."

"Women of this caliber dressed becomingly but modestly and when dealing with young men, they discouraged liberties."

He turned in the saddle in order to give his daughter a good look. Something in her expression suggested that she thought he was completely off base if not demented. "What in the world are you getting at Papa?" she asked.

"What I'm getting at," he said, "is the immodesty of that prom dress. Your mother would not have approved of it, and I don't approve of it."

Josy, eyes flashing, suddenly came alive and sat straight up in the saddle. "I'd like to know why not," she demanded. "Tedde liked it. Miss Mattie liked it. The only person who doesn't like it is that prissy Miss Louisa Jones."

He continued to use the calm and deliberate voice he used in court. "Miss Mattie is getting on in years. She doesn't know what is appropriate for young girls, and Tedde comes from a more sophisticated environment than we know here in the South. Louisa and I both feel the dress is too revealing."

"Papa, it's Miss Louisa who doesn't know what's going on. My friends expose so much cleavage that you wouldn't believe it. My dress isn't low cut at all by anybody's standards."

"Josy, the dress is provocative, and you don't realize how . . . how fiercely the fires of spring burn."

"Papa, I don't know what you're talking about, and I love that dress!"

With the intention of closing out the conversation forever, he said, "Wear it if you like, but do so in the knowledge that your father feels it is inappropriate."

Josy, eyes glaring and teeth bared, turned toward him. "You ruin everything!" she shouted. Then she dug her heels hard into Rosebud's flank so that horse and rider took off like a rocket.

He couldn't believe it. His brave little Indian and companion of so many rides was talking back to him. They had always been such friends, and now she had turned on him when he was only trying to protect her. If only he could be more honest and direct. If only he could say, I can't stand for you to kiss your date good night because I'm afraid something will happen, and the reason I'm afraid is because I know temptation so well. Saint Paul said, "Better to marry than to burn," and Saint Paul knew what he was talking about.

He did not have an opportunity to dwell on the total failure of his lecture because Charley did not take being left behind lightly. He and Rosebud had developed a rivalry about who could get to the river first, and he snorted and danced to show his malcontent. To make matters worse, Blossom suddenly burst out of the woods and began to frantically run around horse and rider, stopping only to jump high enough to lick his master's boot.

Feeling that his whole day was totally ruined, Morgan shouted to his dog, "Down! Down! Get down, sir!" but Blossom continued to jump, and Charley threw white flecks of foam as he wheeled in a circle.

Morgan's voice rose as he berated his dog with a series of "Down! Down! Down!" Finally, thoroughly exasperated, he resorted to language he did not ordinarily use. "Down, you dumb bastard!" he yelled, and he raised his crop to threaten his dog at the same time that his horse commenced to rear. Realizing that he was about to be unseated or go over backward, he gave Charley his head, and horse, dog and rider were off in a thick cloud of red Georgia dust, passing his daughter on a hill. The only satisfaction he got out of the whole ride was the fact that he and Charley got to the river first.

∞∞

Morgan, at Louisa's instigation, began thinking about sending Josy away to a good boarding school. The girl did very little studying, and he was not satisfied with the education she was receiving at the public high school. He would miss her dearly, but he felt the atmosphere of a good all-girl school might be conducive to study. He asked Miss Mattie's opinion on the matter.

"It's been my experience," Miss Mattie said, "that girls who are sent off to boarding school get pimples."

"Frankly," Morgan said, "We might all be better off if Josy got a few pimples. It's her attractiveness that frightens me. She's too pretty and too free and easy in her ways. I don't like the idea of dangling her in front of these high school boys."

Miss Mattie drew herself up to her full five feet and one inch and looked her employer in the eye. "Josy knows where babies come from," she said. "And she is too smart and too good a girl to do anything foolish."

"I am sure you are right," Morgan said, "but Louisa and I feel that the dress for the dance is too provocative. It's this kind of thing we need to watch."

"Of course, if you don't like the dress," Miss Mattie said, "we will send it back."

"I hope," Morgan said, "she will choose of her own free will not to wear the dress. She knows my feelings on the matter. However, regardless of the choice, we will not send the dress back. I have never approved of returning merchandise to stores. It's a difficult thing to run a business, and merchants don't need their customers changing their minds right and left. If she decides to wear something more modest, we can either put the dress away or give it away."

"Very well," Miss Mattie said, "but since I not only sanctioned but also encouraged the purchase of the dress, I would like to pay for it out of my salary."

"That would not be appropriate."

Again Miss Mattie looked her employer squarely in the eye. "You leave me no choice," she said, "except to feel absolutely miserable about the whole affair." Then she turned and left the room.

Morgan wanted to shout after her that if he wanted to make her feel miserable, he would tell her about the little fur muff. However, he restrained himself. The whole conversation had left him with a very unpleasant feeling, and this feeling was magnified when, two weeks later, Josy elected not to go to the dance. Instead she and her date went to the movies, and she wore a sweater that revealed more of her budding sexuality than the evening gown.

Morgan did not know precisely when his home had turned into a hangout for Josy's beaus, but he knew he didn't like it. It seemed boys were forever in his yard, on his porch, or in his living room. And if they weren't physically present, they were tying up his telephone talking with Josy. They reminded him unpleasantly of dogs sniffing a bitch in heat, but he supposed he would have to get used to it. He had fathered a belle, and he was grateful she still rode with him on the weekends.

As for his youngest daughter, she presented problems of a different nature. Agnes had taken to eating all of her meals in the kitchen with Viola and Roxie. He suspected this had something to do with their conversation about the servants coming to dinner, and he decided to leave the matter uncontested.

The farm was his haven and worth all the money he was spending on it. The Laudermilks were good people and competent workers. He liked them so much that he put in an artisan well and installed a bathroom in their house. Even so, the little outhouse with the rose on the door remained standing, leading Sam Laudermilk to say he had surpassed the American dream. He had a two-bathroom home. With the advent of running water, Jane Laudermilk spruced up and got a secretarial job in town. Jane and Sam wanted to send Tim to college, and Morgan planned on helping them as long as the boy kept up his grades.

Meanwhile Morgan's relationship with Louisa remained unclarified. She was an appropriate companion, but she was so self-righteously Southern that he felt he could predict her responses to almost every situation. In short, she was boring. As for the fires of spring, they never seemed to burn very brightly at appropriate times. If they were alone at her house, she was as chaste as a nun, but if they were at his house and likely to be disturbed by Miss Mattie or the children, she was wantonly flirtatious. So he saw her when he needed a date for a party, but he made no move toward anything permanent.

Once, to his great surprise, Tedde called him. It was late at night, and she sounded sad and lost. "Morgan," she said, "They've got Lola."

In the excitement of hearing her voice, he forgot who Lola was, and he was ashamed of the way his heart leapt up in his chest. It took him a moment to steady himself.

"Lola who?" he asked.

Too late he remembered she was the cousin of Tedde's who lived in Berlin and was a singer of some prominence.

Tedde sounded more dejected than ever. "I thought you would remember," she said.

"I remember now. Who has her?"

"The Nazis, They came and pulled her off the stage and took her away."

"What in the world do the Nazis want with Lola?"

"They're taking the Jews away and putting them in camps. Lola is a Jew, and she made fun of Hitler on stage. The next night, they took her away."

"Look here," he said. "The Germans are a civilized people. They are not going to harm your cousin."

"The Nazis are taking Jews away and killing them,"

"Where did you get your information?" he asked. He didn't mean to sound unsympathetic, but he was a lawyer, and he liked facts.

She sounded tired. "I have a friend in Germany who writes letters. I shouldn't have bothered you, but I thought the sound of your voice might comfort me. It hasn't."

"Now give me her last name and address." Morgan said. "I know a lawyer in Berlin. I'll call him. Perhaps he can help us get to the bottom of all this."

"Morgan, I am already at the bottom of it. Lola has been taken away by the Nazis."

She spoke as if she was addressing a child, but she gave him Lola's full name and address. Then she apologized for bothering him and hung up. She didn't even ask about Agnes and Josy.

The next morning, he contacted his friend in Berlin who, when he discovered the reason for the call, appeared anxious to terminate the conversation. Then he called his senator who put him in contact with someone in the state department who, in turn, put him in contact with someone else, and so forth and so on until it became obvious that obtaining information about Lola would be difficult, if not impossible.

He called Tedde back, composing himself beforehand so that she would not detect how emotionally involved he still was. She, however, did not answer her phone, so he wrote a letter and explained that he would do everything in his power to locate her cousin, but the going would not be easy.

Three weeks later, he got a letter from his Berlin friend, stating that the person about whom he had inquired was dead. That was all. The letter contained no details or explanations.

He called Tedde again, and this time, she answered. He explained that he had received a sad message, very incomplete and short.

Before he could finish, she interrupted him, saying, "I know. Lola is dead."

"I'm sorry," he said, "and I'm sorry I sounded so unsympathetic on the phone. It was late, and you startled me, and for only a moment, I forgot who your cousin was."

"Oh, Morgan, believe me. I appreciate your efforts. I had no right to call you, but you came through, as you always do. Now tell me about Josy and Agnes."

He assured her they both were fine.

Her voice took on the old lilt. "And how did you like the prom dress we bought in New York? Wasn't it perfect?"

He didn't tell her that the dress had caused a disturbance in the home. Instead he opted to lie and say he liked it fine.

They chatted politely for a few minutes longer. All the while they talked, he so badly wanted to make arrangements to see her again, but he couldn't bring himself to do it. She had left him once. He had learned his lesson.

Chapter Sixteen

THE STORM

The family viewed Josy's popularity in different ways. Viola was frankly proud and regarded the quantity of Josy's beaus in much the same way an Indian regards the scalps on his belt. Every time the girl went out with a new face. Viola would grin broadly and say to Roxie, "Here comes a heart itching to be broke."

Morgan regarded the young men that hung around the house as an irritant and a worry. His own sexual longings were a constant reminder of just how hot and heavy the fires of spring did burn, and he kept a weather eye out for signs of sin, drawing some comfort in the knowledge that his youngest daughter was a vigilant and self-appointed chaperon. Agnes, hoping for action, stuck close to her sister but saw little.

Miss Mattie enjoyed Josy's popularity more than anyone. It brought back memories of her girlhood when the boys came courting in buggies instead of Model Ts. She attempted to ease Morgan's concern by reminding him that there was safety in numbers.

Josy took all the attention she received for granted and often looked upon it as a nuisance and a bore. Despite Morgan's lecture, she allowed the boys to kiss her goodnight on the third date, but they were for the most part, discreet, sweet kisses and rather boring. She knew her lack of enthusiasm for the goodnight ritual was due to the fact that the one person she wanted to kiss had never asked her out. In fact, he was so unlikely a candidate for her affection that he wasn't even on Morgan's or Agnes's suspect list, but Josy dreamed of him at night and hugged her pillow.

Ever since the Laudermilks had come to work for Morgan, she had liked the look of Tim. He was a tall, redheaded fellow with a mass of freckles and a chin that inspired confidence. Morgan said the Laudermilks came from good blood, and Tim had a hawk-nosed, high cheekboned kind of good looks unusual in a stable boy.

When he first came to the farm, he and Josy shared an open, lively friendship. She taught him how to ride, and they had spent many happy hours tearing through the woods and across fields on Rosebud and Old Tom. But as they grew older, Tim became distant and, if he joined Morgan and Josy on their weekend rides, he seemed more interested in talking to the father than the daughter.

One Sunday afternoon in April, while Morgan worked his vegetable garden, Josy coaxed Tim to ride with her to the river. They started out slowly, walking their horses side by side along the red dirt road that separated the kudzu fields. The skies were blue and friendly when they left the barn, but by the time they were a half-mile away, there was an ominous roll of thunder and a show of rain clouds.

"We're gonna get wet," Tim said. "You want to turn back?"

"Oh, no" Josy said. "I don't mind rain, and Rosebud needs the exercise."

"You're really an outdoor girl," he observed.

"I hate cities," Josy said. "and I hate city clothes. I'd rather be in the country wearing my jeans than all dressed up at the fanciest party."

They rode a few minutes without speaking, but for Josy, it was not a comfortable silence. She wanted Tim to enjoy her company, and she searched her mind for some line of conversation that might be interesting. In desperation, she said, "April is my favorite month."

He didn't say anything, so she began to prattle. "I guess it's my favorite month because I like that fresh green color the first new leaves have, and I like the smell of sweet shrub in the woods. I like everything about April except it's the month my mother was killed in an automobile accident."

Tim nudged Old Tom with his foot so that he would keep stride with Rosebud. "How old were you when it happened?" he asked.

"I was ten. For months, I cried myself to sleep. Then one night Miss Mattie came into my room and said she grieved so hard when Dr. Craig died that her hair turned gray and her face got wrinkled. That scared me so bad, I dried up."

Tim grinned. "So your vanity conquered your grief."

"'So your vanity conquered your grief,'" she mimicked. "Why don't you talk like a country boy? How come you always sound so educated?"

"I guess it's because my father went to college and because he's really an artist, not a farmer. My father can paint a lot more than that rose on the outhouse door."

"I love his pictures," Josy said. "I particularly love the one of the river. I want to buy it for Papa for his birthday."

"And I guess I talk like I do," Tim continued, "because I would rather read than do anything, and because I don't want to be a country bumpkin and eat corn bread and turnip greens all my life."

Old Tom had fallen behind, and Tim gave him a swift kick. "No offense, Old Tom," he said, "but someday I am going to ride a magnificent animal who doesn't have a Roman nose and who doesn't have to be kicked every few minutes to keep up."

When his horse fell in stride with Rosebud, he said, "Miss Louisa was out here looking at the garden with your father. Does she enjoy riding?"

"Yes, but thank goodness it's not fancy enough for her out here. I can't stand that prissy old bitch."

Tim raised his eyebrows. "How come you don't talk like a Southern lady?" he asked.

"I guess it's because I just like to hear those bad words roll off my tongue. I guess I've got an ear for profanity. I know lots worse words than 'prissy bitch.'"

"You'd better not let your daddy hear them."

"He's too worried about other things I might do to worry about how I talk."

"What other things?"

She turned her face toward his and with much rolling of the eyes said, "Oh, dumb things like, and I quote, 'giving privileges to young men.'"

His grin stretched from ear to ear. "You wouldn't do that, would you, Josy?"

She had quoted Morgan's old-fashioned language in an effort to be amusing, but suddenly she was embarrassed. She could feel the heat in her cheeks. When they came to a cut off through the woods, she said, "You go first."

"No, Rosebud likes the lead. You go first."

"All right, but don't let Old Tom run you back to the barn."

"I won't. And when you fall off, get out the way so we don't stomp on you." It was the way they used to joke before Tim became distant.

There was a rumble of thunder as they turned off the road, and a strong gust of wind swept through the woods. Rosebud arched her neck and danced a little, and even old Tom's rather large ears shot forward in a salute to the weather. Josy allowed her horse to start off in a trot, which soon became a gallop, with Tim and Old Tom hard behind. They raced through a forest of pines, not slowing up until the terrain became too steep.

They paid no attention to the darkening sky as they picked their way down a rocky incline. Once at the bottom, they galloped along a flat path by the creek until they reached the river road. However, they were no longer able to ignore the elements. A clap of thunder and a streak of lightning zigzagging across the sky brought them to their senses.

"We better wait it out in that old barn down the road," Tim said. He was referring to a battered, broken-down structure that had once served to house cattle.

Again they galloped, but now thunder and lightning were all around them. Then the rains came, at first gently and then in torrents. By the time they reached shelter and rode their horses inside, their hair was plastered down, water dripped off their noses, and their clothes were soggy.

Josy took stock of herself and became painfully aware that her wet shirt had become transparent and was clinging to her breasts. She pulled it away from her body and hunched over in the saddle so Tim wouldn't see.

Tim dismounted and attached his reins under his stirrups. He put Old Tom in a stall, and then, having tested the ladder, climbed up to the loft. "We might as well sit up here," he said. "It's dry, at least."

She looked at the dirt floor of the barn and decided he was right. Dismounting, she put Rosebud in a stall and climbed the ladder. When she sat down, she folded her arms over her chest and let her legs dangle over the edge of the loft. Tim sat down beside her, leaving a good distance between them.

A clap of thunder seemed to shake the barn, and the rain banged out an angry, erratic rhythm on the tin roof. Josy shivered and moved closer to Tim so that their cold wet jeans touched.

"How long do you think it will last?" she asked.

"Not long. We'll probably be out of here in twenty minutes, if we're lucky."

She hoped they would not be lucky.

"This is like a movie," she said.

"What kind of movie?" he asked. "A Western?"

She widened her eyes and looked up at him. "A romantic movie."

He gave her one of his rare smiles. "I saw a romantic movie once," he said. "It was about a poor stable boy who fell in love with the rich squire's daughter. It was set in the moors, and there was lots of thunder and lightning, and the rich squire's daughter died."

"Wuthering Heights," she said. "I saw it, too." She unfolded her arms and took his hands in hers and examined them closely. Mimicking a disdainful, British accent, she exclaimed, "Oh, Heathcliff, your hands are so dirty—so terribly, terribly dirty." Then speaking in her own voice, she added, "But I like dirt."

He withdrew his hands. "I like Westerns. I don't go in for romance."

"Had you rather kiss the horse than the girl?" she asked.

He looked straight ahead at the opposite side of the barn. "It's more like I don't want to get mixed up with the rich squire's daughter."

She refused to accept the rebuff. Reaching up with her outside hand, she caressed his cheek, turning his face toward hers. "Are you sure about that?" she asked. "Or is it just big talk?"

A flash of lightning lit up the barn so that they could see each other plainly and, for a moment, he looked angry, as if he might push her away. Then he bent toward her and kissed her, and in the space of a second, they were in each other's arms.

She wiggled away from the edge of the loft so they wouldn't fall off. He pushed her down against the floorboards, his wet soggy body on top of hers, and for a moment there was no world outside the feel of their two bodies touching. Then, just as suddenly as they had kissed, he rolled away from her and lay on his back.

"I like you a lot," he said, "but I'm a poor man's son. I don't have a car or any fancy friends. I just go to school with a lot of country bumpkins and take care of horses."

She propped her head up on her elbow so she could see his face. "That's all right. I don't care about that."

"Even if I could have a girl," he continued, "my father works for your father, and this could get him fired. There's a depression out there. Jobs are hard to come by these days."

"Papa doesn't have to know."

He sat up and looked at her straight. "Your father has been very decent to me. He said he would help me go to college if I do my part."

"I can't help it if I like you, too," she whispered.

He took her hands and pulled her to her feet. "It isn't gonna work. We got to get back. The storm is just about over."

He spoke with such authority that there was nothing to do but follow him down the ladder, mount the horses and ride home in the diminishing rain.

The weather had cleared by that time, wet and bedraggled, they arrived back at the barn. On their return, Morgan, dry as toast, emerged from the Laudermilk house, where he had sat the storm out drinking Mrs. Laudermilk's tea by a blazing fire. He seemed vastly amused by their soggy condition but was pleased they had found some shelter in the old cow barn. He sent Josy inside to warm up and to borrow a jacket from Tim's mother while he and Tim rubbed down the horses. Old Tom showed his contempt for grooming by rolling over in the mud as soon as he was turned loose in the pasture.

When Josy came back out, Morgan was waiting for her in the car. She went in the tack room to say good-bye to Tim, and when she handed him the jacket to return to his mother, he barely looked at her. "You're a good kisser for a farmer," she said softly, and she didn't wait for a reply.

During the next week, Tim occupied every corner of her mind. She didn't believe in the finality of his rejection. He was afraid of her father, but there were ways to get around that. The scene in the barn had happened so fast that she hadn't had time to understand it, but of one thing she was sure: kissing Tim was the way kissing was meant to be.

Morgan usually took her riding on Wednesday afternoons, but that week he was too busy at the office. Finally, Saturday came, and Josy was as careful about her appearance as if she were attending a ball. She washed and curled her hair and tried three shades of lipstick before selecting a pleasing one. She wore her favorite faded blue jeans and left enough buttons of her shirt unbuttoned to reveal a crevice. The details of her appearance, which usually bored her to the point of negligence, were suddenly important.

When they drove up to the stables, Tim came out of the house in order to help saddle up. He got Charley out of his stall and began brushing him off. He never even looked at Josy. Morgan asked him if he wanted to ride, and he said, "No, thank you, sir. My father has some chores for me."

He was cleaning stalls, when the riders returned. He put down his shovel in order to wipe Charley off while Morgan checked out his vegetable garden. He neither looked at nor spoke to Josy. After he put Charley in the pasture, he went back in the stall.

Josy cleaned Rosebud off and put her in the pasture. Then she got a shovel and joined Tim. "I can help," she said.

"I don't need any help," he said. "It's too crowded in here."

She put the shovel down and went to Morgan's car. She didn't want to cry in front of anyone.

When Morgan got in the car, he looked at her closely. "You all right, honey?" he asked.

"Sure," she said and turned her face to the window.

Chapter Seventeen

THE SNAKE

After the scene in the barn, Josy pretended to dislike Tim Laudermilk as much as he apparently disliked her. She spoke to him only if necessary, and if Morgan asked Tim to join them on a ride, she took her horse a different route.

The self-doubt his rejection had engendered caused her to look inward and to examine certain aspects of her personality. Her preoccupation had always been with horses and friends and never with books. She lost her homework on a daily basis, daydreamed in class, and barely made it from one grade to the next. She wondered if Tim rejected her because he liked smart girls, and she wondered if she was too far behind to ever catch up. For the first time, an education seemed to have a direct bearing on her life, and she decided to change her ways and give it a try.

She began by pursuing the smartest boy she knew, who was Jay Hightower, Miss Mattie's great nephew. Jay had developed into a tall, awkward fellow who wore thick glasses and usually carried a Hemingway novel or *The Rubaiyat* under his arm. As his peers valued physical prowess above mental, he was not much admired. However, under Josy's cultivation, his self-esteem and popularity rose, and he spent countless happy hours sitting on the Bigley's veranda, drinking Coca-Colas, doing homework, and reading poetry out loud to a pretty girl whose eyes glazed over as he read.

Agnes sat on the porch with them. Liking poetry and possessed of an appreciation of language beyond her years, she rarely let a reading go by without benefit of her evaluation. Once, upon listening to a verse in praise of the grape by Omar Khayyam, she raised her Coca-Cola bottle and examined it wistfully. "I wish this was wine," she said.

"What do you know about wine?" Jay asked. "You've never tasted it. You might hate it."

"I know I would love it," Agnes said. "I love the way it looks in the glass. And I love the way the poet makes it sound. My friend, the actress, drinks it every night."

"Jay," Josy said, "you're leading my little sister astray with those poems and boring me to death."

"Just wait until you hear this next one," Jay said. "I know you'll like it." He read another verse in which the poet asked to have his body wrapped in a winding sheet of vine leaf and buried by a garden.

When he had finished reading, Josy rolled her eyes, and Agnes said, "She doesn't like it any better. You might as well face it. She doesn't understand poetry, and she never will, and she wants to be buried by a stable and wrapped in a horse blanket."

Josy nodded her head in agreement, and Jay had to admit the truth of what the two sisters knew all along. His student was either totally adverse to or incapable of literary appreciation. He went on to other things and, in preparing her for a math exam, was shocked to find she had never mastered the multiplication tables. He spent an afternoon trying to instill them permanently into her brain and then gave her a little quiz.

"We'll start off with the easiest question of all," he said. "What's one times one?"

"Two," Josy said.

Jay groaned. "Two times one is two," he said

"Are you sure?" she asked. "It seems like if two times two is four, and four times four is sixteen, that one times one ought to be two. I thought multiplication was just another horrible form of addition."

"We need to work harder," he said.

Her spelling was worse than her arithmetic. Upon looking over her biography of George Washington, he laughed out loud. "Josy," he said, "this is the most Freudian paper I have ever read."

"What's that mean?" she asked. "I suppose it's another insult to my intelligence."

"Never mind. What we've got to work on is your spelling. In the South, we don't talk the way things are spelled."

"I know. Yankees do that. Personally, I think it's one of their more unattractive traits."

"Well, you had better learn to spell like a Yankee, or you're going to get in trouble. You have misspelled 'Virginia.'"

They were sitting on the porch swing, and she took the paper out of his hands and examined it. "Are you sure?" she asked. "It looks all right to me."

"Believe me; I am sure. Virginia is spelled V-I-R-G-I-N-I-A." He named each letter slowly as he spoke. "And you have spelled it Va-gin-ia. You've got George Washington born in Vaginia, settling in Vaginia, and dying in Vaginia."

He continued reading, laughing, and making corrections as he did so. When he put the paper down, he commented, "You've written an appropriate concluding sentence for a great Vaginian." And he read out loud, "George Washington, a great soldier, statesman, and patriot is known as the father of our country."

"Thank you," she said. "I thought that line had a nice ring to it."

The next day, Jay gave her a pocket dictionary and advised her to use it.

Despite the poor beginning, Josy's grades improved. She began to bring home Cs and Bs instead of Ds, and Morgan was full of praise. "Hard work always pays off," he said, "and you are to be commended for an outstanding effort and for fine results."

Josy beamed, and Agnes said, "I guess she's not as dumb as we thought."

∞∞

Morgan still toyed with the idea of sending his beautiful daughter off to boarding school. He sounded her out about it and was pleased that she was not totally opposed.

"But what would I do about Rosebud?" she asked.

"Tim can exercise her," Morgan said. "Frankly, I would hate to see you go, but a good stiff boarding school might give you an edge in getting into college."

"I'll think about it," Josy said.

She did think about it, and the more she thought, the more appealing the idea became. It would be easy to study if she could get away from the boys who pestered her for attention. Jay had been helpful, but she wouldn't miss him except in his role as tutor. She had taken him riding one afternoon and was embarrassed in front of Tim when Old Tom came roaring back to the barn minus his rider. The look of amused satisfaction on Tim's face infuriated her, and she pretended more sympathy for the hapless rider than she actually felt.

With Jay's help, she finished her junior year of high school with a B average. Morgan was pleased with her effort, and she delighted in his praise. She knew she would never love books the way Agnes did—there was too much going on in the real world for her to be a reader—but she was not turning out to be the dummy everyone supposed her to be. She decided to go off to school and to work hard.

∽∾

That summer she got her driver's license and sometimes drove to the farm alone to ride. Occasionally she caught a glimpse of a tall, redheaded figure working in the fields, but she seldom bothered to wave.

It often took her a while to catch Rosebud because the pasture in back of the barn was large and included a wooded area where the horses went for shade. Sometimes it was hard even to find the horses, and when she did, Rosebud, under the tutorship of Old Tom, enjoyed trotting a teasing distance away just before she was close enough to catch her. If she forgot to bring an apple or a lump of sugar, it might take twenty minutes before she was allowed to slip the halter over the horse's head.

One hot, August afternoon, while she was standing quietly in the pasture looking for the horses and planning her strategy, a cold unpleasant sensation started in her legs and traveled upward. Sensing the presence of something threatening, she stood stock still, rooted to the spot. A buzzing sound caused her to look downward where, close to her feet, lay a large, coiled snake. Its head was up, and a pattern of diamonds ran along its back.

Josy took great pride in her courage, but as she stood there in the pasture in cutoff blue jeans and holding nothing but a halter, she lost the power of movement. She did not like any reptiles, but in the back of her mind, while she was frozen, it had registered that this was a rattler and that he was angry.

The snake made the buzzing noise again, and somehow she forced her legs, stiff with fear, to slowly step backward. When she had put a little distance between herself and the rattler, she turned and ran.

She got back to the barn and sank down on the back steps of Tim's house just as he was coming up from the garden.

"What's the matter with you?" he asked. "Are you all right?"

She was panting so hard, she could barely talk. "I nearly stepped on a rattler," she gasped. "He's in the pasture, and he's big."

"It's probably just a king snake," he said.

She spoke between clenched teeth. "I know he is a rattler because he rattles, and I nearly stepped on him."

"Well, I'd better kill him then." He went into the shed and brought out a pitchfork. "You've got to point him out to me."

"Wait a minute," she said. "You're not going to get all the glory." She got up from the steps, went into the shed, and brought out a shovel.

"What do you think you're going to do with that?" Tim asked.

"Well, after you miss him, I'm going to kill him,"

"In that case," he said, "you can have the first blow."

She shook her head. "No, thanks. To tell the truth, he scared me so bad, I couldn't move."

"That's probably what saved you. That is, if it was a rattler."

Her courage returned as she walked back to the pasture beside Tim. He was tall and strong and looked as if he knew what he was doing. However, when they found the snake, still coiled but with its head down, he said "Are you sure you don't want to strike the first blow?"

"I'm sure."

They were about fifteen feet away from the rattler, and they stood very still while Tim sized the situation up. "I guess I better hit him on the head," he said.

"I guess so."

He didn't seem to be in any hurry. "You'd better give me the shovel, and you take the pitchfork."

She did as she was told, but he kept on studying the lay of the land as if he were a golfer about to make an important shot.

"It's a rattler, all right," he said.

"I told you that. Now when are you going to do it?"

"Do what?"

"Kill it, you fool."

Some intimation of their presence roused the rattler, and it lifted its head and began to buzz. Tim, with his arms held high, walked quickly over to the snake and brought the shovel down as hard as he could. He struck it three times on the head, and then he held the head down with the shovel while the rest of it convoluted in the air. Josy followed with the pitchfork, which she brought down on the snake's tail so that they held the animal pinned between them.

"What do we do now?" she shouted. There was no need to shout, but the urgency of the situation caused her voice to rise.

"I guess we stand here until the damn thing dies," he shouted back.

The snake wriggled up high in its middle, and they bore down hard on the shovel and the pitchfork.

"We could be here all day," Josy said.

"Are you getting bored?" Tim asked.

"No, but if I do, I will leave. My end isn't terribly important."

The snake rose in the middle, and when it fell back down, Tim lifted the shovel and bashed it again. He kept on bashing until the head was destroyed and the body lay still.

When they were absolutely certain the snake was dead, Josy began to giggle. "Well," she said, "You did that real well. I taught you how to ride, and now I've taught you how to kill rattlers."

"You sure did." He drawled his words out casually and leaned on the shovel. "The way you lit into that tail while I took care of the venomous end was real instructional."

"I guess," she said, "I'll make a man of you yet."

Then, as they stood there, the snake gave one last convulsive twitch. They both leapt two feet in the air, dropped the shovel and the pitchfork, turned and hightailed it to the barn where they collapsed on the Laudermilk back steps, laughing.

When they were sober enough to talk, Josy asked, "What are we going to do with him, that is, presuming we get enough courage to go back to the pasture?"

"I don't know about you," he said, "but I've had enough excitement for one day. For the time being, I'm going to leave him there as a warning to his friends and relatives, and I'm going down to the creek for a swim." The sweat was pouring off his face and bare chest.

"Mind if I go with you?" Josy asked. "I'm hot, too."

"It's your creek," he said.

"I'm going off to school in two days, and I'd like to talk to you before I go."

"Well, let me get my bathing suit on."

He went in his house, put his suit on under his jeans, and came back out. They walked back through the pasture, circling the unpleasant looking dead rattler. While they were walking, she told him about all the studying she had done and how she was going off to school in order to work hard and get in a decent college.

"The only thing I hate about it," she said sadly, "is leaving Rosebud. "You'll have to ride her for me and, of course, I know you'll take good care of her."

"I'll take good care of her," he promised. "And I'll be more than happy to ride her."

When they got to the woods, Tim took the lead, and they walked single file along a path that followed the creek.

"Remember," Josy said from the rear, "how we used to come swimming here with our clothes on after almost every ride?"

"I remember how I ripped my pants on the sliding rock," Tim said.

"We haven't been swimming in the creek since I was fourteen and had that birthday party down here, and you wouldn't come," she said.

He turned and glared at her. "Those were city kids, and I didn't fit in."

They walked in silence until they got to the place where the creek widened and the water cascaded over the rocks, forming a foamy pool beneath. Tim pulled off his jeans, throwing them down on the ground, and waded across the creek to the sliding rock. His white legs contrasted sharply with his above the waist tan.

Josy watched as he sat down on the sliding rock and slid into the churning pool. He went under for a minute, and when he came up, he was standing shoulder high in the water.

"You've grown," she shouted. "It used to be over your head."

"What?" he shouted back.

She kicked off her shoes and picked her way over to the sliding rock. "You've grown," she repeated loudly. Then, in her cut-off jeans and white shirt, she sat down and slid, turning on purpose and entering the water backward. When she came up, she stood on tiptoe so that the water came just below her chin. She pulled her hair behind her ears and looked up at Tim, her eyes full of challenge and excitement. "Can you do that?" she asked.

"Okay," he said, "if that's the way you want to be." He got out, climbed up to the sliding rock, lay down on his back and entered the water head first.

She laughed, and the sound of her laughter was filled with a growing excitement.

"That's nothing," she said, grinning widely, and she climbed up the rocks and came back down on her stomach.

"You think that's good?" he said. "Watch this." And he got out of the water and, with his knees bent and hands out for balance, slid down the sliding rock on one foot.

They continued in this vein, each one trying to out do the other. Every time Josy went under and came up, she laughed a little louder and stood a little closer to Tim in the swirling creek.

Now, when she climbed out of the pool, she paused, as if concentrating on a difficult and intricate maneuver. Her wet clothes clung to her body, but unlike the afternoon in the storm, she made no move to pull the wet shirt away from her breasts.

On her last slide, she attempted to come down the rock standing up and backward, so that she faced the rock instead of the water. She crouched down low and leaned forward, but this time she fell, bumping against the rock and entering the water upside down.

Tim pulled her to the surface, where for a moment she looked dazed and uncertain. However, before he let her go, she looked up at him and asked, "Why have you been so mean to me?"

"Because it won't work," he said, and he glared at her angrily. Then he closed his eyes and kissed her. And because it was difficult for her to reach his mouth in that depth of water, she stood on her tiptoes and clung to him, so that they stood there in the current, locked in each other's arms.

When they came up for air, he whispered, "This isn't right."

"I'm leaving, tomorrow," she said softly.

He shook his head. "That doesn't make it right," but he kissed her again. Then they climbed out of the creek and sank down on the rock and this time, when their lips met, they forgot the old rules.

She had not meant for it to come to that. She had not planned any of it. But ever since this boy-man had first come to the farm as a twelve-year-old, she had been drawn to him, and after he had kissed her in the barn and then rejected her, she had hated him by day and dreamed of him at night, remembering always the feel of his body against hers. And now, while they were making love on the flat rock with the back of her head half submerged in a pool of water, she entered a world that had nothing to do with the do's and don'ts of her upbringing, and everything to do with the sun and the air, the rock, and the current.

She didn't know it would be like that. She didn't know that when he kissed into her mouth, she would kiss him back the same way. She didn't know that when he touched her breast, she would feel it deep inside her body, and, of course, she didn't know that when they tore off her jeans and threw them aside, her jeans would land in the current and travel downstream to parts unknown.

When it was over, and the two virgins were no longer virgins, they lay in each other's arms. He raised his head and said, "What have I done?"

And she stroked his hair and said, "Whatever it was, I wanted you to do it."

Then she became increasingly aware the rock was hard, her head was in a pool of water, and she still lived in the same world with her father who, although it was improbable, might at any minute come strolling by. She sat up, hastily put on her underclothes, but could not locate the cut¬off jeans. She looked at Tim, her eyes wide with panic. "They're gone," she said. "My jeans are gone. They must have washed down the creek. You've got to find them."

Tim dressed in a flash and began leaping from rock to rock in the direction of the river, and Josy jumped back into the swimming hole. Now the water seemed cold, and she shook as she waited there and reviewed her situation. She knew she had sinned, but it wasn't God so much as her father that she was worried about. God seemed so far away, but her father was close by and might decide to take an afternoon ride. On the other hand, only God could help Tim to find her pants, and only God could keep Morgan from coming.

"Please," she prayed. "Oh, please, don't let Papa find out, and please let Tim find my jeans. Please God. I'll be a nun and shave my head if You will just find my pants. Oh, please, God."

The sun hung lower in the sky when Tim returned empty-handed. "You'll have to put on mine," he said, holding out the pants he had worn over his bathing suit.

She climbed out of the swimming hole and quickly put on his pants. They were better than nothing but not much.

"I hope we don't see anybody," she said. "I don't know how I'm going to explain why you are wearing your bathing suit, and I am wearing your pants." Her teeth were chattering so that she could hardly talk.

"Hurry up!" Tim said. "Maybe we can get back before Mama gets home from work."

The two sinners walked silently and hurriedly back to the barn, each one pondering the enormity of their sin and the possible repercussions.

Two days later, Josy was enrolled in Miss Barnes's Seminary for young ladies, a school devoted to the elevation of young minds and the preservation of virginity.

CHAPTER EIGHTEEN

DANCING CLASS

The year that Josy went off to school was the year Agnes lost weight. At first, no one noticed, not even Agnes. Then one morning at breakfast, Morgan looked up from his paper and said, "Why, honey, I believe you're slimming down."

"I've been thinking the same thing," Miss Mattie said, "and it's mighty becoming."

Viola, who was passing a plateful of scrambled eggs and bacon, added, "My baby gets prettier every day."

Agnes beamed. She had a deeply ingrained streak of vanity and, now that Josy was not around to poke fun, spent hours in front of the mirror, experimenting with hair and makeup possibilities. Compared to Josy, she was no beauty, but the jowls were going, and she had a pleasant, intelligent face.

"I've been thinking," Miss Mattie said, "that it's time Agnes joined the afternoon dancing class. It gives a girl confidence to learn to foxtrot and waltz early. Josy started early, and she enjoyed it."

All the pleasantness departed from the girl's face. She knit her brows and spoke slowly as if she were addressing a child. "She only went because she was the prettiest and most popular girl there. Just because I'm not fat any more doesn't mean I'm popular. I've only got two friends, and they don't go to dancing school."

"Two friends are enough," Morgan said, "as long as they're nice people. But I'm hoping Agnes will take up riding again. It would be nice to have a companion next Saturday."

Agnes had been thinking about riding with her father even before he mentioned it. She envied the close companionship Josy and Morgan shared and knew she would never be part of it unless she overcame her fear of horses.

"All right, Papa," she said. "I'll give it a try, but I'm not going to dancing school."

That night and every night before Saturday, Agnes got down on her knees and petitioned God for the success of the Saturday ride. "Don't let Old Tom kill me," she prayed, "but if he does, let it be quick and painless. And remember, God, I had rather be killed than maimed. I couldn't stand being maimed, and I am sure you remember that you promised not to give your servants more than they can stand."

When Saturday came, she found an old shirt of Josy's and put it on. Wearing something of Josy's might just possibly bring her luck.

On the drive out to the farm, Morgan talked to her about riding. "If you look between your horses ears," he said, "it gives you balance. And don't pull on the reins unless you want to slow up or back up. Pulling on the reins hurts your horse's mouth, and I know you want to always take good care of your mount."

"I just want to take care of me," Agnes said.

When they got to the farm and she was actually astride, she felt more secure than she anticipated. He legs had grown since her last encounter with Old Tom, and he looked too tired to cause trouble.

Morgan adjusted her stirrups, handed her a crop and advised her to use it if necessary. Old Tom dropped his head and threatened sleep. Agnes envied his relaxed attitude.

Morgan mounted, and they started down the road that led to the river path. They passed Tim working at the far end of the garden, and he shouted to Agnes, "You look pretty good up there."

She was too busy looking between her horse's ears to acknowledge his greeting, but Morgan smiled and waved. "That's a fine young man," he said. "I would trust him anywhere."

They walked a mile without incident. When they reached the path through the woods, Morgan suggested they go a little faster. He put Charley into a slow trot, but Old Tom stood stock-still. Agnes timidly raised her crop and brought it down gently on his back. He dropped his head and bit a chunk out of a bush on the side of the road.

Suddenly Agnes's past flashed before her eyes. She saw herself at seven being thrown from her new pony, and she remembered how she had screamed, "I hate this pony. Sell him, Papa! Sell him!" Morgan had sold him, and Josy had looked at her with such scorn. "That was a good little pony," Josy had said, "and you're just a fat little sissy."

Then she recalled the many times Josy had teased her about being a sissy, and as soon as she began to blubber, Josy would say, "Ha! Ha! You're soft, and I'm hard."

Reviewing those events stiffened her spine and spurred her to action. She took her reins in one hand and jerked her horse's head up. Then she raised the crop and brought it back down with a mighty wallop, and this time Old Tom took the hint. He shot forward, swerved past Charley, and cut away from the path. He galloped hell for leather toward a tree with a low branch and then stopped as suddenly as he had started, dropping his head in an attitude of total boredom.

When Agnes saw the low branch coming at her, she got so low over the horse's withers that she was barely visible to the naked eye. Then, after the horse stopped, she straightened up and looked at her father in amazement.

"Papa," she said, "I think Old Tom wants to kill me."

"Well, honey, he sure couldn't do it. Could he? You were superb! You got down so low that I didn't know where you went. I believe you are going to be a little circus rider."

Agnes applied the crop again but not so hard. Old Tom fell in behind Charley, and they continued along the trail. After a few minutes, Morgan put Charley into another slow trot, and Agnes bounced along behind him without incident. When they slowed down to a walk, Morgan asked, "You all right back there?"

"I'm fine," Agnes replied. "Old Tom keeps trying to break my neck, but I'm taking good care of him. A good rider takes good care of his mount."

Morgan laughed appreciatively. "You're going to be all right, Agnes," he said. "You're going to be all right."

From then on, she was committed. If Josy was her father's little

Indian, she was his circus rider, and she did every thing in her power to live up to the description. She rode at every opportunity and was up to any shenanigan Old Tom initiated.

Often, when they were riding side by side, Morgan talked to her in the same way he had talked to Josy, advising her of his love of the land. "We must hold on to it, honey," he said. "The land will always be there for us, and we must treat it well."

Or sometimes, he spoke to her of his love of the South, its natural beauty, and his hope that it would never become too industrialized. "We have a way of life here," he said, "that has a gentler quality than that of other regions."

He spoke to her as if she were an adult, and she hung on every word.

She wrote several letters to Tedde, telling her about the farm and her experiences with Old Tom. The letters went unanswered, but sometimes the actress was out of town for long periods of time and didn't get her mail.

That year that Agnes learned to ride marked a change in her attitude. She had always lived in a world of books, but now that she was her father's little circus rider, she began to see that life had something to offer outside the printed page. This realization, along with the fact that she was a secret dancer, contributed to the decision to let Miss Mattie talk her into Wednesday afternoon dance lessons.

Viola was the only one allowed to watch when, in the privacy of her bedroom, Agnes would turn on the radio so that she could shimmy, shake, and sway to the rhythm of the big bands. Viola, too, was a secret dancer, and if the music got hot enough, she would roll her big hips and big bosoms in perfect time as she took the little girl's hand and swung her out between the twin beds saying, "Now truck on home, baby. Truck on home." And Agnes's response to the music was so strong, that she tended to agree when Viola said, "Honey, you is some dancer."

When Agnes told Miss Mattie that she guessed she might go to dancing class after all, the housekeeper did everything in her power to make the lessons a success. She observed the class beforehand in order to see what the little girls were wearing, and then she took Agnes shopping in order to buy an attractive and appropriate dress. She showed her how to roll up her straight brown hair and produce curls, and on the Wednesday afternoon of the first class, she pretended not to notice that Agnes had applied a little Tangee Natural to her lips. The result of all this preparation was gratifying, and the little girl marched off to lessons with her best foot forward.

The class was held in the ballroom of a country club, and the minute Agnes entered that room, she began to deflate. She only recognized a few of the students, and they were members of the "in" crowd at school and had never had much to do with her. She wanted to turn around and go home, but Miss Mattie was by her side, happily pushing her toward the teacher. The most she could hope for was to discreetly stay for one lesson and never return.

The teacher, Miss Peabody, had a wide jaw and a big chin. The resolve of a top sergeant was written all over her face. Merely by clapping her hands, she organized the boys and girls into two separate lines. Then she took Agnes by the hand and led her to the center of the room. "Class," she said, "we have a new member with us today. Let us all extend a warm welcome to Agnes Bigley."

There was a flourish of notes from the piano and some perfunctory applause. Agnes knit her brows and scowled

"And," Miss Peabody continued, "we are happy to have our new member not only for herself alone, but also because we now have an even number of boys and girls. That means that no one, absolutely no one, will ever lack a partner."

Something about this last sentence alerted the new member to danger. The scowl on her face intensified as she made her way back to the girls' line.

With the help of a male and female high school student, Miss Peabody drilled the class in the foxtrot and the rumba. The male assistant was a friend of Josy's, and he winked at Agnes. However she had problems closing one eye and not the other and did not wink back.

Miss Peabody counted out the cadence of each step loudly and slowly until each student could execute a perfect square and come out on the correct foot. When she was sure every one had mastered the box step, she went on to something else. Toward the end of the hour, she clapped her hands and addressed the class from the center of the room. "Now, girls and boys," she said gaily, "it's time for the fun part."

The fun part consisted of a game called Choosing, in which Miss Peabody picked out one couple to start off the dancing. When the piano stopped playing, that couple broke up, and each dancer picked another partner until everyone was dancing.

Agnes watched the first couple perform but was not impressed. They could execute a perfect box and even do a cross over, but they watched their feet and had no rhythm. She was sure she could do as well and possibly better, but she suspected she might be the last one chosen. Her father, Miss Mattie, and Viola had noticed that she had slimmed down and grown more attractive, but her contemporaries had not.

Sure enough, the floor filled until finally she and one boy, a freckle-faced runt, were sitting across the room from each other. He and Agnes exchanged glances, and he rose from his chair. She thought he was coming over to ask her to dance, but he headed toward the men's room. Just before he got there, the strong arm of Miss Peabody reached out and grabbed him.

"Stop the music!" she commanded in her best drill sergeant voice. "The dancing will not continue until Agnes Bigley has a partner."

Agnes sank down low in her chair. She didn't mind being the last one chosen if she could do it discreetly, but she didn't want to go down in history as the girl with whom nobody would dance.

The culprit was marched across the room by his collar until he was standing in front of her. All eyes turned in her direction, and there was an audible snicker from one of the girls.

Miss Peabody shifted her grip from his collar to the hair on his head. "This young man," she said, addressing the class and giving his head a jerk, "has behaved badly, and we are all waiting for him to apologize to Agnes and ask her to be his partner."

The boy looked at the floor, mumbled an apology, and almost inaudibly said, "Let's dance."

"Speak so we can hear you," Miss Peabody demanded, "and ask her properly." She gave another little jerk to his head as she spoke.

"May I have this dance?" he asked, almost shouting and obviously in pain.

Agnes wanted to die and disappear but that was not possible. The most viable option was to dance with the boy and hope to never see anyone in that room again. However, a little hard core of something tough and resilient inside herself came to her aid. Her answer was distinct and dignified. "No," she said. "I don't want to dance with him, and he doesn't want to dance with me."

There being nothing more to be accomplished, she rose from her seat and walked toward the arched doorways that led away from the ballroom. The piano player struck up a tune, and Josy's friend grabbed her arm and pulled her onto the floor.

She shook her head and twisted away.

"Come on," he said. Don't let 'em get your goat," and he held her hand firmly and put a steady arm around her waist. "Now smile," he demanded.

"I can't smile, "Agnes said, "but I can dance," and without looking at her feet, she followed him in a foxtrot that wove her in an out around the room.

"You're good," he said, and he swung her under his arm and out and, because of Viola's training, she was able to come on home, in perfect rhythm. The second time he did it, several members of the class stopped to watch.

When that number was over, it was time to go. Miss Mattie, who had been waiting and watching in the wings, already had her coat and hat on and was holding Agnes's coat. It was obvious she was bristling. Agnes thought she was mad at her, but as soon as they were in the car alone, Miss Mattie said, "I didn't know Miss Peabody was a fool."

"Now you find out," Agnes said.

"I wouldn't blame you if you never went back. That little pipsqueak boy was extremely rude, and Miss Peabody only made things worse. But, honey, where did you learn to dance like that?"

Agnes thought for a minute. "I think I was just born knowing how to do it, but Viola taught me how to go out and in."

"Thank the good Lord for Viola," Miss Mattie said.

"I guess," Agnes said, "I'll go back a few more times, just to let 'em know they didn't get my goat."

Chapter Nineteen

CHRISTMAS

Christmas of 1939 was an unsettling one for the Bigley family. It got off to a bad start the very day that Josy came home from boarding school. Morgan, Agnes, and Miss Mattie met her at the station. They arrived early, but to their surprise, Jay Hightower was already there. He held a small gift-wrapped package in his hand.

Agnes asked about the package, and Jay said it was a new edition of *The Rubaiyat* that he wanted Josy to have.

"Oh, yes," Morgan said, "That's that book about drinking and carousing around."

"It's beautifully written poetry," Jay protested, his loyalty to the tentmaker never wavering.

"That's the trouble with these modern poets," Morgan said. "They think they can say anything as long as it's well written." He spoke with such conviction that his remark went unchallenged.

It was a cold day, but their faces were lit with anticipation as they huddled together on the platform. There was a moment's anxiety, however, after the train pulled into the station, and they couldn't find Josy. Then Morgan spotted her at the far end of the track, and he and Agnes broke into a run. When she saw them coming, she ran, too, until she fell into Morgan's arms.

Next, Agnes got a big hug and noted gratefully that her sister actually seemed glad to see her. Miss Mattie rushed up a minute later and received similar treatment, and Jay got a discreet handshake. Then, to the amazement of everyone, Josy burst into tears.

It was both a surprising and unsettling moment. Josy prided herself on never crying, and everyone was puzzled. Was she overcome with happiness to be home or was something terribly wrong? Miss Mattie made sympathetic noises, and Morgan, having decided it was some kind of female thing that was bothering his oldest daughter, gave her a few pats and went off to find the Red Cap. Jay shoved his present into her hand, saying, "Open it as soon as you get home, and I'll call you to see how you like it."

Josy managed to thank him between sobs, and he left, promising to call before lunch. The Red Cap and Morgan gathered up the luggage, and Miss Mattie said, "Come along girls. Let's hightail it out of here. Time is on the wing."

On the ride home, Josy pulled herself together, and Morgan, in an effort to say something cheerful, congratulated her on her B in chemistry. "That's a hard subject," he said, "and I know it took a lot of work to get a B."

"It is a hard subject," she said, "and I didn't get a B. I got B+."

This animated reply reassured them all and, as she seemed fully recovered by the time they reached the house, they almost forgot about the strange outburst at the station. However, when Roxie and Viola ran out to greet Josy with open arms, she bursts into tears again.

"What's wrong with this sweet baby?" Viola asked, as she held the unhappy girl in her strong embrace.

Since Morgan, having picked up the bags and headed inside, was out of earshot, Miss Mattie spoke her mind. "I'll tell you what's wrong!" she snapped. "Her nerves and brain cells are frazzled from the rigors of those exams they give them. It's wrong to feed a young girl's brain cells with information she will never use. She ought to stay right here with us where she can have a good time and be happy."

Viola went upstairs with Josy to help her unpack. Agnes followed, but when they got to the bedroom, Viola firmly closed the door in Agnes's face.

That afternoon, Josy, Morgan, and Agnes went riding. Agnes, having gone through several contentious rounds with Old Tom during her sister's absence, could now handle him with some authority, and she was anxious to show off this new-found ability. However, she knew, by the time the ride was over, that something was terribly amiss. Her sister was much too kind: Josy complimented her on her horsemanship, gave her a few gentle pointers, and treated her like an equal.

This new attitude was so troubling that Agnes urged Old Tom up beside Charley and said in an aside to Morgan, "Papa, she hasn't called me a fat sissy yet. She must be sick."

"Well, you are not fat, and you have proved you are not a sissy, and she probably missed you very much," Morgan said.

But Agnes knew that something was wrong, and she kept her eyes open. And one of the things she noticed was the urgency in Tim Laudermilk's face when he first saw Josy, and the polite coolness with which she greeted him. He's got it bad, Agnes thought, just like all the boys in town.

When they got home after the ride, word had gotten out that the local belle was back, and the phone was jingling on the hook. From then on until after Christmas, Josy was caught up in a social whirl that kept her on the run.

The day before Christmas, Miss Mattie's sister died. Miss Mattie was stoic, but every now and then her eyes watered over. "We were not a thing alike," she said. "She was shy and retiring, and I never missed a good time in my life. I was a bridesmaid in thirty weddings before I married. Sister only had a few friends and was sickly to boot. But she was my own blood, and I shall miss her more than I can say."

The family was very supportive, but Agnes couldn't help noticing that as Miss Mattie grew older, the number of weddings in which she was a bridesmaid grew larger.

Of course, the prospect of the funeral on the twenty sixth put a blight on Christmas Day. But aside from that, Agnes didn't like her presents, and Josy could hardly be aroused from bed to share in the festivities.

Morgan started things off gracefully enough by asking Viola and Roxie to join the family in the living room while he read chapter two, verses one through twenty from the book of Luke. Then he wished everyone a merry Christmas as he passed out white envelopes containing crisp ten-dollar bills. He followed this procedure annually, but everyone always looked forward to it with fresh anticipation—there being the possibility of more ten dollar bills in each envelope than the year before. Nevertheless, everybody had the grace to abstain from immediately counting except Agnes, who came up with the exact same number as the previous year.

After that, Viola and Roxie went back to the kitchen and the family opened their presents. Morgan tried hard to look pleased over new socks and ties, and Miss Mattie feigned pleasure over Irish linen handkerchiefs, wryly commenting that it was good to have something pretty to weep into at the funeral. Agnes thanked everyone politely for books she knew she had outgrown, and Josy's gratitude for a cashmere sweater was lukewarm.

The holiday didn't get much brighter when Abigail Bigley and her mother came to dinner. Old Mrs. Bigley was now almost totally deaf, and conversation was difficult. Just after they sat down at the table and just before Morgan closed his eyes to say the blessing, Abigail asked him to pray for peace.

Morgan bowed his head and launched into a prayer in which he castigated Hitler and entreated God to endow Roosevelt with large quantities of courage, honor, and wisdom. He prayed for the British, the French, the peoples of the Netherlands, and all those who by their proximity to the barbarian dictator were in danger of losing their freedom or had already lost it, and he prayed for German refuges and victims of the Nazi state. He wound up with "May the true meaning of Christmas touch the lives of all the suffering peoples of the world. Amen."

"What did he say?" old Mrs. Bigley asked.

"He said 'Amen,'" Abigail shouted.

"Praise the Lord! Now we can eat."

"Was that blessing for peace?" Agnes asked.

"No," Morgan said. "That was for the country doing the right thing, and I don't know whether that's war or peace. Now let's all have a little dinner."

As Morgan began carving the turkey, the old lady turned to her daughter and audibly whispered, "I hope it's not cold. A long blessing makes for a cold dinner."

"Hush, Mama!" Abigail said. "And try to be polite."

"Mind your tongue!" her mother said. Then she looked sharply at Morgan and asked, "What happened to that pretty little Jew you were planning to marry?"

"Mother!" Abigail admonished. "It's none of your business."

"She ditched me," Morgan said, and his grip tightened on the carving knife.

ᙡᙠ

Josy took sick two days after Miss Mattie's sister's funeral. Miss Mattie was so busy sorting out her sister's things that she didn't realize how ill the girl actually was. Morgan was kept in the dark, too, because Josy managed to pull herself together for the evening meal.

One night at supper, Morgan commented on the paleness of his oldest daughter. "Maybe you had better see a doctor," he suggested. "I don't want to send you back to school in poor health."

"I'm fine, Papa," Josy said. "I just have a little upset stomach. Everybody in town has got it."

"She couldn't be too sick," Agnes said, "because she's gaining weight. Maybe she'll turn out to be the fat one, and I'll be the pretty, skinny one." The minute she said it, Agnes was sorry. Josy looked at her with real suffering in her eyes, and Viola, who was passing the vegetables, glared so ominously that Agnes sank down in her seat.

"Everybody who goes to boarding school either gains weight or gets pimples," Miss Mattie said. "Thank goodness she doesn't have pimples. They are harder to get rid of than a few pounds."

Josy's health was dismissed and, as the days went by, only Agnes, Viola, and Roxie knew that by day the girl behaved as if she were poisoned. Viola brought her cup after cup of her special tea, but it only seemed to make matters worse. She hung over the toilet, pale and wretched, unable to disgorge whatever was turning her stomach inside out.

Agnes was worried. "Maybe you had better call the doctor," she said.

Josy vomited into the toilet and then rested her head on the bowl. When she had gathered strength, she said between clenched teeth. "No! No! No! NO! And you keep out of this, you little idiot."

Agnes felt better immediately. It was the first normal thing her sister had said to her since she came home.

After a few days, Josy's health improved, and she seemed to be almost her old self. On her last day at home, she and Agnes took a long ride together and tore through the woods like wild Indians. Then, as they were walking their horses the last mile home, Josy gave Agnes the ultimate compliment. "You are riding Old Tom real well," she said, "and when I'm gone, I want you to ride Rosebud, and if anything ever happens to me, I want Rosebud to be yours."

"What do you mean if anything happens to you?" Agnes asked.

"I mean if anything bad happens to me. Suppose my train goes off the track and turns over or the school burns down and I'm in the fire . . ."

"Maybe you better not go back to school; maybe you better tell Papa you are still sick."

"I have to go back."

She left the next day, looking so lovely in her new cashmere sweater that Morgan gave her a lecture about speaking to strangers. "You never know what kind of low-down person you might meet traveling," he said. "Just read your book, and if anyone bothers you, tell the conductor or the porter."

Morgan and Agnes got on the train to help find her berth. "Keep up the good work," Morgan said, as he kissed her good-bye. "I'm mighty proud of you, honey."

Josy's eyes watered over. "Yes, Papa," she said.

They got off just as the train began to move, and they jogged along the platform with it, waving wildly. Agnes kept on running until she reached the end of the platform and Josy's car was too far away for her to see the beautiful face in the window. "Good-bye," she shouted, "Good-bye," even though she knew her voice was lost in the sound of the engine.

"Well," Morgan said, as they were driving home in the car, "You and your sister seemed to get along very nicely this Christmas. Are you going to miss her?"

"I feel as if I will never see her again," Agnes said.

Chapter Twenty

STOLEN MONEY

As soon as Agnes got home from the station, she forgot she was sad to see Josy go because her Christmas money was missing. She had left it under the book that she was currently reading, and the book was still on the table by her bed, but the money was gone. She searched high and low but to no avail. By the time dinner was ready, such a storm cloud had settled over her face that Morgan added an addendum to the blessing. "Kind Father," he entreated, "Grant that we partake of thy bounty with a spirit of cheerfulness as well as thanksgiving."

His request was ignored.

"Somebody took my Christmas money," Agnes said. "It was on the table by my bed, and now it's gone."

"Perhaps," Morgan said, "Josy took it by mistake."

"Josy didn't take it. She knew that was my money, and she wouldn't take it. But somebody took it," and she looked ominously around the room.

"Don't get worked up about it now," Morgan said. "We would like to digest our food in peace and look for it after supper."

Agnes folded her arms and knit her brows even closer. "We're going to have to search everybody that's ever been in this house. I didn't even have a chance to spend any of that money, and it was my best present." She paused a moment before adding darkly, "By far my best present."

Viola, who had just brought in the lamb chops, quietly spoke. "I took it," she said, and she passed the lamb chops to Morgan, Miss Mattie, and Agnes without saying another word.

This information was received in silent amazement, but as soon as Viola went back to the kitchen, Miss Mattie said, "I wasn't going to mention it, but my Christmas money disappeared several days ago."

Viola reentered the dining room majestically bearing the potatoes. "I took yours, too," she said. "I aim to pay you both back out of my paycheck."

She continued to pass the vegetables, offering no excuses and walking as straight and proud and silent as her Indian grandmother. The good and faithful servant of so many years had taken money belonging to someone else, and there were no questions. The resolute set of her jaw and the dignity of her bearing forbade questions. The meal was finished in a puzzled and uneasy silence.

After dinner, Morgan lit the logs in the living room fireplace, and he and Miss Mattie settled down with the evening paper. Before he started to read, he got out his glasses, wiped them off, and looked thoughtful. "What do you make of it?" he asked.

The housekeeper wadded and unwadded her little white handkerchief. "I don't know what to make of it. I'm utterly flabbergasted."

"Well, I don't like it one bit," Morgan said, "but I'm not going to push her. In all the years she has been with us, I have never known her to do anything hurtful or dishonest. I'm sure there is some logical explanation and that you and Agnes will get your money back."

"Yes," Miss Mattie agreed. "I'm absolutely certain of it. It's very strange, but I trust her completely."

"We'll wait for her to bring the subject up again," Morgan said. Then he put his glasses on and opened the paper.

A few minutes later, Agnes joined them in the living room. "Papa," Agnes said, "I don't think you ought to get mad at Viola."

"Is that so?"

"Papa, she must have needed that money bad, and I don't care if I never get mine back."

∞∞

The following afternoon, Miss Mattie received a call from Miss Willette, headmistress of Barnes Hall, inquiring if Josy Bigley were ill. Classes had begun, and Josy had not arrived as scheduled.

At first, Miss Mattie was unable to grasp what the headmistress was saying. "Josy's at school," she said. "We put her on the train yesterday."

The voice on the other end of the line was firm. "She is not here. Our bus has met every train. Could someone have driven her?"

"I tell you," Miss Mattie said, "We put her on the train. She is at school."

Miss Willette spoke gently. "I know this is very, very worrisome, and it requires prompt action, but you must understand that Josy is not here."

The impact of what the headmistress was saying finally hit Miss Mattie, and the shock of it took away her power to function. She sank down on the chair by the phone, unable to speak. Finally, she found enough voice to say very slowly, "You must call Mr. Bigley at his office."

∞∞

Morgan was called out of an important meeting to receive the phone call, and he could hardly keep the irritation out of his voice. However, when he heard the message, he turned white but remained calm.

"Do you know of any reason why your daughter would not want to return to school?" Miss Willette asked.

"No! I know of no reason. I was under the impression she was happy at school."

"She was well liked and doing well," Miss Willette confirmed, "which makes me think we must promptly turn this matter over to outside authorities."

He spoke carefully. "I am going home to speak to each member of my household to see if anyone has any knowledge of the whereabouts of my daughter. After that, I will contact you, and we will decide what course of action to take."

Driving home, he reviewed the events of the past weeks. Were Josy's tears on arrival more significant than he had imagined? Was her illness more serious than she indicated? Did Viola's strange admission last night have anything to do with her disappearance? He had no factual answers—

only vague suspicions that he did not want to face.

Agnes had just come from school when he arrived at his house. He told her to round up Viola, Roxie, and Miss Mattie. "Tell them that we are having a conference in the living room, and that it's urgent."

When everyone had gathered, he told them of Josy's disappearance. "All I know," he said, "is that I put her on the train myself, and that I waved good-bye to her as the train was moving. So what I want to know now is whether anyone here knows where she might be, because if not, I've got to call the FBI." He made a fist of his right hand and beat it into his left palm both for emphasis and to control the trembling.

Agnes began to cry, and Morgan said, "Hush, Agnes. We don't have time for tears."

Miss Mattie was also tearful, and her voice was shaky. "I don't know where she is, but I feel so guilty. I was so busy with Sister's funeral that I was out of touch. Something may have been the matter, and I didn't know it."

"She told me," Agnes said between sobs, "that if anything bad were to happen to her, I could have Rosebud."

Morgan turned even paler. "What kind of bad thing?" he asked.

"If the train had a wreck or the school burned down."

"At least we know that hasn't happened," Morgan said. Then he turned to Viola and Roxie. "You two know as much as anybody about what goes on in this family. Can either of you shed any light on the whereabouts of my daughter?"

"She ain't said nothing to me," Roxie said.

"Viola?"

Before Viola could answer, the phone rang, and she started toward the front hall to answer it, but Morgan stopped her. His eyes had become intensely blue and piercing. "Before you pick up that phone," he said, "you had better tell me if you know where Josy is."

Viola could not be hurried. "Yes, sir, I know. And I 'spect that's Miss Theodosia calling now to say Miss Josy's done arrived safe and sound at her apartment in New York."

"Damn!" Morgan exclaimed.

He walked to the phone and picked up the receiver. Theodosia's warm, husky voice greeted him.

"Morgan, dear," she said, "I know you must be worried and upset, but Josy is with me."

He spoke through clenched teeth. "You girls are experts at disappearing acts."

"Of course, you are angry," she said. "You have every right to be. But I had nothing to do with this disappearing act. I've talked Josy into letting you know where she is, and you need to come here. We need to talk face to face."

"First, will you do me the kindness of telling me what is going on? I would very much like to know what to expect. Is that too much to ask?" The edge in his voice was undiminished.

"No, Morgan, I can't tell you on the phone. I need to look into your eyes. Please come right away."

"I will come tonight, and I will expect the worst." He put the receiver on the hook without saying good-bye.

As soon as he hung up, he confronted Viola, his words coming out like bullets. "You're in on this. You took the money from Agnes and Miss Mattie to finance this runaway trip to New York."

She was as imperturbable as a mountain. "Yes, sir," she said. "I did."

He pointed his finger into her face. "That makes you a thief and a conspirator."

"Yes, sir. I see it that way, too."

He turned toward Miss Mattie. "Will you call the station and get me a berth on the Southerner? If there aren't any berths, I will sit up."

"You are going to see Tedde," Agnes wailed. "I want to go. Please, Papa, take me."

"No!" Morgan said.

"But . . ."

"No! No! No!" he shouted, and he went upstairs to call Miss Willette and to pack.

∞⁓∞

That night on the train, Morgan tossed and turned in his berth. The only explanation he could think of for Josy's behavior was that she was pregnant and that the father of the unborn child was Jay Hightower, Miss

Mattie's great nephew. She had been seeing more of him than anybody else, and it was Jay who had given her that book of unfit poetry. The boy came from a broken home, and his values had suffered. Morgan remembered he had taken Jay to Maine the summer his mother and father were divorcing, and it was a kindness he now regretted.

He couldn't understand how a girl who was so beautiful and popular could throw herself away on Jay. He supposed it was the poetry that did it. She had left the book in the living room, and he had glanced through it, noting its sensual appeal. He recalled something about a book of verse, a jug of wine, and a loaf of bread. It had reminded him of an afternoon in Maine when Tedde had read a book of verse to him, and there had been a line about a shining castle built upon the sand. He remembered the passion with which he had said, "I'll build you a shining castle that stands upon a rock." But in the end, she had not wanted his shining castle.

He did not think that Josy was evil or what she had done was evil. It was just that she had shown such a surprising lack of character and good sense. It was shameful to throw everything away, and particularly when, for the first time, she was making good marks at school, proving she was bright as well as beautiful. Neither the South nor, as far as he knew, the world had a place for a bright, beautiful unwed mother.

He tried to remember everything he had ever heard about Jay. His grandfather, old Martin Craig, had been a highly respected judge in town, but his daughter had married poorly so that Jay came from both good and bad blood. Miss Mattie had told him Jay was going to Princeton on a scholarship, and that, of course, was to his credit. If he were only four years older, he might be a decent-enough catch. As it was, they would have to put as good a face on the situation as possible. Jay and Josy would have to swear before God they would cleave to each other until death did them part with everybody knowing they were too dumb to come in out of the rain.

And then there was the biggest question of all. If the girl were in trouble, why had she gone to Tedde when she could have gone to Miss Mattie? Why did his children keep bringing back into his life someone who had, with no explanation, jilted him at the altar? He wanted to forget Tedde. He wanted to forget her merry face and the feel of her body in his arms.

He tossed and turned until he could no longer tolerate the confinement. He put his clothes back on and parted the heavy, green curtains of his berth. Apparently, all passengers were bedded down and sleeping. He grabbed his coat, hurried past the unmade berth where the porter was gently snoring, and opened the heavy door to the platform.

It was good to get out of cramped quarters. The steady rhythm of the engine and the blast of January wind against his face suited his mood. He put on his coat, hugged himself with his arms and, planting his feet apart for balance, stood between the two cars. Outside the open window, he could see a night full of stars, cold and steely against the sky.

Despite the cold and despite his burdens, his spirits rose. He remembered how as a child he had walked home from evening worship with his grandfather on starry winter nights. His grandfather had held his hand and quoted scripture: "When I consider thy heavens, the work of thy fingers, the moon and the stars, which thou hast ordained; what is man, that thou art mindful of him?"

The wind whipped at his face and the cold was painful, but he didn't want to go in. He felt he was part of the speeding train and the earth that rose up to meet it. His problems became almost weightless in the vastness of the night.

He recalled a fragment of another verse his grandfather was fond of quoting: "Whatsoever things are pure, whatsoever things are lovely, whatsoever things are of good report; if there be any virtue, and if there be any praise, think on these things." And for some reason, his thoughts turned to Josy racing her horse on the path by the Chattahoochee River—a beautiful, high-spirited girl who was as much a part of the wind and the river as he was now a part of the racing train.

Soon the cold became unbearable, and he went inside and sat across from the snoring porter. He leaned back against the seat and fell asleep.

∞∞

Even though Morgan had been to New York many times, the hustle and bustle always amazed him. He grabbed a cab immediately upon his arrival and gave the driver detailed instructions on how to get to Tedde's apartment. He had the outsider's distrust of cabbies and didn't want to be driven around the same block three times. As usual, while riding down Fifth Avenue, he marveled that so many people, even under the best of circumstances, could live so close together without killing each other.

The doorman at Tedde's apartment greeted him with both surprise and appropriate pleasure. "It's been a long time, Mr. Bigley," he said, and there was a question in his voice.

"Yes," Morgan responded, and out of courtesy he added. "Too long."

In an effort to steady his nerves, he took several deep breaths on the elevator. In happier times, when the elevator was slow, he had raced up the three flights of stairs to Tedde's apartment, knowing she was waiting for him with open arms. Now, he was afraid of what she had to tell him, although he realized his anxiety over his daughter was coupled with the mounting excitement of seeing his ex fiancée.

The elevator doors opened. He walked to the door of Tedde's apartment and paused. He inhaled deeply and rang the bell. The door opened and he stepped into the large, familiar foyer.

CHAPTER TWENTY ONE

BACK TO NEW YORK

Morgan had thought that either Josy or Tedde would open the door. Instead, a skinny, dark-haired girl of about fourteen stood before him. She had the look of a waif, and he supposed she was some sort of servant. She spoke to him in German, but before he could respond in any way, Tedde rushed out to greet him. Her arms were wide open as he knew they would be. Whatever her faults, she did not have a cold bone in her body. As they embraced, he was able to forget for a moment the miserable little note under his door. He only remembered how she used to say, "Don't you ever let me go."

Reluctantly, they drew apart, and she introduced him to the girl. "This is Lisle. Lisle, meet Herr Bigley."

Lisle extended a thin hand and curtsied. The hand was so cold and damp that he almost winced as he took it.

"She has just arrived from Germany," Tedde said, "and she doesn't speak English." Then she said something in German, and the girl curtsied again and left them alone.

"Is Josy here?" he asked.

"Yes, she and Lisle are sharing the guest room, and she is in there now, shaking in her boots. But I promised her I would talk with you before she sees you. Let's have coffee first."

He followed her back to the kitchen where the smell of fresh coffee permeated the air. He had always loved her kitchen. The teapot on the stove, the tin canisters on the counter, and the crockery showing through the glassed-in shelves exuded a comfortable atmosphere that ran counter to the modern paintings and grand piano in the living room.

He sat down at the little table in the alcove. He could see a bit of Central Park from the window. The last time he had sat there, the leaves had been a brilliant red and gold, but now the trees were bare. Only the traffic remained the same. The angry, intolerant sound of a horn broke the silence.

"I dislike cities," he said.

"You didn't when we were courting," she reminded him.

"No, I didn't dislike much of anything then."

"And you won't again. You're not a querulous person."

She handed him his cup of coffee. "It's extra strong. And now I'll fix you an egg."

"No," he said. "No egg." He looked directly into her eyes. "Theodosia, spit it out. She's pregnant, isn't she?"

"Yes."

He groaned and put his head in his hands. "She had everything in the world," he said, "and now it's gone. How could she be such a damn fool? I thought she had more character—more good sense."

Tedde put her hand on his head and gently stroked his hair. "Morgan," she asked, "have you forgotten how it is?"

He removed his hands from his face and looked at her hard. "No, I haven't forgotten."

"But now," she said, sitting down opposite him, "we have to talk about what to do about this situation; she could stay here until the baby comes, and then she could put the baby up for adoption."

"Adoption?" Morgan said indignantly. "That baby has my blood. I'm not putting my own blood up for adoption. She will just have to marry the father and Viola will raise the baby just like she raised its mother—only better."

"Morgan," Tedde said, "you've got to let Josy enter into the decision. Right now, she won't even tell me who the father is."

"I know who it is. It's that gawky, pasty-faced fellow who helped her with her homework last year. He met her at the station when she came home from school and gave her a book of questionable poetry."

"What kind of poetry?" Tedde asked.

"Questionable! Poems of the 'eat, drink, and be merry' variety. There's one about a jug of wine, a loaf of bread, and copulating underneath a tree."

She smiled. "That sounds like Omar Khayyam."

"That's the one. No doubt he's some modern poet with no scruples. I'd like to wring his neck."

Her smile broadened. "Oh, darling, I wish you could if it would make you feel better, but Omar Khayyam died five hundred years ago."

"In that case, I hope that five hundred years ago his demise was untimely and painful. Now I suppose I will have to vent my spleen by wringing the neck of the baby's father, but right now, we need him to take up his paternal duties. My grandson needs a father."

"Morgan, darling, the baby might just possibly be a girl and marriage may not be the right thing. You haven't even spoken to Josy. You're putting the horse before the cart."

Despite his temper, a glint of humor played around his eyes "My learned Theodosia, you know much more about poets than I do, but I know more about horses. That's just where he belongs, right up there in front of the cart. But then you always had a little trouble with horses."

She laughed, her eyes crinkling up at the corners, and he noticed how her wonderful, merry lips matched the red of her sweater.

Taking a sip of coffee, she asked, "How is that miserable beast you keep in your stable to torment your women with?"

"Old Tom? Agnes rides him very well."

"That little girl has courage. She just had to find it out. And how is my beloved Agnes otherwise."

"Your beloved Agnes is very independent and still heavily under the influence of a likewise independent actress. She eats half of her meals in the kitchen with Roxie and Viola and wants to know why, in the name of fairness, they can't eat the other half in the dining room with the family."

Tedde's eyes sparkled. "Agnes is going to bring light into dark places."

They were interrupted by Lisle who came in the kitchen and, looking very earnest, said something in German. Tedde responded in kind, and Lisle went back to her room.

"Who is that skinny, sad-looking child?" Morgan asked.

"She is a little German orphan whose parents were friends of Lola's.

She and Josy have become quite friendly, even though they can't understand a word they say to each other. She just told me Josy was going to expire of nervousness."

He put his head in his hands again. "I dread seeing her," he said.

"Don't let her know that. She needs your support, not your condemnation. She's made a mistake; that's all."

"Well, let's get it over with. Tell her to come in."

Tedde excused herself and came back leading his daughter by the hand. Josy's head was down, and she seemed barely able to look at him.

"Papa?" she said, and the word was both a question and an entreaty.

He knew she wanted him to put his arm around her and say that everything would be all right, but he wasn't up to it. His disappointment was too great, and he felt something akin to repugnance when he looked at her—his sixteen-year-old daughter, who should be innocent and pure but instead was pregnant.

She sensed his rejection and her shoulders drooped perceptibly.

"Stand up straight," Tedde whispered gently. "Hold your head up high."

Josy tried to straighten up, but her spirit wasn't in it.

"Pull up a chair," Morgan said, "and join us."

Josy sat down at the table, and Tedde poured her a cup of coffee and gave her an affectionate pat. "I know you two have lots to talk about," she said. "I'll just excuse myself so you can have some privacy."

"You sit down, too," Morgan said. "You know more about this than I do."

Tedde sat down, and she and Josy waited patiently for Morgan to speak. He took his time, and the silence was close to unbearable. He cleared his throat, folded and unfolded his hands, and looked thoughtfully off into space. Finally, he addressed the matter at hand.

"It seems," he said, "we have a situation here in which a young girl has gotten herself in the family way without the benefits of marriage."

He looked meaningfully at Tedde before continuing. "I believe that constitutes a classic case of putting the cart before the horse. I don't see any solution to this predicament except to rearrange the positions of the horse and cart. That means that the young girl must marry the father and give the baby a name."

"I can't do that, Papa," Josy's voice was barely above a whisper.

"What are your reasons?"

"It was my fault. I led him on. And if anybody found out who he was, it would destroy him and his family."

"If you don't marry him," Morgan said, "it will destroy you and your family."

Josy put her head down on the table and wept. Tedde reached over and stroked her hair, and Morgan, seeing his brave little Indian in such distress, felt something akin to tenderness. He cleared his throat. "Now see here," he said, "things may not be as hopeless as you think. I know who the young man is, and he's a likely enough young fellow—quite an intellectual, I take it, since his head is always in a book. This marriage may temporarily interfere with his education, but its consequences are not necessarily tragic."

Josy raised her head, her eyes wide. "You know who he is and you don't hate him or his parents?"

"This is a very unfortunate turn of events, but, no, I don't hate anybody."

She got up from her chair and flung her arms around him. "Oh, Papa!" she said. "I've loved him since I first met him. You're the most fair-minded man in the world, and if he'll marry me, I'll marry him. We can live in one of those little empty houses at the farm."

Morgan was not about to turn miserable circumstances into a celebration. "Let's hope he likes the country," he said stiffly.

"Papa, you know he likes the country. He was born and bred in it, just like me. The only problem is that he doesn't want to get married. He wants to go to college and be a great man like you."

"I really know very little about him, other than he did a credible job of helping you with your studies last year, and I believe he has a scholarship to Princeton."

Josy looked as if she had been struck and the breath knocked out of her body. She sat back down in her chair and stared at her father. "You think it's Jay Hightower," she gasped.

Morgan's heart missed a beat. "It isn't?"

His daughter looked at him as if he were out of his mind. "I wouldn't let that skinny, uncoordinated runt kiss me goodnight."

"Then tell me who it is." His voice was harsh.

"I can't," and she put her head back down on the kitchen table.

Morgan looked at Tedde. "I'm back where I started."

"I'm confused, too," Tedde said, "but Josy seems to think that if you knew who the father was, it would destroy him and his family. Isn't that right, Josy?"

The girl raised her head high enough to nod and then put it back down on the table.

"Perhaps," Tedde said, "if you exacted a promise from your father that he would do nothing to hurt the baby's father or his family, you would tell us who he is?"

Josy remained silent with her head on the table, but Morgan sensed that Tedde had made some progress. "I am not in the habit of destroying families," he said, "but if it would make you feel better, you have my word."

"It's Tim," Josy said.

Morgan searched his mind, but he didn't remember a Tim. "I don't believe I know him," he said.

"Tim Laudermilk."

It was Morgan's turn to look as if the wind had been knocked out of him, but he examined the information in silence, trying to get a handle on it. Strange, he thought, how a man worked hard to maintain a position of prominence in the community so that his daughters would know the best people, and then his beautiful, popular, and talented eldest daughter makes love with the hired hand. He thought of how he had promised to help educate Tim, and he felt betrayed by the Laudermilks, whom he had always tried to treat fairly.

"Who is Tim Laudermilk?" Tedde asked.

"My farmer's son," he said dryly.

Josy looked up from her place of woe. "Are you going to fire Mr. Laudermilk?" she asked.

"No, I'm not going to fire him. In fact, I guess I'm going to promote him, but I just can't think of to what. We must put as good a face on your situation as humanly possible, but I don't know how we are going to do it."

Tedde's eyes twinkled. "If only this were England; you could make him a squire. Then you could call him Squire Clabbermilk."

"Laudermilk," Josy groaned, not raising her head. "Not Clabbermilk."

Morgan scowled at Tedde. She had always had the ability to turn even the darkest situations into comedy, and sometimes it was irritating. "Right now," he said, "I could call him any number of things, the least of which would be Clabbermilk, but, in fairness, I don't suppose he knew any more about these events than I did. He's a cross between an artist and a farmer, and I can't think of a more economically hazardous combination. However, I have always liked him, but I never expected to be his relation."

"Papa, Tim could refuse to marry me."

"Josy, you and Tim both made a mistake, and it's a mistake with consequences. You bring a baby into the world, and it's your baby, but it's my grandchild and is connected by blood to my father and my father's father and your mother and your mother's mother. And it's the same with Tim's family. And that baby has a right to be loved and cared for by its own blood. You come from people who care for their own, and we pass that down to our children and our children's children. You and Tim will have to understand that."

Josy raised her head from the table just long enough to sigh heavily and say "Oh, brother! I don't know whether I'm up to all of this," and Morgan refrained from pointing out that it was too late to wonder if she was up to facing the consequences.

∞ ∞

That night Tedde and Morgan left Lisle and Josy at the apartment and went out to dinner at a small, Italian restaurant a few blocks from her apartment. It was a quiet place they used to frequent because they enjoyed the ambiance. Red checked tablecloths covered the tables, candles burned low in Chianti bottles, and extravagant oil paintings of canals and gondolas hung on the walls. The waiter gave them their old corner table and immediately brought Tedde a Pinot Noir. Morgan, feeling that the tension of the last few days warranted something stronger than usual, ordered a Scotch. He did not become light-headed, but the liquor intensified his desire to find out exactly why she had left him three years ago. Nevertheless, he was halfway through his dinner before he asked, "Has the theater been good to you? Is it as fulfilling as you expected it to be."

"Oh, Morgan," she said. "I didn't leave you for the theater. I made it look that way, but the theater was just a front."

"Was it that you changed your mind about me?" he asked.

"No! No! No! I never changed my mind."

"What was it then?"

Instinctively they reached across the table to hold each other's hands. It was something they used to do and had forgotten.

"It was too perfect. You and I loved each other, and I loved your girls, and they loved me. I would have been safe, and loved, and protected. And all the while I kept getting these letters from Lola telling me what a nightmare it had become in Germany and reminding me that there, despite my father's conversion, I was a Jew and the Nazis were killing my people. And she always said, `You can help. You are an actress. You speak German and French like a native. You can do things and go places that are not open to other people. Her letters preyed on my mind, and I felt the pull of those blood ties—the same blood ties you spoke to Josy about this afternoon."

"Couldn't you have helped as my wife?"

"I don't think so, my darling. You had your own noble causes. You didn't want a house full of refugees speaking a foreign tongue or a wife who traveled and met people in clandestine places. You wanted a wife who was there for you, and I don't blame you."

He withdrew his hands and idly pushed a little spaghetti around his plate. He knew there was some truth in what she said. He didn't want to play second fiddle to his mate. Nevertheless, he deserved better treatment than he had gotten.

"Look," he said, raising his voice. "You could have talked to me. You could have sounded me out. We might have reached some accommodation. You didn't have to just walk away without a word. I deserved more than a little note under my door. I was devastated, as were my girls. Why poor little Agnes couldn't even eat for weeks."

"Morgan," she asked, "do you remember how I used to beg you not to let me go?"

"Yes, I remember."

"I meant it. I prayed you would come down to the railroad station and get me. I prayed you would come to New York and get me before I met Lola in France. I prayed you would come to my play and get me before I got in too deep. I know it was terrible to leave you just before the party, but it would have been worse to do it later. I don't ask you to forgive me; I just ask you to try to understand how torn I was."

He regarded her closely. She spoke passionately, but the trouble with falling in love with an actress was that you never knew when she might be acting. The strain of the last few days suddenly hit him. He felt tired and deflated. It was one thing to be deserted for the glamour of the theater and quite another to be dumped for a noble cause. He felt outclassed, the way he might feel if a woman were to oppose him in court and win.

"Exactly what do you do?" he asked, and his tone was resentful.

"One of the things I do is find jobs and homes for Jewish immigrants, but I keep quiet about it. I don't want to draw attention to it because it would interfere with other things, and I can't talk about those things. But right now I am looking for a home for Lisle."

"What happened to her parents?"

"Murdered!"

"By the Nazis?"

"Of course."

He reached for her hand again. "Are the other things you do dangerous?"

She smiled. "A little risky. I was in Germany, and I was frightened, but I am an actress and didn't show it. The only living thing I haven't been able to fool is that miserable horse of yours."

"Well I am glad that the Nazis are not as perceptive as my horse."

They were silent for a moment. It seemed odd and bizarre that his ex-fiancée was mixed up in foreign intrigue, but no more odd or bizarre than the fact that his daughter was pregnant by his farmer's son. He would never understand women, but he was aware that he had underestimated them in the past.

"I think," he said, "that I was and am too simple a fellow for you."

"No," she said, "but you don't have my problems and you can't understand the issues I'm facing."

A sadness descended on him, weighing down his spirit, and it had less to do with Josy's predicament than the truth she had just hit upon.

When she spoke again, there were tears in her eyes. "Morgan," she said, "we each have problems. Mine must remain secret, but yours must, to some degree, come out in the open. People will talk about Josy. Help her to hold her head up. Don't make her feel any worse than she does. And always remember, eyebrows don't stay up forever."

"We'll brazen it out," he said, but he didn't feel like brazening anything out. The prospect of going home, confronting the Laudermilks with the problem and the solution, putting as good a face on the situation as possible to friends and neighbors, seemed overwhelming. He hated to think of Tedde in danger, but he knew she was right. He wouldn't be any good at aiding and abetting a wife who was saving the world. If anybody saved the world, he wanted it to be him.

"I need to talk you out of the dangerous part," he said, but he was so tired that he could barely suppress a yawn.

"Morgan," she said, "you look exhausted, and it's time to go home. I don't want any coffee, so let's call it a night."

They walked back to her apartment holding hands. They said goodnight at the door, and he caught a cab to his hotel.

The next morning, he and Josy took the train back home.

Chapter Twenty Two

THE WEDDING

Agnes knew something was not right at home. An atmosphere of gloom had settled over the house, and people were constantly whispering. She knew it had something to do with Josy's leaving school, and she wondered if her sister had contracted some dread disease and, if so, was it contagious. Except for a short trip to the farm with Morgan, Josy stayed in her room with the door closed. Viola brought her a sandwich on a tray and tried to coax her to eat. However, the girl showed no interest in food or anything else.

The night after Josy and Morgan returned from New York, the family ate dinner together in almost total silence. Morgan appeared absorbed in his thoughts, Josy only played with her food, and Miss Mattie's eyes brimmed over with tears. After they rose from the table, Josy and Miss Mattie retired to their rooms, and Morgan invited Agnes to join him in the living room for a private conversation. They sat down on the sofa across from the portrait, and Morgan began by saying, "I expect you have been feeling kind of left out."

"I don't know what's going on," Agnes said, "but I don't think it's right that you went to see Tedde without taking me, and I don't know why Tedde gave you a ring for Josy and didn't give me anything, and I don't know why everybody is so miserable."

"Honey, Tedde did send you a present! I have been so preoccupied that I forgot to give it to you. Just as we were leaving her apartment, she gave me the ring for Josy and also something to give to you. It's upstairs on my bureau, and you can get it as soon as we've finished our conversation."

He paused for a minute, glanced at the portrait of his late wife, and continued. "I want to talk to you about your sister. She is getting married to Tim Laudermilk this Saturday."

Agnes thought her father had just made the most ridiculous statement she had ever heard in her entire life. Josy was much too young to get married and Tim Laudermilk was the farmer's son. Marriage between the two was unthinkable and downright silly.

"I don't believe that," she said, her voice rising in righteous indignation.

Morgan spoke gently. "I'm afraid it's true."

Agnes looked at him closely and saw that he was serious. If he had told her that Miss Mattie had shed her clothes and walked downtown naked, she could not have been more stunned.

"Papa," she wailed, "you can't let her do that. She's only sixteen."

"I agree with you. She is too young, but sometimes the course of true love makes demands of its own without regard to age. Your sister claims she has been in love with Tim since he first came to the farm."

"That's nonsense," Agnes said. "She's never been in love with anybody more than two weeks."

Morgan smiled and in so doing managed to look more tired than happy. "Nevertheless," he continued, "they are getting married the day after tomorrow in this house. No one knows about it outside of the family, and no matter what we think, we must try to make it a cheerful occasion."

Agnes was quiet for a moment in order to better organize her thoughts. She knew that she was not getting the whole story. Nothing her father said explained Josy's running away to New York, and she knew he was leaving out something important. "Why," she asked, "did Josy go to see Tedde?"

He paused. "I think," he said, "it was because Tedde is a wise person and a good family friend. I think she needed and valued Tedde's advice."

Agnes looked straight into her father's eyes. "Papa," she asked, "Did Josy commit a sin?"

"A sin? What do you mean by a sin?"

"Did Josy and Tim commit a sin together?"

"I'm not sure I know what you mean by sin," he said. "Everybody commits sins every day, and it's our place to look for it in ourselves, not in other people. The world would be a dull and pointless place without the struggle between good and evil, and if Josy and Tim have committed a sin together, God will forgive them, and it's up to us to help them live with it. Now go look on my bureau and get the present that Tedde sent you."

Morgan took his glasses out of their case, wiped them off, and put them back on. He settled back on the sofa and opened up the evening paper. The private conversation was officially over, but Agnes, had figured out two things: one was that Josy and Tim had committed a very big sin together and the other was that the sin was one her father did not wish to discuss in great detail. She was afraid that any more probing questions might lead to a long and tedious prayer session, and she was anxious to see what Tedde had sent. She excused herself and ran upstairs to Papa's room to look on his bureau.

∞∞

When Agnes got home from school on that Friday before the wedding, she realized that the atmosphere in her house had changed from somber and sad to a flurry of almost-hysterical activity. She heard Miss Mattie talking enthusiastically on the phone to someone at the Women's Club about arranging an exhibit there of Sam Laudermilk's watercolors. After finishing that conversation, she immediately picked up the phone again and called the society editors of both the *Atlanta Constitution* and the *Atlanta Journal* to give them particulars about the wedding. In so doing, she described the groom's father as a prominent watercolorist who was having an exhibit at the Women's Club at the end of the month and possibly another one at the High Museum later on. Her voice was unusually animated.

As Miss Mattie was busy, Agnes went in the kitchen where Viola was polishing silver, and Roxie was baking. When she asked Roxie to fix her something to eat, the cook said, "I'm cooking the first wedding cake I ever cooked, and I ain't got time to be studying after you." However she handed Agnes the bowl she had used to make the cake because Agnes liked the dough better then the finished product. When the bowl looked as if it had been scraped clean, Viola said, "Everybody is busy trying to give your sister a fine wedding. The best thing for you to do is lie low until tomorrow."

Agnes went upstairs to Josy's room and knocked timidly. When she heard no answer, she cracked the door. Her sister was lying in bed but not sleeping. Something about her expression prompted Agnes to ask if she wanted her back scratched. "I'll do it for you free," Agnes offered. "You don't even have to pay me back."

When Josy nodded, Agnes climbed up on her bed and gently scratched until the two of them fell asleep.

That night at supper, Agnes quizzed Morgan about the extent of Mr. Laudermilk's fame as a watercolorist.

"I didn't know he was a watercolorist," Morgan responded.

Miss Mattie, sounding very flustered, broke in. "I'm afraid I got carried away," she stammered. "His pictures are really very good, and the Women's Club is going to exhibit them. I am afraid I just let that slip out when I was talking to the society editor about the wedding announcement. I hope you are not upset."

"It appears," Morgan said, "that you were trying to make a silk purse out of a sow's ear." Then, suddenly and inexplicably, he began to laugh. The rest of the family, not knowing exactly why, joined in, and the tension that had pervaded the house since Josy's return evaporated.

"Tomorrow," Morgan announced, "is going to be a happy and cheerful occasion," and everybody, including Josy, nodded in agreement.

☙❧

The wedding went off pretty much as planned. The silver gleamed, and the house was full of camellias. The O'Brians and the Laudermilks were the only invited guests. As soon as it was over and they were gone, Agnes sat down and started a long letter to Tedde. She wanted to make it a particularly good letter because the actress had always complimented her on her vocabulary and writing. The letter was so long that it took her several days to finish it and get it right. It read:

Dear Tedde,
I hope you are well. Thank you so much for the locket you sent

me. It is very pretty.

This has been an exciting week. Josy got married to Tim Laudermilk this afternoon, and I know why. The wedding took place at noon in our living room, and nobody came except the Laudermilks and the O'Brians. Mrs. O'Brian brought champagne. Josy wore a loose silk blouse over a skirt, and I know why. The Laudermilks wore their Sunday best, but they still looked like poor people. Tim wore a suit that didn't fit, and he looked so scared and skinny that I can't imagine why Josy committed that sin with him.

After the ceremony was over, Mrs. O'Brian kissed both Josy and Tim and told Papa it was time to break out the champagne, which he did. Everybody had some including Roxie, Viola, the minister, and me. I thought it was very good, and when Josy put down her glass, I picked it up and finished it. Papa didn't seem too interested in drinking his, so when he put it down, I drank his, too.

We were just about to go in the dining room for dinner when the doorbell rang, and it was Miss Louisa who hadn't been invited. Papa asked her in, and she acted real surprised about the wedding, but I could tell that just like me, she knew why. She asked Josy where she was going to live, and when Josy told her they would live in one of the little houses at the farm, she asked Tim if he was going to paint a rose on the outhouse door like his father did on his.

Then Josy said something so funny, that I couldn't stop laughing. She said that instead of a rose, they were going to paint a skunk on the outhouse door. I laughed so hard that Papa told me to pull myself together or leave the room. I pulled myself together, but every time I thought about that skunk, I got the giggles again. When she left, we sat down to a real good dinner with a fancy cake for dessert, but I couldn't eat because I was still giggling about the skunk. After dinner, Josy and Tim left to spend the night in a hotel. Papa gave them an old secondhand Ford for a wedding present, and when Tim drove it out of our driveway, he knocked our mailbox over.

When they were gone, I heard Mrs. O'Brian ask Papa how he was holding up. Papa said that for the father of a pregnant bride and an intoxicated adolescent, he was doing real well.

The next day after church, Papa, Roxie, Miss Mattie, and I went out to the farm to clean up the little house. The Laudermilks helped, too, and together we got it ready for Tim and Josy to move in. I don't know how Josy is going to stand it without running water, but between you and me, she doesn't care that much about washing, anyway.

Lots and lots of love,

Agnes

P.S. Tim did paint a skunk on the outhouse door. Josy painted "PHEW" underneath it. Papa made her paint over the "PHEW," but he let the skunk remain as he said it looked more like a squirrel, anyway.

Chapter Twenty three

TIM AND JOSY

Morgan had given the newlyweds a secondhand Ford for a wedding present so that Josy would have a way to come to town when she felt like she needed a bath or a good meal. As soon as dinner was finished, he handed the keys to Tim. Then the bride, carrying her clothes in an overnight bag and the groom, carrying his in a paper sack, went outside to claim their new possession. They were off, courtesy of Morgan, to a one-night honeymoon at a hotel.

The car was facing the street under the porte cochere. Tim gave Josy the keys, but she shook her head and handed them back, indicating he should drive. Obediently he got behind the wheel but did not seem to be in a hurry to start.

"We have a problem," Tim said.

"Tell me something I don't know," the girl responded.

"I've only driven the truck once. I don't know how to drive."

Her jaw dropped and her eyes widened. "I thought everybody knew how to drive."

"You thought wrong."

"It isn't hard," she said. "Any fool can do it. You know where the clutch is?"

"Yes."

"You know where the accelerator is?"

"Yes."

"Well, push in the clutch, and turn on the key."

He looked at her imploringly. "Can't we do this sometime when your father isn't watching?"

"No, I don't want him to know I slept with somebody who doesn't even know how to drive." She leaned over him. "Now I'm going to put it in first while you let out the clutch and push down on the accelerator."

Tim did as he was told, and the Ford shot forward and then abruptly stopped.

"You let the clutch out too fast," she said.

"I expect," he said coldly, "that if your father is watching, he is now aware you slept with someone who doesn't know how to drive."

"Just try it one more time. If it doesn't work, I'll drive." Tim tried again, and this time the car started forward, bucked a few times and threatened to stall.

"Keep going," Josy shouted. "Stop at the end of the driveway. Then turn."

"Which way?" he shouted back.

"Right! Take a right!"

The car picked up speed, and Tim didn't even pause at the end of the driveway. Instead, he took a wide turn and in the process knocked over Morgan's mailbox. They raced down the steep Muscogee hill and crossed Rivers Road without acknowledging the stop sign except for honking the horn. It was not until they almost reached the crest of the next hill that Tim, realizing he had confused the brake with the accelerator, was able to stop the car. Then, accusation and hatred written all over his face, he turned toward Josy.

"You almost made me have an accident," he said.

Josy glared back and enunciated her reply slowly and carefully. "I did not knock over Papa's mailbox, and I did not know you did not know where the brake was located. I thought everybody knew that."

"You drive, and I'll walk," he said, and with that he got out of the car, slammed the door, and started off.

"I'm glad you know how to walk," she shouted, and she slid behind the driver's seat and took off. Morgan had made reservations for the newlyweds at a lovely old hotel near the Fox Theater. Feeling lonely, deserted, and foolish, Josy drove up to the entrance and turned the car over to the valet, not knowing if the correct procedure was to tip then or later. She decided on later. On entering the lobby, she walked over to the reception desk and identified herself.

The clerk looked at her closely. "I don't believe we have any guest by that name," he said.

"It's Bigley," Josy said. "Josy Bigley and Tim Laudermilk. I know my father made the reservations."

He looked at the registration book again and then eyed her even more carefully than before. "Ah yes. That would be under Mr. and Mrs. Laudermilk."

"No. That's his mother and father." Too late she saw her mistake. A wave of heat rose from her body and settled in her face, turning her cheeks the color of a ripe peach. The clerk must think her a perfect fool, and he was right. She was a perfect fool. She was no longer the pretty popular girl who lived in a pretty house in the best neighborhood. She had, for better and most certainly for worse, turned into a Laudermilk—a Mrs. Laudermilk. With a sickening sense of loss and eyes that threatened to brim over, she took the pen proffered by the clerk and acknowledged her new name. When she got to her room, the phone was ringing. It was Morgan, checking to see if she had arrived safely. He didn't mention the mailbox.

She thanked him for the accommodations and told him how pleasant it was when all she wanted to say was "Papa, let me come home. I want to sleep in my own bed."

The hotel room had twin beds, two comfortable chairs, and a desk loaded with stationery. She started to write a letter to Tedde and Lisle, but her heart wasn't in it. A good movie was playing down the road at the Fox Theater, but the thought of being alone and running into some of her friends on her honeymoon night was too horrible to contemplate.

She switched on the radio between the two beds, lay down, and closed her eyes. The soft tender notes of "I'll Never Smile Again" pervaded the room. How appropriate, she thought.

Tim arrived an hour later. Neither of them spoke. He took off his good clothes and left on his shorts and undershirt. He washed up in the bathroom, got a book from his paper bag, lay down on the empty bed, and commenced to read.

Presently, Josy began to giggle. "I'll always remember the way you honked that horn when you ran the stop sign," she said.

He didn't look up from his book.

Her voice became conciliatory. "We can nail the mailbox back up, tomorrow. Then we can go out to the country where there's no traffic, and I'll teach you how to drive. It was crazy of me to think you could just get in the car and do it right off the bat. I'm sorry."

He didn't answer.

"I mean I'm really sorry."

He still didn't look up from his book. "I never had the opportunity to learn to drive," he said. "My dad didn't want to teach me in your dad's truck. Besides, whenever he wasn't working, he was always painting. He likes to paint like I like to read."

"Well, reading is a good thing to do."

"I know that."

Encouraged by a slight indication of forgiveness in his voice, she attempted to make him laugh. "Of course, I wasn't really scared when you were speeding. I knew you would either find those brakes or we would run out of gas before we got to South Carolina."

He smiled slightly and turned his attention to his book.

After a while, she went in the bathroom and pulled her pretty new nightgown over her head and slightly rounded belly. Then she got into the other bed. He put his book away and turned out the light.

∞∞

They had breakfast at Josy's house the next morning. To their relief, no one was at home except Roxie, who greeted them cheerfully and heaped their plates with eggs, bacon, and grits. However, the newlyweds spoke little and ate sparingly.

After breakfast, Tim fixed the mailbox. Then Josy drove them to the farm. She parked the car in front of the stable, and he made her get out while he practiced driving. She mucked Rosebud's stall while he manipulated the Ford backward, forward, and in circles. It didn't take long for him to get the hang of it, but when his new wife congratulated him, he glared but did not comment.

That afternoon, they moved into their new home, which Agnes, Miss Mattie, Viola, and the Laudermilks were in the process of getting ready for them. It was a dark, cold, and drafty little house. It had a bed-room, a kitchen and living room combination, a big porch in front and a smaller one in back. The wood stove wasn't working, so a large mattress was temporarily placed in front of the fireplace in the living room. One window had been boarded up, but Mr. Laudermilk said he and Tim would fix it the next day. The outhouse and the well were in the back. Someone had put flashlights on the mantle and a chamber pot in the bedroom closet.

"It doesn't look like much now," Jane Laudermilk said, "but at least it's almost clean. It takes time to fix a place up, but we'll help you. In the summer, those big trees on either side of the house will be beautiful, and they'll give you lots of shade. I'll get Sam and Tim to build you some window boxes, and we'll screen in the porches. Pretty soon this place will be as sweet as can be."

Josy nodded dumbly.

"The wood walls are so much nicer than plaster," Miss Mattie said. "And Sister's house has some nice furniture you can have. Pretty soon this place will be cozy."

Josy nodded again.

"And," Agnes added cheerfully, "the outhouse isn't too far away. You'll be just like a pioneer woman."

Josy gave her such a menacing look that Miss Mattie said reproach-fully, "Your little sister has worked her heart out."

"And it's not my fault she has to live in a dump," Agnes muttered.

"We ain't finished cleaning yet," Viola said, "and there's more scrub brushes in the kitchen."

∞ ∞

That night Josy and Tim ate with his parents. The Laudermilk's warm little cottage seemed like a paradise compared to the honeymoon house down the road. The fire burned cheerfully on the grate, dinner was good, and Jane had lit candles and put them on the table. Josy commented on how nice the house was and how charming Sam's watercolors looked on the walls.

"I hated the house when I first saw it," Jane admitted, "but after your daddy gave us the electricity and the bathroom, I learned to love it."

"I was gonna give you a couple of watercolors for a wedding present," Sam said, "but I thought you might think they were too poor a thing. Then a friend of Miss Mattie's came out the other day and gave me a good price for six of them, so when you get your house fixed up, pick out whatever you want."

She thanked him and then looked at Tim. "It may take more than pictures to cheer our place up," she said.

Before they went home, Jane promised to leave some breakfast out for them. "That's the nice thing about not having a stove," she said. "You don't have to cook."

When they got back to their house, the fire had almost gone out. Tim built it back up, while Josy, flashlight in hand, visited the outhouse. The temperature had dropped, and the wind whipped around the little privy as if it wanted to blow it into the next county. It was cold and uncomfortable, but at least it wasn't raining. Realizing that things could be worse, she swore a solemn oath to herself that no matter how bad it got, she was never going to use that chamber pot.

When she got back in the house, the fire was blazing away. However, due to the lack of electricity, there was nothing to do except go to bed. Tim had drawn some water from the well, and they stood on the steps of the back porch to brush their teeth. Josy, feeling that she would freeze to death, brushed vigorously and hurriedly spat out the rinse water. In doing so, she missed the ground and splattered Tim's foot.

Without saying a word or changing expression, he stooped down and slowly wiped the spit away. Then rising and looking at her from his superior height, he commented, "I thought you knew how to spit. I thought everybody knew how to do that."

She wasn't sure if he was mad or if he was kidding. "I'm sorry," she said. "I know I can learn."

The gleam in his eye was unmistakable. "I certainly hope so. I would hate for my mother and father to find out I had to sleep with somebody who couldn't spit."

She smiled slightly.

The mattress was placed lengthwise in front of the fire so that one side of it would stay warm. Tim, wearing a sweater over his pajamas and wool socks, took the cold side and turned toward the far wall. Josy, also wearing a sweater, got the warm side and turned toward the heat. At first, she was too hot. She tossed off the covers so that the fire was her only warmth. Tim's restless turning and twisting kept her awake, but she maintained a stoic silence. Finally she dozed off.

She awoke several hours later. Only a few embers glowed in the fireplace, and her teeth were chattering. The comforter now felt like ice against her skin, and it was too cold and dark to get up and look for her coat. She burrowed down in the mattress, but it didn't help. Finally she turned toward Tim, who was still on his side, facing the wall, and gave him a nudge.

"What's the matter?" he asked.

"The fire went out. I'm cold."

"You want me to build a new one?"

"No. I want you to move closer to me and let me get some body warmth."

He sighed audibly, as if he had rather get out of bed and fix the fire than share his own, personal heat.

"Tim," she said, "I know it is my fault we're in this fix."

"The fault goes both ways," he said.

She moved closer to him. "And I'm sorry I was so mean about the driving."

"I guess I'll forgive you when I get my license."

"Well, I know it's my fault, but I thought that since we're in this predicament, we might make the best of it."

"How?"

"Well, if you don't hate me too much, you could start off by sharing your body heat."

He sighed again, but he moved closer.

∞∞

The next morning, Tim was up first. He made a fire, drew water from the well, and grabbed one of several apples his mother had left on the kitchen table. Then he walked out into the cold to catch the school bus.

Josy got up later and drove to the Laudermilks' house. Jane had left coffee, rolls, bacon, and directions on how to boil an egg in the kitchen. After she had eaten, she watered the horses and cleaned stalls. Morgan had agreed to pay her a modest fee to perform these tasks as long as she was able. Then she drove into town and announced to Miss Mattie that she wanted to learn to cook.

"As I live and breathe," Miss Mattie said. "I never expected to hear those words from you."

"Well, I don't have any stove, so we have to eat either here or at the Laudermilks.' And as Tim's mother works, I think I ought to help her. I could cook a couple of meals a week over at her house if I knew how to do it."

"As I live and breathe," Miss Mattie repeated. "I guess you better go in the kitchen and watch Roxie."

CHAPTER TWENTY FOUR

VIOLA PLOTS

Josy came to town two or three times a week to have lunch and to see if she had received any telephone messages. She always found a sandwich but rarely a message. It was obvious that her friends, once they heard about the little house, the mattress on the floor, and the privy, had decided that Josy Bigley had gotten her just desserts. Only Miss Mattie's nephew, Jay Hightower, remained loyal. He often dropped by the Bigleys to leave a book or a box of chocolates for her.

One day, while Josy was in town having lunch with Miss Mattie, the housekeeper said, "Honey, you look so healthy and rosy cheeked. I believe you must be happy."

"I guess," Josy said. "I'm too stupid to be unhappy." She didn't know how to explain that she had entered some strange in-between territory with this new life, and she had found things she liked about it. She missed her friends, but she enjoyed being in the country and working with the horses, and she had adjusted to the bare little house with its few sticks of furniture. And most importantly, she looked forward to the return of the school bus every afternoon at four.

"The only thing that bothers me," she said, "is that Papa hasn't forgiven me. He's been good to us, but he hasn't forgiven me. Maybe he never will. But I miss the way his eyes always lit up when I came in the room. Now he almost cringes when he sees me. I guess I am adjusting to the fact that I've ruined my life and Tim's life, but I hate it that I've ruined Papa's, too." She sighed deeply and took a large bite of her second sandwich.

"I'm glad to see you haven't ruined your appetite," Miss Mattie remarked. "It's hard to imagine a person who has ruined so many lives having such a good appetite."

"Tim and I will be alright. It's Papa I'm worried about. I just wish he'd forgive me."

"Everything will change when the baby comes," Miss Mattie said. "Then his heart will melt. Wait and see."

"But he seems so depressed, and he's always tired."

"Perhaps," Miss Mattie suggested, "he's still carrying a torch for Theodosia."

"I wish he would marry her," Josy said. "I'm so afraid he'll marry Miss Louisa. That woman is taking over. He brings her out to the farm, and she rides my horse. And she is helping him look for a horse for Agnes. I ought to be the one doing that."

"Well, if he does marry her," Miss Mattie said, "we will all have to accept it as cheerfully as possible."

Josy stared at her plate as she toyed with the last half of the second sandwich. Finally, she said, "Tim's had a real hard week. A boy at school said 'I hear you knocked up the boss's daughter,' and Tim hit him. Then Tim had to stay after school in the principal's office just like a little boy."

"That must have been very humiliating," Miss Mattie said.

"And that's not all. He went to the public library to get a book, and the librarian wouldn't give it to him."

"My goodness!" the housekeeper exclaimed. "That's unusual. What kind of a book was it?"

Josy paused and, looking very sheepish, launched bravely ahead. "It was a book about sex—when to have it and when not to have it and all that kind of thing, but the prissy librarian said he was too young to concern himself with those matters."

Miss Mattie barely suppressed a smile. "My goodness!" she exclaimed again. "I hope Tim didn't hit the librarian."

"No. Tim thinks the librarian is right and that he is too young, but we need the information."

Miss Mattie's eyes brimmed over with tears. "Honey," she said, "I'm afraid I've failed you in many ways, but there is something I can do. I'm an old lady, but I'm going to the library this afternoon and take out as many

sex books as I can carry at one time, and I'll get them to you and Tim before supper. And if I can't get them all in one load, I'll go back tomorrow.
That ought to give the most liberal of librarians pause for thought. And
if there are any questions that I can remember the answer to, I'll be glad
to answer them."

Josy was moved by Miss Mattie's kindness. "Sometimes," she confessed, "I can't believe I'm having this baby. But I know I am, and I know
it's got to get out of my body. But what really bothers me is what in the
world am I going to do with it once it does?"

Miss Mattie spoke firmly. "You and Tim are going to love the baby
with all your heart, and you're going to take care of it, and you're going to
show your father that when push comes to shove, you know how to act
responsibly."

"I just hope that will make him happy," Josy said. "I hate to see him
so sad."

∞∞∞

Josy and Miss Mattie were not alone in expressing a concern over Morgan's state of mind and his relationship with Miss Louisa. The servants
worried, too.

"He done give up eating," Roxie complained to Viola. "I try to fix
what he likes, but he doesn't eat it."

"He ain't well," Viola said. "He's sick in his head."

"You think he's taking Miss Josy and the baby that hard?" Roxie
asked.

"That ain't it."

"Well, what is it?"

"He's sick in his head because he's got the honey britches for Miss
Theodosia, and he's about to marry Miss Louisa."

"Oh, Lord," Roxie groaned. "I guess I got to find me a new job."

"I been thinking that way myself," Viola said, "but I ain't gonna
leave Agnes. Right now she is all excited about getting a new horse, and
Miss Louisa acts like she's crazy about little girls, but I ain't sure how she's
gonna act once she gets her hooks in Mr. Morgan."

"Then, we're all in trouble," Roxie said.

There was a long silence before Viola said, "I done called Miss Theodosia."

Roxie's mouth dropped wide open. "You done called Miss Theodosia in New York?"

"I done called her in New York and told her Mr. Morgan's sick in his head, and this family's in a heap of trouble."

"Fool, you don't know what's your business and what ain't."

"You're right," Viola said, "but I been deep in this family's business for a long time. After Miss Emily passed, I done showed Mr. Morgan the wisdom of hiring Miss Mattie for a housekeeper. I done raised Agnes, and I done helped Miss Josy out when she got herself in the family way. Now I done called Miss Theodosia in New York and told her something she can stew on."

"You done everything but marry Mr. Morgan yourself," Roxie said.

Viola chuckled. "Now, I believe that might be carrying things too far. Besides, he ain't my type."

∞∞

The family was right about Morgan's depression. He felt low and tired all the time. His heart wasn't in his work and riding over his land every weekend no longer invigorated him. All he wanted to do was sleep, but when he went to bed he couldn't.

His club gave a gala spring party every year. Louisa was supposed to be his date but, when the time came around, he was too tired to take her. He called her up and apologized. "I feel awful," he said. "I have a headache, and I feel like I can't move. I must be coming down with something, and I wouldn't want you to catch it."

She was lovely about it. "I'm so sorry you don't feel well," she said. "And, of course, you shouldn't go to the party. It's important that you get some rest. Besides, I've been going to that same party for twenty years."

Grateful for her understanding, he sank down in the easy chair in his den and closed his eyes. He had fibbed about the headache, but the rest of the story was all too true.

A few minutes later, the doorbell rang. Viola answered it and, to his consternation, he heard Louisa's voice. Viola ushered her into his den and, as he rose to greet her, she said, "Don't move, dear. I just came over to rub your head and see if I can't make that headache go away."

Feeling trapped, he sank back in the chair. Louisa stood behind him and massaged his forehead, sometimes running her soft fingers over his closed eyelids. After a while, the trapped feeling left.

She didn't stay long and, on leaving, advised him to go to bed and get some rest. He did as he was told and, when he lay down on his four-poster bed, he felt like a child who had been comforted by a loving mother.

He thought a lot about Emily during this low period of his life. One weekend, he drove the girls to the little town where she was buried, and the three of them stood solemnly by her grave, speaking in whispers as if they might rouse her.

Viola had arranged a basket of new daffodils for the occasion, and Morgan knelt down and gently placed it on her stone. The old cemetery with its huge shade trees and sprinklings of flowers was pleasant, and he looked longingly at the vacant spot beside Emily. It would be nice to lie down by his first love—his truest love—and rest there through eternity. It took effort to shake himself free of these thoughts and drive the girls home.

On weekends, he made himself go to the farm and often took Louisa with him. She was a fine equestrian who knew more about riding than he did, having shown three- and five-gaited horses since she was a child. Even now, she owned a saddle horse named Adonis who usually placed in the local show. Adonis was much too fine to bring out to the farm and ride on Morgan's rough-hewn trails, but the high-stepping black horse and his elegant blond rider made a striking picture in the show ring.

Morgan couldn't help comparing Louisa's horsemanship to Tedde's. Louisa looked neat and put together even when mounted on Old Tom, whereas Tedde, due to her generosity of build and lack of experience, had resembled a sack of potatoes. They were both beautiful women, but, as he constantly reminded himself, he and Louisa came from a similar background. Passion was for young people. At his age, like values and shared traditions were more important.

☙❧

One Saturday afternoon, he and Louisa cut their ride short because he was so tired that he didn't think he could stay on his horse. They came back to his house where he sank deeply into his chair while she ran her cool fingers over his forehead.

"You're so good to me, Louisa," he said gratefully.

"Oh," she assured him, "It's my pleasure to make you feel better. I enjoy taking care of you."

"I don't know what's wrong with me. I've always had so much energy."

"You're just worried about Josy. Worry wears people down more than anything."

"Well, I'm not much fun, and I appreciate the way you've stood by me."

She leaned over and kissed him on the cheek. "I'll always stand by you, Morgan. After all, we have so much in common. We're Southerners, and we're Christians, and we love horses and the outdoors, and the South. Our heritage is almost the same. We know who our grandfathers and our great-grandfathers were, and we are proud of who we are."

He was almost asleep and aware of little outside the gentle stroking of her fingers and the soft comforting drone of her voice. She spoke of the pleasure it gave her in taking care of him and the happiness they were meant to share. He heard her words but, in his fatigue, missed their meaning.

"Yes," he said drowsily. "We're two of a kind." and he slumped deeper into his chair.

The phone rang, but its noise was faint and far away. He was aware only of Louisa's hands on his brow and his desire to rest. His peace, however, was shattered when Viola came in the room and announced that he was wanted on the telephone.

He groaned audibly. "Take the message for me, Viola. I'm just too tired to talk to anybody."

"It's long distance," Viola said.

"Take the number and tell them I'll call back."

"Yes, sir. I'll tell Miss Theodosia you gonna call her back as soon as you gets the time."

Louisa's fingers suddenly froze. "Tell her he can't come," she said quickly.

"No," Morgan said. "Don't tell her that. I'm awake now. I'll take the call."

He was not only awake, but he felt a sudden surge of vigor. He got out of his chair, overtook Viola in the hall, and said, "Hang it up for me, please. I'm going to take it in my room."

He tore up the stairs like a schoolboy but, in the privacy of his bedroom, paused for a moment to compose himself. Then, in a tone as matter-of-fact as he could manage, he spoke into the receiver.

"Theodosia?"

"Morgan, darling," she said, and her voice was as rich and warm and husky as ever, "I'm calling to ask a favor of you, and it's a big one, so steel yourself against me. Don't let me take advantage of you."

He was silent. He was wary of favors.

"Are you there?" she asked. "Are you steeling yourself?"

"I'm in the process. There. Now I'm steeled, or, at least, I hope I am."

"Morgan, I'm only asking this because you are the best and kindest—"

He cut her short. "Just tell me what's on your mind? Then you can see if I'm the best and kindest."

"I want you to take Lisle," she said, "and I don't know for how long. It might be for just a short time or it might be longer."

"How long is longer?"

"Well, I think you might want to enroll her in school down there."

He cleared his throat. "You mean you want Lisle to come live with me."

"Yes. Exactly."

He sank down on the edge of his bed. It was shock, not fatigue, that weakened him.

"And where will you be living while Lisle is living with me?"

"I have a new assignment, and it involves travel. That's all I can tell you at the moment."

He exploded at that. "Good God, Almighty! Woman! If you are still trying to get Jews out of Germany, it's too late! All of Europe is at war. Stay home!"

"This will be my last trip, but I have to see that Lisle is taken care of before I go."

His voice, ordinarily so calm and deliberate, rose to a shout. "In the first place, I don't know where in hell you're going, and you probably aren't going to tell me, but wherever it is, I don't want you to go! In the second place, Lisle would probably be uncomfortable here for a long period of time. She would probably be more at home with people of her own heritage—her own religion. But the important thing is that you are needed here. Lisle needs you!" He almost added, "I need you," but caught himself in time.

"Oh, Morgan, I know it's too much to ask, but Lisle wanted me to ask you." Her voice was subdued.

"And," Morgan continued, "you can't just make people love you and then leave them. It's not right. It's not right to try to save the world while killing the people who love you."

He had never talked to her this way before. He had accepted her rejection with outward grace. But now that he had begun to reproach her, his resentment poured out of him, unstoppable.

"Agnes loved you, and you left her. I loved you, and you ran out on me with no explanation—only a little note under my door saying you were in a new play. What do you think this does to people? How can you justify treating the people who love you this shabbily? It's a terrible thing you do to us."

"Oh, Morgan," she gasped, "I had no right to call you. I don't know what I was thinking of."

The release of tension had cooled him off. "You were thinking of finding a home for Lisle. And you knew that if you left her with me and Miss Mattie and my girls and my servants, she would be with decent people who would care for her, and you could leave in good conscience."

"Yes, you see right through me, except you don't see that I don't want to go. I'm not going on a picnic, and I may be back soon unless . . ." she paused.

"Unless what?" he asked.

"Unless I'm dead," she said, and she hung up.

He called her back immediately, but there was no answer. Then he called again in case he had dialed the wrong number. He let it ring fifteen times before he gave up.

"God damn!" he said out loud. "God damn!"

He was angry, frustrated, and frightened. "Unless I am dead," she had said. What did she mean by that? Was she going to try to do some damn fool thing like getting into Europe? Didn't she know there was no safe way to get there, and no safe place to be once there? Yes, she knew. Of course, she knew. That's why she had said, "Unless I'm dead."

"God damn!" he said again, and he picked up the phone and dialed. Again Tedde did not answer.

He had forgotten Louisa was downstairs until he heard her voice from the hall below. "Morgan, dear, are you all right?"

He wished she had gone home. He was no longer in the mood for soothing fingers. He was in the mood for action. He walked briskly downstairs and found Louisa rearranging a vase of flowers that Viola had put on the hall table. She had removed some fern-like greenery from the vase and was holding it in her hand.

"Well," she said, and she arched her brows and widened her eyes.

"Let's take a walk," he said, "so we can talk without interruption."

"Yes, I think we should," she agreed and, still holding the greenery in her hands, she passed through the front door that he held open.

They walked out the driveway and were halfway down the hill before the conversation began.

"Well, what did she want?" Louisa asked. "I think I'm entitled to know."

"She wants to send a little fourteen-year-old girl to visit me," he said. In the silence that followed, he made no attempt to clarify his remark.

"I find that a rather odd request," she said.

"She's a little Jewish girl whose parents were killed by the Nazis."

"And she wants to pawn her off on you. What a lot of nerve that takes. And how long does she want her to stay? A week? Ten days?"

"She wants to send her here to live."

Louisa's mouth dropped open. She stopped dead in her tracks and faced Morgan. When she was able to speak, she did so slowly and with great feeling. "Only" she said, "a Yankee or a New York Jew could make such a ridiculous request."

"I don't think it's ridiculous. I've got plenty of room. Four bedrooms, and one is empty."

Louisa stiffened. "I assume you are having a little fun with me. What did you tell her?"

"I told her I thought the child would be happier with people of her own religion."

"Well, of course, she would. Anybody of any sensitivity knows she would be happier with her own kind."

Morgan spoke quietly. "It seems the girl likes us. She wants to live with us."

"Well, I hope you told your actress friend that she has a lot of nerve." And to emphasize her indignation, Louisa shook the fist that held the greenery.

Morgan looked at her carefully, almost as if he had never seen her before. "Louisa," he asked, "what are you holding in your hand?"

"Just weeds," she said. "I forgot I had them. Your Viola mixed these weeds with forsythia and put them in Emily's beautiful Waterford vase. I just did a bit of rearranging."

He looked at her incredulously. "You rearranged Viola's flowers."

"Darling, I simply took out the weeds. That darkie doesn't know a flower from a thorn bush."

He continued to examine her closely. Suddenly the perfection of her appearance held no attraction for him. The golden hair was too tidy, the complexion was too sun starved, too milky white, and the thin, aristocratic mouth was too cruel.

"I can't believe you rearranged Viola's flowers," he repeated.

"Darling," she said. "You seem upset. It can't be because I took weeds out of Emily's vase. It must be the phone call. Let's go back to the house. You can tell me all about it while you're resting."

"I'm not tired anymore. I've been lying around for too long." He looked at his watch. "Besides, it's four thirty, and I've got to be on the Southerner at six."

"You're going to New York?"

"Yes." He couldn't help himself: he was smiling.

"To see your actress friend? Why don't you send her a telegram and tell her you can't take in the little Jewish girl."

"I'm sorry, Louisa. You've been good to me, and I've taken advantage of your kindness. I didn't mean to, and now I don't even have time to apologize." His smile was lighting up his entire face.

He turned and began to run back toward the house. Her voice followed him up the hill. "It will never work," she called after him.

"I'm sorry!" he shouted over his shoulder. "I'm really sorry!" And he ran faster.

Chapter Twenty Five

MORGAN AND TEDDE

Morgan ran back to his house and up to his room, taking the stairs two at a time. It was close to five now, and the Southerner left at six. He threw some clothes in his suitcase and was on his way out the front door when Miss Mattie came in from shopping. "Come on!" he shouted, "Drive with me to the station, so you can bring the car back."

"Just let me put my groceries in the kitchen," she said.

"No time for that. We've got to make tracks." He grabbed her packages and put them on the stair. Then he hustled her outside and into the front seat of his car. "Hang on to your hat," he said, as he drove out of the driveway and on to the road. "I've got to get to the station by six."

Miss Mattie's voice quivered with alarm. "Is something terribly wrong?" she asked.

"No. I have some business in New York with Theodosia that's just come up." He was driving fast, and the housekeeper put her foot forward as if to brake.

"It must be urgent," she said.

"Yes, it's urgent."

She closed her eyes as Morgan honked his horn and passed another car on a blind curve.

"I love her," he explained, "and I'm going to do everything in my power to get her to marry me. I want you to call her and tell her I'm coming. If she doesn't answer, send her a wire."

"How wonderful!" she exclaimed. "I'll call her the minute I get back, that is if I do get back."

"And by the way, there's a fourteen-year-old girl who is going to live with us for a while. Could you see that the beds in Josy's room are ready?"

They approached a green light turning yellow, and Miss Mattie braced with her hands against the dashboard as Morgan stepped on the gas.

"Is that all?" she gasped as they came to a screeching halt in front of the Peachtree station.

"That's it for now," he smiled, and turning toward her before jumping out of the car, he did something unheard of. He leaned over and kissed her good-bye. "Wish me luck," he said, and his face glowed with a youthful eagerness unknown to him since Tedde's visit so long ago.

She patted his shoulder. "Tell her we'll be waiting with open arms."

∞ ∞

He got a compartment, but its confines were too small to contain his excitement. He left it in favor of the club car, where he sat down by a young lawyer he knew slightly. After they had exchanged greetings, his acquaintance offered to share his paper, and Morgan was eager, for the first time since his great fatigue, to read the news.

"Strange war, they're having over there," the young man commented as he handed over the front section. "Nothing much has happened since the Nazi's took over Poland."

"Do you think it's the lull before the storm?" Morgan asked.

"I hope so. I hope all hell breaks loose, and we join in, and together with England and France we kill every God damn Nazi in Germany."

"Strong words," Morgan said.

"Strong feelings!" his companion answered. Their conversation was interrupted by the waiter, who brought a scotch and soda to the young lawyer. Morgan, in order to calm his excitement, ordered one, too. When it came, he sipped it slowly and listened carefully as the young man elaborated.

"I'm part Jewish on my father's side. It's not on my baptismal certificate or on my application to the country club, or on any of those other fine things. In fact, I've enjoyed every benefit a Christian nation can bestow on a Christian. But now that robbing and torturing and killing Jews has become a national pastime for Germans, I feel my Jewish blood rising to the fore."

"I have a friend who shares your heritage and your passion," Morgan said.

"Wouldn't you share it, too," the young man asked, "if Hitler and his gang persecuted and killed all the Christians in Germany, and then, not content to stay within German borders, went into Austria and Czechoslovakia and Poland and did the same? Wouldn't that raise your hackles?

"Yes," Morgan said. "It would."

He spread out his paper and pretended to read. The young man's passion had brought to mind the difficulties he would face in dissuading Tedde from taking the trip she had spoken of on the phone. Her Jewish blood had come to fore, and in some way she was secretively fighting her own war against Hitler. He wished she were not so brave nor so talented. If only she were content to be that bright spirit who brought so much laughter and happiness to him and his family.

The young lawyer gave him the second half of the paper and excused himself. Morgan nursed his drink and read. When he had finished reading, he went to the dining car and ate alone. Something childlike in his nature responded to the novelty of eating on moving vehicles. He imagined sharing this pleasure with Theodosia on the trip home. It might take all his strength and all his horse-dealing powers of persuasion, but he would bring her back.

That night in his berth, he went over his arguments. He knew he would have to rely heavily on need—not just his need for her but that of Josy and Agnes and Lisle. Perhaps they would adopt another little Jewish refugee who would need her, and somewhere between wakefulness and slumber, he pictured his house as a haven for all sorts of children who, like a nest of clamoring baby birds, waited to be fed by their mother. Then, to the rhythm and blues of the Southerner, he dreamed his woman was with him.

∞∞

New York was cold, and he had forgotten his overcoat. The chill, however, was not foremost on his mind as the taxi sped up Fifth Avenue. In the common-sense light of day, this trip seemed overly dramatic, and he was afraid she would take him for a fool. Nevertheless, he set his jaw. This time he would bring her back.

The doorman of her apartment building was his usual studied, cheerful self. "Good morning, Mr. Bigley," he said. "It's a pleasant sunny day, but a wee bit chilly out."

"Yes, and I've forgotten my coat," Morgan said.

"Well, if you would like my job, you can have mine." He laughed heartily at his own joke.

Morgan punched the button for the elevator. It was slow in coming, and he decided to take the stairs. "I guess I'll just go up on my own steam," he explained. "It might warm me up."

"If it doesn't kill you first," the doorman said.

Morgan half ran up the stairs and, when he reached the third floor, he was breathless. He took a second to compose himself before ringing the bell. There was no response and, after a few minutes, he rang again, keeping his finger on the buzzer. Then an anxious, husky voice from within asked, "Morgan, is that you?"

"It's me, all right."

She kept him waiting for a full minute. When she unlatched the door, she was wearing a terry cloth robe. Her hair was damp, and her face looked freshly scrubbed.

"Oh, dear," she said. "You're early, or I'm late. I just got out of the shower. I guess I'll never learn what time that train goes north or south." And then she took him in her arms, and her familiar fullness made him tremble.

"You're cold," she said. "Your face is cold. Your hands are cold."

"I forgot my coat. I didn't notice the weather." He devoured her face with his eyes as she took his hands and rubbed them. She looked younger and more vulnerable without makeup.

"Morgan," she said. "it's good to see you, but.... Stop ... stop looking at me that way."

"What way?"

"As if you loved me."

"I do," he said, and he sank down on his knees and buried his head in her body. And she, who was never stingy in her affection, sank down beside him.

Later, when he had time to think about it, he would wonder if she had timed the shower and worn the robe as a deliberate enticement, there being nothing underneath the terry cloth except her own fresh, sweet-smelling body. It was all so reminiscent of that night three years before when she had come to him in his own four-poster bed with the scantily veiled excuse of a bad dream.

They made love in her front hall. The rug was soft, and if she minded the hardness of the floor underneath, she gave no indication. Her body opened up and welcomed him in such a way that afterward, lying beside her, he was almost completely happy. Only the old nagging question marred his contentment. Did she really love him or was she acting? Was she simply using him as a way to provide a home for Lisle and, if that were the case, was it such a bad thing? Could he live with it? Yes, he thought he could.

Suddenly an alarming thought crossed his mind, causing him to sit up straight. "Where is Lisle?" he asked.

"I sent her to a friend's house. When Mattie called and said you were coming, I thought we might need time alone, but I didn't know we would need it so soon."

"How long will she be gone?"

"Two days."

He kissed her again until she said, "Morgan, my darling, I'm getting to an age when I don't think I can bounce around on the hall carpet again. Can we go to my bedroom and get into my bed?"

He got up and pulled her to her feet, marveling at the beauty of her body. He didn't know much about art, but she reminded him of one of those full-bodied, pink-complected nudes he had seen on canvasses adorning museum walls. In contrast, he knew he looked ridiculous with his shirt and socks still on and his pants twisted around his legs. He grinned self-consciously and kicked off his pants.

"Darling," she said, "you're still half-dressed. We need to take off the other half."

She led him into the bedroom, helped him out of his clothes, and pushed him down on the bed. Something about her touch made it so easy to forget he was the son of missionaries and the grandson of a Presbyterian preacher. She knew how to find the urgent secret places of his body and to guide him to the urgent secret places of hers.

After they were both satiated and lying in each other's arms, another appetite prevailed. He realized he was hungry. "Come on," he said. "Let's get up and get something to eat before I grow donkey ears. I believe I've worked up an appetite."

"Donkey ears?" she asked.

"Pinocchio got donkey ears. I used to read about it to Agnes."

"No. No. He got a long nose for lying. Have you lied to me, my darling?"

"He got a long nose for lying, but he grew donkey ears when he went to Pleasure Island and got everything he wanted. Right now everything I want is you, and you've given it to me."

"And Odysseus went to Circe's Island. His crew got everything they wanted, and they turned into swine."

He pretended irritation. "All right! All right!" he said. "So your reading is more advanced than mine."

"Morgan, my dearest Morgan," she said, her voice rich with tenderness, "We've got two days to love each other, and if we turn into donkeys or pigs in the process, who cares?"

A strand of her dark hair lay across his face, and he took it in his fingers and kissed it. "Yes," he said, "who cares?" And then he added, "but I'm hungry."

That afternoon he bought a new overcoat and, holding hands, he and Tedde walked in the park. The sun was out, and the promise of spring was in the air. Vendors sold soft drinks and pretzels and bare-legged children, free from the confines of snowsuits, played tag and shouted to each other in high-pitched, excited voices.

"We'll go home in two days," he said. "We'll adopt Lisle, and we'll be an old married couple by the time Josy's baby comes. We'll take that baby walking in the park, and everybody will think you're the mother."

"I can't come right away," she said. "I have a job to do. I'm committed. There's no way out."

"Tell me about this job."

"I'm uniquely qualified for it, and the less I talk about it, the better off I am."

"Then it's dangerous. How dangerous?"

"As dangerous as a Saturday afternoon ride on Old Tom."

"I don't want to joke," he said. "I know you speak French and German fluently. I know you are an actress, I know your grandfather was a rabbi, and I know the Nazis killed your cousin. And the thing you are doing now, I don't know but I can speculate."

They stopped walking, and she took his hand and kissed it. "Don't speculate," she pleaded.

"Will you tell me how Lisle got out of Germany? At least, tell me that."

"I can't tell you that. I won't tell you that. Please just stay with me for two days, and we'll both grow donkey ears."

"That was a stupid thing I said. I made it sound as if loving each other was an overindulgence."

"No Morgan, it wasn't stupid, and I love your sense of Presbyterian propriety. We can't stay in bed all day. But for two days, we can love each other as much as the body can stand."

"I assume," he said, "that your mattress is substantial."

∽∾∍

Despite the impending crisis, they did a lot of laughing and talking during that time. She showed him the letter from Agnes describing the wedding, and he told his version of the event. She was particularly interested in anything he had to say about Louisa, and she was righteously indignant when he told her how Louisa had redone Viola's flower arrangement. "If I haven't done anything else right in this world," she said, "I've saved you from that woman."

"You've done a lot more than that for me. You've restored me," and he told her about how depressed he had been.

"I have a job to do," she said. "And I have to go away to do it. After it's done, we'll marry, and you'll never be depressed again."

"I'm not going to let you go," he said. "I will tie you up, if I have to." Their conversations always came back to that, and the trouble was he didn't know how he was going to stop her from leaving. Somehow he would have to find the right words and the right time. On the second night, after they had made love and were lying in each other's arms, he reminded her that he had once admitted he didn't want a wife whose causes were bigger than marriage.

"That isn't true anymore," he said. "I've changed. I don't care how many causes you have or how important they are. If I can just have you, I'm happy. We can fill the whole house with refugees. All I ask is that you be there with me."

"Oh, my darling," she said. "You may rue those words."

∞ ∞

Lisle arrived back at the apartment on the third day, looking as solemn as ever. Tedde explained to her in German that she and Morgan were getting married, and that Lisle would live with them in the South. The girl seemed to accept the idea and answered in her native tongue.

"She says," Tedde explained to Morgan, "she will help Josy with the baby."

"Tell her," he said, "that Josy will need all the help she can get."

That night, Tedde cooked spaghetti for supper, and when the three of them sat down to eat at the little alcove off her kitchen, she impulsively kissed first Morgan's hand and then Lisle's. "We're part of a family," she said. "We must drink a toast."

"You know I'm not much of a wine drinker," he said.

"I know, but this will be for luck." She got up from the table and got three wine glasses from the cupboard, carefully filling each one. "To us and to our happiness," she toasted.

"And to welcome Lisle into our family," Morgan said, and he gallantly drank.

"You have to finish it, or it's not lucky," Tedde said, and Morgan obediently drained his glass.

Suddenly Tedde's eyes filled with tears. They flowed, unstoppable, down her cheeks, into her spaghetti and onto her lap. "I'm sorry," she said. "I can't seem to help myself."

He leaned over to gently pat her back. He knew she must be planning her departure and somehow he had to stop her. He said a silent prayer, reminding God that he had loved two women and lost one.

They ate their meal in silence. Tedde's tears continued to flow and Morgan, fearing he would lose her again, lost his appetite and had to force himself to eat. Lisle, however, devoured her spaghetti in the manner of one who has seen tears before.

After dinner, Lisle went to her room, and Morgan and Tedde decided to walk in the park. However, before they were out the door, Morgan was suddenly dizzy.

"I've got to rest a minute," he said, and he stretched out on the living room couch. Tedde sat on the floor and rested her head on his chest. He reached out to play with her hair, and that was the last he remembered of that particular evening.

CHAPTER TWENTY SIX

MAX

When Morgan awoke, his mouth was dry and his head hurt. He would have to get it through Tedde's head that he had no capacity for wine. He looked at his watch. It was eight o'clock so he figured he had been asleep for about twenty minutes. He went in the kitchen to get a glass of water and to find Tedde.

A shaft of light streamed through the alcove window and settled on the dinette table. That was odd. The sun had no business being out. He checked his watch again and then compared his time to that of the kitchen clock. They both said eight. "I've lost my mind," he said out loud. He looked out the window and saw the sun rising in the east and realized he had slept through the night.

A cold dread encircled his heart. Knowing she wouldn't be there, he went to her bedroom. The bed was made, and the room was immaculate. He looked in the bathroom. There was no sign of use at all. The sink was dry and clean, the towels hung neatly on their racks, and all was in order. However, when he ran a finger over her toothbrush, he noted it was still damp.

He searched her closet, but nothing seemed to be missing except her coat. Perhaps she had gone out for a walk. In that case, the doorman might have seen her. He picked up the phone beside her bed and called downstairs.

The doorman was as professionally cheery as ever. No, he had not seen Miss Boyd. He had come on duty at seven o'clock and had nearly frozen to death. But now the sun was out, and it was a beautiful day though still chilly. And then he asked, "Will you be leaving today, Mr. Bigley?"

"I don't know when I'm leaving," Morgan said gruffly. "Why do you ask?"

"I promised Miss Boyd I would send the cleaning crew in before the new people come."

"What new people?"

"The friends of Miss Boyd's who are staying here while she travels. They should be here in a few days."

"I see," Morgan said and hung up. He sat down on the bed and put his head in his hands. The cold dread encircling his heart had settled in, but he was also angry. The doorman knew more about Tedde's plans than he did.

He needed coffee, and he went back to the kitchen to make some. She had left the pot sitting on the counter with the coffee grains and water already measured. All he had to do was plug it in. There were two letters on the counter, one for him and one for Lisle. He had forgotten about Lisle. She must be still sleeping in the guestroom. He tore open his letter, even though he was sure he would not like its contents. With a sinking heart he read:

My darling Morgan,
Forgive me. I have grown wise in the ways of deception, and I hate it. I put a pill in your wine so you would sleep because I could not say good-bye. It would have hurt too much, and you might not have let me go. When I come back, I will quit this nasty business, forever. I am enclosing Max Waldheim's card. He is my lawyer, and he will talk to you about Lisle. A family from Berlin is staying in my apartment. They will take her, but you have a warm home, and she would be happier with you. I love you. I love you. I love you.

Tedde

He read the letter twice. It occurred to him that perhaps he was not too late. Perhaps with more information, he might find her before she was out of the country. Shamelessly, he tore open Lisle's letter, but it was written in German.

He dashed to the phone and called Max Waldheim's number, but he was too early. The lawyer wasn't in. He tried to get him at his home, but the two other Max Waldheims in the Manhattan phone book were a dentist and a plumber.

Morgan knew he had to act fast. He raced to Lisle's room, pounded on the door, and when there was no answer, opened it. The girl was just waking up. He remembered Tedde had given her the wine, too.

"Get up," he shouted. "Put your clothes on."

Lisle looked terrified and pulled the covers over her head. For God's sake," he growled, "I'm not going to hurt you."

Realizing she didn't understand a word he was saying, he went to her closet and pulled out a dress. Then, jerking the blanket away from her head, he said in a calmer voice. "Put this on. We're going to find Tedde."

∞⌒∞

Lisle and Morgan arrived at Max Waldheim's office at ten to nine. Morgan had given the doorman five dollars to get a cab immediately, and the money had done the trick. In less than an hour after he had awakened, he found himself explaining to Max Waldheim's secretary that his business was urgent and that he didn't have time to have a seat.

"You have no choice," she said rather crossly. "He isn't here yet."

Morgan and Lisle sat down. The secretary offered to take their coats, but they both declined. He was aware that the two of them looked a little bedraggled. He had not shaved, and Lisle had not combed her hair. He handed her Tedde's letter and watched closely as she read it. She appeared unmoved by its contents.

A few minutes later, Max Waldheim arrived, and Morgan was on his feet before the lawyer had time to remove a rather worn fedora.

Waldheim looked to be about seventy-five, and his appearance confirmed Morgan's conviction that lawyers never retire. He had a deeply lined, kindly face and carried a briefcase as battered as his hat. He shook hands with first Morgan and then Lisle.

"I meant to be early this morning," he explained, "but my train broke down. However, I know who you are and why you're here. I've been expecting you."

They followed him back to his small inner office, which was lined with books. As soon as he closed the door, Morgan blurted out, "Where is she?"

"Have a seat," Waldheim said.

Morgan and Lisle remained standing.

"I don't mean to be abrupt," Morgan said, "but last night I was with Theodosia Boyd. This morning she's gone. If I can figure out where she is and we don't waste time, maybe I can catch her."

Waldheim looked at his watch. "I expect she's bouncing around in a plane somewhere over the Atlantic," he said.

Morgan and Lisle sat down, and the lawyer took a seat behind his desk.

"Mr. Waldheim . . ." Morgan began.

"Max," the lawyer said.

"Max, if you would just tell me everything you know about Theodosia."

The older man's eyes twinkled. "I know she's in love."

Morgan leaned forward in his chair. "Please," he pleaded. "Tell me about this trip she is on."

"I don't know. I can only surmise."

"Then surmise," Morgan demanded.

The lawyer hit a buzzer on his desk, and his secretary appeared. He asked her for coffee and bagels. Then he opened his briefcase and pulled out a photograph and handed it to Morgan. "This is a snapshot I took about thirty years ago. I thought you might like to see it."

Morgan examined the photograph carefully. It was a picture of a beautiful little girl standing between two men; one was young and handsome, and the other was elderly and bearded. It was taken in front of an apartment house somewhere in the city. He handed the snapshot to Lisle, who pointed to the little girl and said, "Tedde?"

"Yes," the lawyer said, "that lovely child is Tedde. The young fellow is her father. He was a friend of mine since school days. The old gentleman is her grandfather. She was extremely close to him, and it's my feeling that he's one of the reasons she's up on that plane."

Morgan studied the picture again. The apartment house did not look as if it was located in a particularly affluent neighborhood, but the little girl was beautifully dressed. Her expression indicated she was extremely proud to be standing between the two figures.

"Please," Morgan pleaded, "tell me everything you know about the grandfather and her reasons for leaving."

"He was a wonderful fellow," Max continued, "full of humor and good will just like his granddaughter. My conjecture is that Theodosia has always felt a little guilty about accepting her mother's faith. I think she felt she had let her grandfather down. So when things got hot for the Jews, she wanted to help."

"I know she's helping," Morgan said, "but I don't know to what extent."

"I don't know either. It started with her cousin, who convinced her of the seriousness of Nazi intentions. She became involved with finding sponsors over here for refugees. Then, after her cousin was killed, she became more dedicated. Because of her language skills, her career, and her knowledge of the country, she was able to travel freely throughout Germany without raising suspicion. She could, secretly, of course, channel money to people and organizations devoted to getting Jews out quickly. She was very effective. A cousin lives with me whose papers were expedited because of money I sent and Tedde delivered."

"How dangerous was this?"

"It was risky. She didn't talk to you about that?"

"She joked about it. She said the danger was no greater than an afternoon ride on my horse, Old Tom."

"A horse that is as dangerous as a Nazi," Max interjected, "I do not care to ride."

Morgan wanted to get the conversation back on track. "But now there's a war going on. She can't fly over to Germany any time she pleases."

"I told you what I know," Max said. "Anything I say about what she's doing now or how she's doing it is guesswork. However, since Theodosia is an entertainer, a linguist, and she's . . ." He stopped in mid-sentence.

"And she's what?" Morgan said.

"She's attractive."

Morgan's pulse quickened. His antenna had risen to full capacity

"Are you telling me she is some kind of Mata Hari?"

Max shook his head. "I'm not telling you anything because I don't know anything. All I know is she is on some kind of mission, and it's dangerous. It's dangerous for anybody to travel now. She knows this, and she's anxious to get whatever she's up to over with and come home. But in the event of anything untoward, she's left a will which provides for Lisle."

"She asked me if Lisle could stay with me and my family while she's away," Morgan said.

"Is that agreeable to you?" Max asked. "It is a heavy request,"

"I don't know how she'll manage. She can't speak English."

Lisle, who had sat solemnly and silently through out the conversation, suddenly sat up. "I speak some," she said.

Max's eyes twinkled. "She speaks some," he repeated. Then he spoke to the girl in German, and she laughed.

"Why is she laughing?" Morgan asked.

"She's laughing because my German is lousy," Max said.

The secretary returned with coffee and bagels. She poured three cups and put them on the table. It was good strong coffee, and Morgan was grateful.

"Do you know how Lisle got out of Germany?" he asked.

"I'll ask her about that," Max said. He spoke to Lisle and translated her reply. "She says it's a secret she shares only with Tedde. You must remember that everything we say in this room is secret. Nothing would be more hazardous to Theodosia's health than for your friends or mine to learn she is involved in possible..." He paused.

"In possible what?" Morgan asked.

"In possible espionage."

"Good God!" Morgan said, and he took a large swallow of coffee.

"Have a bagel." Max said. Morgan declined, but Lisle took one. Something about the way the girl wolfed down food caused Morgan to wonder if at some time in her life she had known real hunger.

"Theodosia indicated to me," Morgan said, "that she would return in a week. I wonder if I should stay in New York or go home and wait?"

"You should go home," Max said. "If I hear from her first, I will call you immediately."

Morgan slowly sipped his coffee. He felt Max knew more than he was letting on, and he wanted to draw him out.

"Tell me about her father," he asked. "What kind of man was he?"

"He was a tortured man," Max said. "He was torn between his Christian conversion and his Jewish heritage—or perhaps torn between his Christian wife and his Jewish heritage."

"And her mother?" Morgan asked.

"A woman who forced people to make choices they shouldn't have to make."

"There's something I don't understand," Morgan said. "and it's this. I don't understand how Tedde could run off and risk her life when we need her so much. I need her here. My children need her, and this poor little orphan sitting here needs her. It's noble to try to save people, but not at the expense of the people who love you. I don't understand how she could do it." He paused before adding, " You know she ran out on me once before."

Max drew a deep breath. "It's my job to know legal from illegal," he said. "It's much harder to know right from wrong. I think our Tedde got in deeper than she had planned, and I'm sure she wishes she were here. But she is a single woman—childless—and she found a way to make a difference. She told me this would be her last trip."

"How the hell does a person get to be a spy?" Morgan asked.

"Again, I don't know she is one," Max said. "I think it is more likely she is a courier and was tapped for the job. It's not often the government comes across someone with her qualifications. My conjecture is she's struck some kind of deal with the powers that be. She supplies them with information, and they help her get a Jew out of the country. However, this may simply be the speculations of an old man's romantic fancy."

"It's my fault," Morgan said. "If I had just come sooner."

Max spoke kindly. "It wouldn't have made any difference. Now, go home young man and wait. And you and I will pray to whatever gods that be for Theodosia's safe and prompt return."

Morgan took out his card and wrote his home phone number on it. "You'll call me night or day?" he said. "It doesn't matter what time."

"If I hear first, I'll call you night or day."

"We're going to be married as soon as she returns," Morgan said. "However we were to be married once before, and she left with no explanation."

"You must forgive her," Max advised. "She has treated you badly, but forgive her. She has the passion and courage and conviction to risk her life for a cause. These are the qualities inherent in the great martyrs and saints but not much seen in ordinary people."

Morgan looked Max dead in the eye and spoke slowly. "To hell with martyrdom! I'll forgive her, but that's because I love her the way an ordinary man loves an ordinary woman."

"That's fair enough," Max said. "And what about Lisle?"

"Lisle comes with me. We'll be going home this afternoon." Morgan stood up as if to leave, but he wasn't quite ready. "I know Tedde's grandfather lived in New York. If you could tell me where, I would like to look at the house before I leave. I know so little of Tedde's beginnings. We saw a lot of New York together, but we never saw where he lived."

"That's because all that's left of his home is in this picture. It was torn down in order to make room for a modern apartment complex. But if you would like to have the snapshot of Tedde and her father and grandfather, I'll give it to you."

"Thank you," Morgan said. "If you can part with it, I'd like very much to have it." He took the picture and assured the lawyer that he would keep in constant contact. The two men shook hands and Max patted Lisle and spoke to her in German.

"Come on Lisle," Morgan said. "We're going to pack our things and go home."

He guided the girl toward the door and, if she felt fear or apprehension, she did not show it. They took a cab to Tedde's apartment where Morgan put in a call to Miss Mattie who was breathless with anticipation. However, when she heard Theodosia was not coming but that Morgan was bringing home a little German girl who didn't speak a word of English, all she said was, "Well, I declare!"

CHAPTER TWENTY SEVEN

BIRTHING

Josy met Morgan and Lisle at the station. Now, in her seventh month, she was large and awkward. Morgan, despite the fact that the emotional upheaval of the last twenty-four hours had left him drained, felt a surge of sympathy and affection for her. He gave her a bear hug and she, gratefully, hugged him back.

When they got home, Miss Mattie acted as if it were perfectly normal for the master of the house to bring back a fourteen-year-old German refugee instead of a wife. The girls had obviously been primed to do the same. Nevertheless, feeling that some explanation was due them, he called for an evening meeting in the living room in which he explained that Lisle was an orphan from Germany whom Tedde had adopted and who would be staying with them indefinitely.

"But where is Tedde?" Agnes asked.

Morgan took his glasses out of the case and put them on. Then he unfolded the evening paper as a clear indication the conversation was about to end. "I don't know where she is," he said. "Her job is of a confidential nature, and she is at an undisclosed location. For her well-being and the well-being of all of us, this is something I don't want discussed either within or outside the family." Even as he spoke, he realized his explanation was clumsy.

"What do we tell people about Lisle?" Josy asked.

"Simply tell them she is the daughter of a friend of the family and that she has lost her parents."

Agnes fixed him with her bright blue eyes. "I know why we can't talk about it," she said. "Tedde's a spy; isn't she?"

He looked at his youngest daughter reprovingly, inwardly marveling at how she caught on to something immediately that had taken him years and a glass of drugged wine to fully comprehend. "You read too many dime novels," he said.

∽∽

Everyone tried hard to make Lisle feel at home. They gave her Josy's old room where, in the beginning, she spent most of her time, emerging voluntarily only for meals. Morgan was much moved by her dark tragic eyes but had no idea what to do with her. He knew she ought to keep busy, but it was too cruel to send a foreign-born, non English-speaking orphan to a new school in the middle of the year. She needed a period of adjustment and, feeling that working with animals in a rural environment was a cure for most afflictions, he turned her over to Josy. Every morning, Josy drove into town, picked up her charge, and brought her back to the farm to spend the day.

Tedde did not return within a week's time. Morgan contacted Max, who assured him again that he would call the minute he had something to report and advised him to be patient. Not content with this, he contacted the German Jews who had already moved into her apartment. They denied any knowledge of her whereabouts.

Living in a state of desperate anticipation, he regularly called home from the office to inquire about the mail, and when at home, he was the first to answer the phone. But as the weeks wore on, and there was no word, he gradually became resigned to his situation. It pleased his fancy to start a journal in which to record the significant happenings of his days. It was almost as if he were writing to Tedde and, in the event he might someday show her these scribblings, he wanted to give a good account of Lisle's activities. He had hired a tutor to help the girl with the English language and to determine her grade level. It was his great hope that once she learned the language, she might shed some light on his sweetheart's activities.

One Saturday afternoon at the farm, an event occurred that temporarily took his mind off the actress. Having returned from a ride with Agnes, he walked over to his garden to inspect his plants. It had been a warm spring with gentle rains, and the new growth, pushing through the soil, gave him a sense of the rightness of things. His strawberries, peeking through the pine needle mulch, were large and ready to be picked. He easily filled two paper sacks and took them to the barn where he kept cardboard containers in the tack room. Lisle and Tim were mucking stalls, and Agnes, her head in a book, sat with Josy on a bale of hay. He was about to ask if anybody wanted a strawberry when something about Josy's expression gave him pause. Her mouth was pulled down in a frown, and she was pale.

"Do you feel all right, honey?" he asked.

"I've got a little stomach ache," she said," but it's nothing much. I've had it all day."

"Are you sure? That baby's due here pretty soon."

Josy smiled. "If it came while I was sitting on this hay, it would be just like you know who."

"Who?" Morgan asked.

"Jesus," Josy said.

Agnes looked up from her book. "I suppose," she said, "when that baby's born, there will be a bright star right over our house."

"Of course," Josy retorted.

Morgan went in the tack room to separate the strawberries so that he could distribute some to his neighbors. While he was thus engaged, a sudden, sharp shriek split the air. He put the strawberries on the floor and dashed out to where Josy was sitting. Tim and Lisle, both holding shovels, had emerged from the stalls, but Josy was still sitting calmly on the straw. "I had a pain," she explained, "but it's gone now. It's probably nothing."

Morgan tried not to convey the anxiety he felt. "Tim!" he said calmly, "get some towels. Put some in the car and bring some here. We're taking this young lady to the hospital."

Tim ran to his parents' house and pulled two towels off the bathroom rack. His mother and father were gone for the day, and he pulled a quilt off of their bed. When he got back to the barn, he and Morgan attempted to help Josy on her feet, but she screamed again in protest. They both watched dumbly as she sank back down on the hay with her knees drawn up. When the pain went away, she glared at the onlookers.

"It's coming!" she announced. "Do something!"

Recovering from a panic that had momentarily paralyzed him and aware that speed was of the essence, Morgan ran into the Laudermilks' house and grabbed the phone off the hook. Two ladies were on the party line. They were discussing the sorry state of their health. One was talking about her feet.

"You'll have to hang up," Morgan said. "There's a medical emergency here."

"I declare," the lady said in a conversational tone. "That's exactly what my doctor said about my bunions."

"Get off the line, please. I'm trying to get the hospital."

"Is there any thing I can do?" the female voice asked.

"Yes. Get off the phone."

There was a welcomed click, and the line cleared. He sent an urgent prayer straight to God beseeching Him to make Richard Simms, who was both Josy's doctor and his friend, available and not on the golf course. His prayer was answered, and in a fairly steady voice he managed to communicate his predicament.

"How many fingers is she?" Dr. Simms asked.

"What?" Morgan said.

"How dilated is she?"

"For God's sake!" Morgan responded. "I'm her father. You're her doctor."

"Well, where are you?"

Morgan took a deep breath and began a detailed description on how to get to the farm. He ended with "About five miles after you cross the river, you take a right at a dirt road called Winding Creek. When you get to the Baptist church with "Jesus Saves" spelled out in rocks on the lawn, take another right until you cross the bridge. Then take a left and drive about three miles through the woods until you see some pastures on the left and a little white house with a barn in back on the right. That's us."

The doctor asked him to repeat the directions and to identify the dirt roads by name, but Morgan didn't think they had names.

"We're twenty five miles outside Atlanta," he said, "These are just roads. They don't have names." The doctor groaned. "How about flares or rockets? Or do you do smoke signals?"

A flash of brilliance crossed Morgan's mind. "I'll meet you at the church."

After extracting a promise from Dr. Simms that he would leave immediately, he put down the receiver. On the way out, he saw a pitcher on the kitchen counter. He filled it with water and took it with him to the barn where Josy was writhing on the hay and Tim was trying to put a towel around her. Agnes and Lisle appeared to be frozen, the apprehension they felt written in their eyes.

The sweat on his oldest daughter's brow and the sound of her voice in pain pierced his being to the core. He didn't know what to do or why he had brought the water. It was just something he had heard was necessary to have at a birthing. A feeling of inadequacy and faintness threatened to disable him. He knew the doctor was on his way, but what if he dawdled or had a flat tire?

"Tim," Morgan said, "go inside and scrub your hands and hurry back."

"Yes, sir," Tim said.

Josy's pain abated long enough for her to say, "I'm sorry I hollered, Papa."

"You holler all you want to, honey. I talked to the doctor, and help is coming. Holler your head off if you feel like it."

His helplessness felt overwhelming. When Tim came running back, he summoned up the last bit of authority he had left. "Son," he said, "I'm going to meet the doctor down the road. If the baby comes before I get back, wrap it in a towel."

"Sir," Tim said, "don't you think you ought to stay with Josy while I meet Dr. Simms?"

Morgan looked his son-in-law in the eye and spoke firmly. "No. Absolutely not!"

"But . . ." Tim gasped.

"You got her into this, and it's your job. I'm sure you know as much about this business as I do, but if the head shows, pull the rest of it out."

Tim gulped before he managed to ask, "What is the water used for?"

"I have no idea," Morgan said. He bolted out of the barn as Josy let out another blood-curdling scream.

He had a forty-five minute wait at the church. There was an old newspaper on the floor of his front seat, but he couldn't read it because of mud stains from his boots. He got out of the car and paced up and down. He absentmindedly picked up a rock from the "Jesus Saves" formation and appeared to examine it closely. Then he picked up a handful of rocks and, in the same abstracted, manner, commenced to throw them, one by one, into the woods. As he did so, a farm truck lumbered down the road and turned in at the churchyard. A big, burly farmer leaned out the window, spat some tobacco juice on the ground, and addressed Morgan. "You got something against salvation?" he demanded.

"No! No!" Morgan stammered. "I'm a believer. I didn't realize what I was doing."

"I done laid those rocks down myself," the farmer said.

"I'm sorry. I didn't mean to desecrate your sign." He began picking up rocks and putting them back, but he was spared this chore when the doctor, followed by a shrieking ambulance, arrived on the scene.

"I'm out of here," he said to the farmer. Motioning for the doctor to follow, he leapt back into his car, gunned it, and took off, destroying as he did so all sense of bucolic peace. Birds took to their nests, and rabbits to their holes as the three vehicles tore across dirt roads. A cow, discarding its usual lethargy, trotted off the road just in time to prevent catastrophe.

Tim was waiting for them outside the barn. He motioned for them to come in and to hurry. Dr. Simms and ambulance driver rushed inside with a stretcher, but Morgan was momentarily frozen. He had just about screwed up his courage, when Josy and a very angry carrot-topped baby were carried out and whisked into the ambulance. Tim jumped in with them, and the three vehicles set off again, this time with the ambulance leading the way. The doctor followed, and Morgan, accompanied by two very quiet and sober girls, brought up the rear. No one spoke in Morgan's car until Agnes said, "I don't know if it's a boy or a girl. Tim was just pulling it out when the doctor came. I didn't get a good look. If it's a girl, we could name it after Tedde."

"It's a boy," Lisle said.

"Do you think Josy and the baby are all right?" Morgan asked.

"I think so," Agnes said, "but there was a lot of noise and confusion in there."

At the hospital, they were ushered into the waiting room. Lisle looked at a magazine while Morgan paced and Agnes bit her nails until Tim joined them. He was grinning from ear to ear.

"Josy's fine," he announced, "and we got us a seven pound boy named Morgan Bigley Laudermilk."

"I think you ought to name him after the man who stood by and brought him into the world," Morgan protested, beaming as he did so and clapping Tim on the back.

"No, his name is Morgan Bigley Laudermilk—only by the way he yells, his last name ought to be Loudermouth."

"I know the perfect name for him," Agnes said. "Let's call him Pigley Wigley Bigley. That's what they used to call me in third grade."

Dr. Simms joined them to offer congratulations and to escort them to the nursery where they viewed a number of babies through a glass window. One of them was terrifyingly small, redheaded, and still angry.

The doctor smiled broadly and asked, "Which one of you midwives wants to hold that little bundle of joy?"

Nobody did. Shortly afterward, they were allowed to visit Josy who, looking fragile against the white sheets of the hospital bed, appeared to be sleeping. However, she opened her eyes and smiled when she heard them come in the room. "Well," she said, looking at her father, "you didn't stick around very long."

"You did all right without me, and a fine-looking redheaded boy was born on a haystack."

"I told you so," she said.

Josy looked so tired that the group did not stay long. Morgan drove back to the farm to drop off Tim, who immediately picked up his own car and returned to the hospital. Then Morgan and the girls drove home to break the good news to Miss Mattie, Viola, and Roxie.

That night before he went to bed, Morgan recorded the events of the afternoon in his journal, giving Tim full credit for the successful outcome. And the next day, he gave away the strawberries as if they were solid-gold cigars.

CHAPTER TWENTY EIGHT

CHANGE

Morgan wrote a lengthy account of his grandson's birth in his journal and, whenever he reviewed his writings, he smiled when he came to that part. In fact, he smiled every time he saw the little red head, which was often, as Josy shared her motherly responsibilities with all takers. The baby's nickname was shortened from Pigley Wigley Bigley to Big and, despite his angry beginnings, he was a good-natured baby.

No one knew if or how much Josy missed the friends who used to swarm the house in town. Miss Mattie drove Lisle out to the farm almost every day, and the two girls depended on each other for companionship. Lisle helped with the baby and did things to improve Josy's house that Josy would never have thought of doing. She made curtains and pillows for the living room, hung Sam Laudermilk's watercolors, and used her own personal trunk as a coffee table. The girl seemed to have a talent for almost everything except happiness. Unless she was with Josy or the baby, her demeanor was always downcast.

There was no word from Tedde. Max sent money that she had left for Lisle's room and board, but Morgan put it away for her later use. Even though he appreciated the girl's helpfulness with Big and her friendship with Josy, he couldn't help feeling used. His sweetheart was off doing something heroic for the country and had left him, for God knows how long, in charge of a despondent teenager with whom he had nothing in common, not even a language.

One afternoon while Morgan, Josy, and Agnes were saddling up for an afternoon ride, Morgan noticed that Lisle wore a wistful expression as she watched. He led his horse over to the Laudermilk steps where she was sitting with the baby. "Lisle," he asked, "Have you ever been on a horse?"

The girl nodded, but he couldn't tell if she understood him or was just pretending.

"I tell you what," he said. "You get on Old Tom, and the girls will take you through the woods. I'll take care of Big."

Agnes and Morgan switched horses, and Morgan gave Lisle a few pointers on mounting. She listened politely before swinging smoothly into the saddle. He led her around the barn for a few minutes and, as she seemed comfortable and secure enough for a short ride, he asked Josy and Agnes to take her on the easy trail through the woods.

"Go slowly," he cautioned his daughters. "Remember, this is her first time up. Be careful." He was pleased to note, as the riders left the barn, that Lisle looked remarkably confident for a beginner and that she was smiling. He sat down on the Laudermilk steps and jiggled the baby carriage as he waited.

Considering Old Tom's past behavior with Agnes and Tedde, it was not too surprising that within ten minutes after departure, the horse came galloping back with the bit clamped between his teeth and his head down. What was surprising was Lisle's reaction. She remained steady in the saddle and showed no sign of fear. However, her normally soft voice rose to a harsh pitch as she unleashed a river of German rhetoric that could not have been flattering. Hiding a crop behind his back, Morgan approached the gate where Old Tom had stopped short.

"What manner of names are you calling my horse?" he asked.

Lisle took a deep breath and blew the hair out of her eyes. Jerking Old Tom's head up, she replied, "I call him 'dirty Nazi pig' and 'dirty Nazi son of a bitch.'"

"Well," Morgan said, as he handed her the crop, "if he is all those things, you had better take this."

Lisle took the crop, turned Old Tom around, whacked him good, and started off toward the trail at a trot. It became obvious that the girl was no stranger to the saddle. But the most amazing thing about the incident was that someone so young and so new to the English language could roll "son of a bitch" off her tongue so deftly. He hoped it was not a talent she had acquired from Agnes whom he suspected of having a nose for sin and an ear for profanity. He had previously examined a book Agnes was reading and noted that it was not the usual little Nancy Drew mystery. It was a novel teeming with male detectives, swear words, and curvaceous blonds whose legs just didn't stop.

That night he wrote in his journal:

> We're getting long on riders and short on horses. I'm going to buy Lisle a horse. She is a gutsy girl, and I like her. I think she will get over her childhood traumas. Theodosia would be happy to know this.

Riding turned out to be only one of Lisle's hidden talents. Before the Christmas holidays, the school music teacher contracted flu and was, at the last minute, unable to play for the annual caroling in the auditorium. This was an event involving both the upper and lower school, and the students had put in considerable beforehand practice. A sprinkling of parents sat in the audience, and Morgan was among them because Agnes was singing the first verse of the "We Three Kings" solo. Lisle, who was not in the choir, sat beside him. They were both nervous. They had heard Agnes practice at home.

The caroling did not start off well. Without accompaniment and direction, the voices did not stay together and wandered in an out of tune at their leisure. When Agnes's turn came, she was so far off-key that she stopped and began again. The second time was worse than the first. Morgan, in the audience, opened and closed his fist in a male version of hand wringing, and Lisle bit her nails. On the third try, Agnes produced only a frog-like croak. A few students giggled, and Morgan closed his eyes as if in prayer.

It was then that another of Lisle's talents came to the fore. The little German girl walked to the front of the hall, sat down on the piano stool, and played "We Three Kings" so that Agnes could follow vocally. She continued to play as another little girl sang the second verse, and so it went until the song ended.

At its conclusion, everyone cheered, and the principal stood up and addressed her audience.

"Students," she said, "today we have witnessed a Christmas miracle and an answer to a prayer." She asked Lisle if she could finish out the program. Lisle nodded, and the caroling was successfully completed. No one had known until then that Lisle could play the piano.

Morgan was mightily impressed by the incident. He no longer thought of his ward as a skinny, helpless orphan who talked little and ate a lot. She had become, instead, a courageous person whose talents ought to be mined. That Christmas, the living room furniture was rearranged to make room for an upright piano, and two palomino ponies showed up at the barn, one for Lisle and one for Agnes. Lisle's smile became less of a rarity.

One night in early spring, Morgan took Lisle and Agnes to the movies and thought he saw Tedde in a newsreel. There was a picture of Hitler giving a speech at a dinner in Berlin, and in the background, an attractive, familiar-looking brunette sat at a table with a German officer. The brunette resembled Tedde, but it was a blurred image, only on screen for a split second. Agnes and Lisle did not appear to notice anything unusual, and Morgan didn't bring it up. Lisle shied away from any conversation about the actress anyway, and Agnes had been good about not asking questions. He returned to the movie two nights in a row in order to check again. There was no way to be sure.

He did not give up hope that Tedde would return. If that was her in the newsreel at a dinner for Hitler, she had gotten to the top. She was in a position to gather valuable information, and she might get away with it. She might be alive.

The news from abroad was all bad. No one could believe how easily the Germans had breezed around the Maginot line and how quickly Paris had fallen. And no one knew how long the British could hold out. There was no safe haven in Europe except Switzerland, and if Tedde were there, he would have heard. Still, there was always the possibility she was in hiding or still with the German officer he had seen on the newsreel.

Then one night something happened that put a damper on his hopes that she was alive. It was after midnight, and he had dozed off while reading in bed. Suddenly he was awakened by a woman's scream, and, in his sleep-befuddled state, he thought it was Tedde. He got out of bed and cracked the door to the girls' rooms. Lisle and Agnes were peacefully sleeping. He went downstairs and listened outside Miss Mattie's room. Only the sound of gentle snoring broke the silence. He returned to bed but not to sleep. Over and over, he rebuked himself for letting Tedde go. He had been so ineffectual . . . He should have kidnapped her and brought her home. He should have slipped a drug in her wine. He should have done something. Finally he gave up on sleeping and got out his journal. This time he wrote:

I think she is dead. I feel it in my bones. Max says to be patient, but I think she is dead. For a while, I could feel a current between us that spanned the ocean, but I don't feel it any more. Tonight, I heard her scream, and I think she is dead.

He did not fall into a depression or even consciously grieve. Being a lawyer, he dealt in facts, and he did not know for a fact that she was dead. Besides, so much was happening to the world that grief would have been an indulgence. With the Nazi conquest of so much of Europe, and the ships Roosevelt was sending to Britain, Americans were feeling closer and closer to war. Against this background, the time he had spent with Tedde took on a gossamer quality.

∮

On the afternoon of December 7, 1941, Morgan, Lisle, Josy, and Agnes were putting their horses up when Tim came speeding up go the stable in his Ford. He screeched to a stop and jumped out of the car, his face radiant with excitement. "Hot damn! We're in it," he shouted. "The Japs have bombed Hawaii. We're finally in it."

The news was received in different ways. Josy turned pale and reached up to touch her husband protectively. Then she rescued Big who, in the excitement, had been left in his booster seat and was indignantly screaming. She held him close, as if he might be forcibly snatched away. The girls were bewildered and didn't know what to think and didn't know why Tim was acting so happy. War was supposed to be a terrible thing.

But Morgan understood that Tim saw the war as a way to get out from under the family umbrella and establish himself as his own man. He walked over to his son-in-law and shook his hand. "It's good to be off the fence," he said. "We're committed now."

Morgan was right about Tim. He joined the air force immediately and seldom was the uniform worn so proudly. He didn't exactly swagger, but there was a confidence in the way he carried himself. With his red hair, straight back, and lean good looks, he had the air of a hero. He and his young wife were such a striking pair that the mothers of Josy's friends forgave them their earlier indiscretions. When Tim was on leave, they were the focus of many invitations. Parties were given for them as if to make up for the lack of wedding festivities. Except when she could join her husband at his base, Josy moved back in her old room with Lisle, where she generously shared the responsibilities of motherhood.

"She might as well give Big to us," Agnes commented one night when her sister was off with a girl friend and everybody else, including the baby in his high chair, was sitting around the dinner table.

"If she does," Morgan responded, "we'll take him."

Lisle nodded and Viola, who was passing the potatoes, muttered. "I done raised two Bigley girls. I might as well raise a Bigley Laudermilk boy."

Morgan felt guilty because he had no active role in the war. His son-in-law had volunteered, and his sweetheart had disappeared into the darkness of war-torn Europe. All he could do was to meticulously carry out all the things the government asked of its civilian patriots. Accordingly, he bought bonds, took the bus to work, walked the two miles to church, and used his gas coupons only for driving out to the farm. But even the farm was losing its sense of bucolic comfort. The government was building a bomber plant just five miles south of his land, and high paying jobs were attracting people from all over the South. There was traffic where there had never been anything but dust and gullies in the roads. Eventually the roar of the mighty B-29 split the silence of the skies, startling every living thing underneath.

Morgan wondered if the world would ever resume its normal pre-war pace, but it was not until Roxie quit that he realized the South, as he knew it, was disappearing. Ironically, she got a job in the bomber plant that produced the planes whose noise, as Sam Laudermilk put it, soured the cow's milk.

"Roxie," Morgan said reproachfully, when she informed him she was leaving, "you've been with us so long. Haven't we been good to you?"

"Yes, sir," Roxie said. "But I got to go where the money is."

She gave two weeks notice at the end of which she cooked the family as splendid a meal as rationing allowed, using her own coupons to add to the splendor.

"Remember," Morgan said, as Roxie headed out the back door for the last time, "you can always come to me for help if you need it."

"I ain't planning on needing it," she replied, and Morgan sensed that the old South, which had been so good to him and his kind, was going with her.

He was afraid Viola would leave him, too. He called her into the living room for a conference and was relieved when she said, "I promised Miss Emily I would take care of her baby, and I ain't leaving until Agnes is grown. But now that Roxie's out there making a heap of money, things around here got to change. Miss Mattie's too old to do much except fuss, and that's just what I want her to do. I want her to fuss at them girls until they start making their own beds and picking up their own clothes. Miss Lisle ain't much trouble, but Agnes makes more mess than she's worth, and when Miss Josy ain't following Mr. Tim from base to base, she's moved back here where she can drop them dirty diapers on the floor. That was all right when Roxie was in the kitchen, but now I'll be doing the cooking and the maiding both, and things around here got to change if this family plans on eating."

Viola put the full force of her height and width and years with the family behind her words, and Morgan assured her he would institute a new routine in which everyone contributed. Miss Mattie would fuss, and if that didn't work, he, personally, would lay down the law. He added that, from that moment on, he would make his own bed and, on weekends, change his own sheets.

Shortly after his conversation with Viola, it became obvious that his girls were terrible housekeepers with no desire to improve. Only Lisle was cheerfully cooperative. Agnes tried to beat the system by sleeping on her spread so she didn't have to make her bed, and she performed household tasks as if she were brain dead. However, it was not until he came home one afternoon and found Josy on the sofa reading a novel while an extremely soiled diaper lay on the living room carpet that he lost his temper.

"What," he asked, "is that very dirty diaper doing on the rug?"

Josy looked lazily up from her book. "I'll take care of it as soon as I finish this chapter," she said.

"You will take care of that diaper now, and you will rinse it off in the toilet. When it is thoroughly rinsed, you will put it in the pail, and you will follow that procedure every time your son needs a change."

"I don't know why you're so fussy," Josy said. "It's all in the family."

He had spoken through clenched teeth, but suddenly his voice rose to a bellow. "And," he continued, "you will clean up that mess that appears to be embedded in the rug, and you will do it willingly because there is a war on and your husband is serving and because you are a mother with responsibilities and obligations."

He had rarely spoken to her so sharply. She had conceived a child out of wedlock and he had been kinder, but there was something about a dirty diaper on the living room carpet that struck a bellicose chord.

The next morning at the office, he recounted the incident to O'Brian, concluding with, "There is a popular conception in the South that blacks and white trash are naturally slovenly. Is there a black or a poor white alive who compares unfavorably with my girls?"

O'Brian grinned. "What you need," he said, "is a young, strong, efficient wife—maybe a Yankee." Morgan smiled and said nothing. He didn't feel like talking about it, but there would be no women in his life until he found out what happened to Tedde.

BIG

Morgan held Pigley Wigley Bigley Laudermilk, otherwise known as Big, on his knee, and read the funny papers out loud. The little boy was fretful, and Morgan bounced a little as he read. He was baby-sitting while Josy, Lisle, Agnes, and Miss Mattie went to the movies.

"Guess you don't like Li'l Abner," Morgan said. "We'll read this one about Steve Canyon. Steve's a pilot like your daddy. That's Steve, right there. He's climbing out of the cockpit."

"Ain't," Big said, as he slid off his grandfather's knee.

"Ain't" was his favorite word, and Morgan figured that like all Southern well-bred little boys, he talked like his cook. Only Big didn't really have a cook since Roxie had gone to work for the bomber plant. However, he had ample opportunity to pick up Viola's grumblings as she tried to feed, nurse, and advise his family.

Big went to the bookcase and began taking out all the books on the lower shelves and putting them on the floor. Morgan let him clear off two shelves. Then he squatted down beside him so that he was eye level and said, "We'll put those back where you got them."

"Ain't," Big said, and he reached for some books on the third shelf.

Morgan recognized a losing cause when he saw one. He looked at his watch and gratefully noted it was almost Big's bedtime. He didn't mind taking care of the little fellow, but tonight he wanted time to himself in order to digest some bad news he had received from Max.

He used his cheeriest tone of voice. "Sleepy time, young fellow.

sleepy time."

"Ain't."

"Don't ain't your grandfather," Morgan said, as he picked up the little boy and carried him upstairs. Before he put Big in his crib, he felt his diapers and decided they were more damp than wet, and he would let well enough alone.

The minute the baby hit the crib, he began to cry, and Morgan marveled that a child so handsome could screw his face into such malevolent expressions. He had Tim's red hair, and sometimes red hair indicated a temper. Tim had one, and Morgan was glad because that was something he would need in handling Josy. He didn't know if their marriage would last, but he had seen hopeful signs, the most hopeful being that Tim had emerged from a nervous, reluctant bridegroom into a dashing young man with a mind of his own. The change began before the uniform, but, no doubt about it, the uniform helped. It was hard to believe that a boy who couldn't drive a car two years ago was now piloting a plane.

The baby continued to scream, and Morgan decided he had been too abrupt. He picked him up and patted him on the back as he walked around the room. "Hush, little fellow," he crooned. "Your mama's at the movies, your daddy's fighting Germans, and your Grandpa's feeling low."

It took fifteen minutes but it worked. He gently eased the sleeping baby into the crib and then took a moment to admire him. By all standards, he was a healthy, handsome specimen.

Gently running his hand over the child's head, he whispered, "Your grandfather is glad you are here." Then he tiptoed downstairs and got his mail off the hall table and reread Max's letter. Max's letter was to the point:

> Due to her silence, you and I have long suspected Theodosia was either imprisoned or dead. This was confirmed today by a friend of hers and mine who has just come to this country from Switzerland. My friend reports that in the spring of 1940, Theodosia arrived in Germany to visit a colonel in the army. He was a man whom she had met during that summer she spent with her German cousin. After the United States entered the war, the German officer very

quietly turned her over to the Gestapo. It was done completely without fanfare, and she simply disappeared.

The German officer is now a general, and it is believed Theodosia walked into a trap about which not much will be known until after the war. There is little likelihood she is alive. I write you this in hopes that you can now get on with your life as she would surely want you to do.

Morgan had felt for a long time that Tedde was dead. For several months after her departure, he had felt his longing for her returned, as if somehow they were telegraphing their need for each other across the ocean. However, this feeling had long since dissipated, and he had sensed she was dead. Someday he would go to Germany and find out, as best he could, the details of her death. However; for the present, he did not want to think about either her capture or the Nazi officer.

Max had enclosed another letter written by Tedde, and if he had not felt heavy of heart, its contents would have made him smile. It was addressed to the dean of admissions of Vassar College, and keeping in mind his blundering remarks about Vassar on their first meeting, he could picture the mischief in Tedde's eyes as she wrote it. This letter read:

In the event I am not alive when Agnes Bigley is old enough to attend college, I take this opportunity, as an alumnus, to recommend her for matriculation at Vassar. She is a person of integrity, intellect, and enormous imagination and, with the help of a great education, she will bring light into dark places.

Morgan sat back in his chair and closed his eyes. He had discovered, by the loss of the two women he loved, that the high pitch of fresh grief is unsustainable. Eventually, it becomes sadness, and sadness waxes and wanes according to the circumstances of life. He would keep busy. He would not think of how Tedde might had died. For the time being, he would think only of the good times and of what a woman she had been, having almost more love to give than he could handle.

In his mind, he reviewed their romance, starting with their first meeting at the party in New York when the merriness of her expression had first caught his attention. He had snapshots of her in the drawer of the table by his chair. He got them out and studied them closely. In every picture the gift of happiness was written on her face.

He heard the girls and Miss Mattie returning, and he put the snapshots away. He would not upset them with news of Tedde's death until he had more information.

They had seen a war movie, and they came in brimming over with patriotism. Agnes was the most vocal of the four and went into long tirades against the Nazis ending with, "We should send all the Nazis that we don't kill to the veterinarian and have them spayed,"

"They only do that to female dogs and cats," Josy said.

"Then I would have all the female German dogs and cats spayed and shoot their owners."

"Agnes's own final solution," Josy commented.

Then Josy went upstairs to check on Big and Lisle followed, as was her custom. Agnes went to her room to read, and Morgan was left alone with Miss Mattie.

"Sit down," he said, "and tell me about the movie. Was it too much for Lisle?"

Miss Mattie sank down in Emily's chair and leaned back. "I don't think so," she said, "although there were plenty of Nazis in it, and they were always beating up people."

"I think Lisle is happy here," he said. "She is beginning to lose that haunted look."

He was tempted to tell her about Tedde but decided bad news could wait, and he turned to something more mundane.

"Is everything alright without Roxie?" he asked.

Miss Mattie closed her eyes for a moment to convey fatigue. "Viola is about to work herself to death, but we all try to do our bit. Lisle helps more than anyone. It's as if she wants to pay us back for taking her in. Josy has her hands full taking care of Big, and Agnes is improving. But my! Oh my! I'll be so glad when this terrible war is over and things get back to just the way they used to be."

"We'll win the war," Morgan said, "but I'm not sure things will ever be the same. We'll have to try hard to hang on to what is best about us."

"If it's not going to be the same," Miss Mattie said, "then I'm glad I'm getting toward the end of my days. And when I'm gone, I want you to put on my tombstone, `She never missed a good time, and she was a bridesmaid in thirty-two weddings.'"

"I thought it was twenty-two weddings."

"To tell you the truth," Miss Mattie admitted, "I don't remember how many it was." She smiled and rested her head on the back of the chair.

Josy came downstairs to chat, and Morgan asked her if she thought Lisle was happy.

"I think so," Josy said. "I know she loves Big, and she loves horses, and she loves to play the piano. She really adds a lot. We never had music in the house before."

"Has she ever told you how she got out of Germany?"

"She's told me a little, but she made me swear not to tell."

He tapped his foot impatiently. "I wouldn't have you break your oath, but is there any information at all that you could give me—some clue that would help me put it all together?"

"I think," Josy said hesitantly, "that Tedde didn't want you to know because she had a friend in Germany. He was someone she used to know when she lived with her cousin, and she used him to help her get Lisle out of the country. He was a Nazi, and he was . . ." She paused as if searching for the right words. "Well, I think he was sort of an old boyfriend, and that's why you aren't supposed to know."

Miss Mattie suddenly interrupted. "I'm getting very tired. You must excuse me but it's my bed time."

Morgan, appreciating her tact, called after her, "Miss Mattie, I'll put thirty-two weddings on your tombstone."

"Thirty-two or twenty-two. It really doesn't matter. There were a lot of weddings and a lot of good times. Good night, everyone."

After she had gone, Josy said, "Lisle thinks that Tedde really loved only you."

"Yes, I hope that's true. And I know about the German boyfriend, and it's all right."

"Lisle and Agnes saw a movie in which the newsreel showed Tedde and the Nazi boyfriend at a dinner for Hitler. You were with them, but you didn't seem to see Tedde, and they didn't want to tell you."

"I saw her. I went back to the movie three times to be sure it was her. I was never really certain because Agnes and Lisle never said anything. I had no idea they were trying to spare me"

There was a silence between them that Josy finally broke. "Do you think," she asked, "that if Tedde had stayed with us, she might have found us a little settled in our ways? A little too Southern in our thinking?"

"No, but she would have kept us on our toes."

"Papa, Lisle thinks Tedde is dead."

"I think so, too. If she were alive, we would have heard from her."

"I'm sorry, Papa,"

"Yes, I am, too."

"Papa, if anything happens to Tim, I don't think I could stand it. But I know I would have to because of Big."

"Yes, you would survive," Morgan said. "And you would fulfill your responsibilities. That's all there is to do. Now let's go to bed. It's getting late. I hope you get a good night's sleep, and Big doesn't wake you up."

"It doesn't matter if he does. Lisle will put him in bed with her."

She bent down to kiss him good night, her dark hair gleaming under the lamplight and falling partly over her face.

"You're mighty pretty," he said, "because you look just like your mother."

She smiled. "God knew what he was doing when he made me pretty, because he also made me so lazy. Good night."

Morgan knew his oldest daughter was only lazy about things that bored her. She could work as hard as a field hand around a barn. And he knew she would survive anything the war dished out. Her brand of courage was not meant to topple.

He got out of his chair and gathered up his mail to take upstairs. But before he turned out the last light in the living room, Agnes appeared in her pajamas.

"Papa," she said, "something terrible happened this afternoon."

He sat back down in his chair. "I guess you had better tell me about it."

Agnes, looking very serious, recounted her story. "I was taking the bus to go over to a friend's house, and Viola got on the same bus to go to town. It was almost empty and, since I sit in the kitchen with Viola all the time, I got up and sat down beside her. I would have felt like a fool if I didn't. Then, when I got off, the driver gave me a terrible look. He said I was a nigger lover, and he looked so mean he scared me."

"What did you do?"

"I just stuttered and stammered. I think I said that Viola worked for my family, and I got out of there as fast as I could."

Morgan exhaled a sigh of relief. "I think that's about all you could do."

"No!" Agnes shouted, "I was a coward! I should have stared him down and looked as mean as he looked. I should have scorched him to the ground with my eyeballs."

Morgan thought of Tedde's remark that Agnes would bring light to dark places. "Honey," he said, "knowing you, I expect you will have plenty of opportunities to scorch people to the ground with your eyeballs."

"What would you have done?" Agnes asked.

"I don't know. I used to know those things, but I don't anymore." Inside, he knew he was lying. He knew exactly what he would have done. He would have sat in the front of the bus the way white people of his ilk had done for generations.

"But, Papa, it was Viola!"

Morgan thought for a moment before answering. He removed his glasses, wiped them off, and put them back on. "You know," he said, "I've served on the school board, and I've done my best to see that both black and white schools have quality education. That's my answer to the race question. Now go to bed."

Agnes didn't bother to disguise her contempt, and her response was surly. "Fat lot of good an education is if you have to sit in the back of the bus."

Morgan ignored her, and she started to leave the room. Then she stopped and confronted her father again. "Papa, what would my mother have done?"

"I don't know where she would have sat, but your mother would have dressed anybody down who insulted Viola, and she would have done it without raising her voice."

"What would Tedde have done?"

Morgan smiled. "I expect she would have sat by Viola, and if the bus driver had the nerve to insult her, she would have scorched him to the ground with her eyeballs."

"That's just what I should have done." Agnes said.

"You did all right. Now go to bed and get some sleep."

Agnes started to leave and then turned and said, "This is what I should have done. I should have scorched that bus driver to the ground with my eyeballs, and then I should have said, 'Tis a far, far better thing I do today than I have done before.'"

"Yes, that would have fixed him, all right," Morgan said. "Now go to bed."

"Good night, Papa."

"Good night, Agnes."

He gathered up his mail, put the lights out, and went upstairs, smiling as he went. His daughters were a lively pair and their good company eased his loneliness. He sat on his bed and reread his mail. Then he opened his diary and wrote:

> Max writes that Theodosia is dead. Tomorrow I will call him and get more details, and perhaps then I will have the courage to tell Agnes, although perhaps she already knows. She saw Tedde on the screen and didn't say a word. Remarkable!
>
> It's strange. I have known she was dead for a long time, but tonight, in talking to Josy and Agnes, I felt her presence in much the same way I once felt Emily's presence in her portrait. Tedde changed our lives and our way of thinking. She inspired my sixteen-year-old Josy to face up to motherhood and marriage with courage and, for better or for worse, she has turned my Agnes into a fire-eating liberal. As for me, she took me into her arms and made me feel like a god. Then she broke my heart and changed me forever, so that I don't know where I would have sat if Viola and I got on the same bus and there was an empty seat beside her.

Morgan put his diary away, lay back on his bed, and thought about Agnes's question. Before the war, he never took the bus, but the war had turned everything upside down. In view of Tedde's example, how could he not sit by Viola on the bus? He supposed he was a man who would be forever haunted and hounded by his grandfather's faith and his sweetheart's courage, and with Agnes and Josy on his tail, he knew there would be no end to the changes he would undergo.

ACKNOWLEDGMENTS

I would like to thank Helga Harris and Bill Andrews, who together run a great creative writing class at the Lifelong Learning Academy in Sarasota. I would also like to express my appreciation to Nancy Shepard, who as a captive audience, laughed at all the right times when I read the manuscript to her. I also offer thanks to Perry Monroe, who read my book twice and liked it better the second time. Finally, my deep gratitude goes to both Margaret Ottley and Betty McKay, for without them, *Goodbye, Miss Emily* would still be a batch of loose, typewritten pages moldering in my desk drawer.

ABOUT THE AUTHOR

※

Martha Sibley George was born in Atlanta, Georgia in the days when that city's population numbered about 300,000, and the term, the New South, was still an incipient dream.

She spent her formative years reading constantly, avoiding her homework, and riding horses on her father's farm. When she was eighteen, she attended a two-year college specifically tailored for academically disinclined girls. Her education took a bump up when she received a B. A. from Oglethorpe University, and later, an M.A. from Long Island University.

In 1953, she met and married a gentleman from Brooklyn and moved to New York where her children were raised. When her husband retired, the couple moved to Longboat Key, Florida, and later, to Sarasota where, in what seems to her a blink of an eye, she finds herself an old, widowed lady who writes.

Made in the USA
Charleston, SC
14 August 2015